ERLE STANLEY GARDNER

- Cited by the *Guinness Book of World Records* as the #1 bestselling writer of all time!

- Author of more than 150 clever, authentic, and sophisticated mystery novels!

- Creator of the amazing Perry Mason, the savvy Della Street, and dynamite detective Paul Drake!

- **THE ONLY AUTHOR WHO OUTSELLS AGATHA CHRISTIE, HAROLD ROBBINS, BARBARA CARTLAND, AND LOUIS L'AMOUR *COMBINED!***

Why?

Because he writes the best, most fascinating whodunits of all!

You'll want to read every one of them, from
BALLANTINE BOOKS

Also by Erle Stanley Gardner
Published by Ballantine Books:

The Case of the
Substitute Face

Erle Stanley Gardner

BALLANTINE BOOKS • NEW YORK

CAST OF CHARACTERS

Chapter 1

Perry Mason stood leaning against the rail as an inky ribbon of black water widened between the side of the ship and the dock. The hoarse whistle bellowed into noise as spectators on the pier waved hats and handkerchiefs in farewell. Propellers churned the water into yeasty foam, then subsided.

The strains of *Aloha Oe*, snug by the soft voices of Island women, reached the ears of suddenly silent passengers.

Minutes later, as the shore noises drifted astern, Mason, watching the Aloha tower shrinking into the background of city lights, could see the black outlines of the mountains rising in silent sihouette against the stars. The hiss of water streaming past the ship's side became increasingly audible.

Della Street, his secretary, clasped strong fingers over the back of his hand where it rested on the rail. "I'll never forget this, Chief. It's big and quiet and solemn."

He nodded, fingering the flowered *leis* which circled his neck with bands of red, white and purple.

"Want to stay?" he asked.

"No—but it's something I'll never forget."

Mason's voice showed his restlessness. "It's been a wonderful interlude, but *I* want to start fighting. Over there—" waving his arm in the general direction of Waikiki Beach—"is something which civilization has commercialized but can't kill, a friendly people, a gentle warm climate, where time drifts by unnoticed. I'm leaving it to go back to the roar of a city, the jangle of telephones, the blast of automobile horns, the clanging of traffic signals, clients who lie to me and yet expect me to be loyal to them—and I can hardly wait to get there."

She said sympathetically, "I know, Chief."

The engines throbbed the big ship into vibrant speed. A breeze of tropical air ruffled the flower petals around their necks. Mason watched the fringe of lights along the dark shoreline, glanced down at the churned white of water where it streamed along the side of the boat.

From the lower deck, *leis* sped outward, to hang poised for a minute in circular color against the black of the water, then collapse and drop rapidly astern, as passengers sought to comply with the age-old Hawaiian custom.

Mason said, with the tolerance of one who has long since learned to accept human nature as an established fact, "Those are the newcomers, the *malihinis*. Those *leis* drift right back into the harbor. Passengers should wait until they're opposite Diamond Head."

Elbows on the rail, they looked down on the heads and shoulders of people leaning over the rails on the lower decks.

"There's the couple we saw last night in the Chinese restaurant," Mason remarked.

Della Street followed the direction of his gaze. "I'm to have her for a roommate," she said. "She was in the cabin when my baggage came aboard."

"Who is she, Della?"

"Her name's Belle Newberry. Her father and mother are in three twenty-one."

"Who's her boy-friend?" Mason asked.

"Roy Amboy Hungerford," Della Street said, "and he's not *her* boy-friend."

"Don't fool yourself," Mason told her. "I saw the expression in his eyes when he was dancing with her last night."

"You'd be surprised at what men can do with their eyes in the tropics," she told him, laughing. "Have you noticed

2

the tall, brown-haired girl with blue eyes and the white sharkskin dress, who was weighted down with *leis*—the one who was standing with her father up there on the . . ."

"I noticed her," Mason said. "What about her?"

"I think she has some claim on Hungerford," Della Street said. "She's Celinda Dail. Her father's C. Whitmore Dail—if that means anything. They're wallowing in wealth, have a big suite on A deck."

"Well," Mason said, smiling at her, "you *do* get around, don't you? How about dropping our *leis*, Della?"

She nodded. "I'm going to save one for the night of the captain's dinner. I'll have the room steward put it in the ice box."

They performed the ceremony of consigning their flowers to the dark waters. "Why is it," Della Street asked, as Mason's last *lei* vanished into the darkness, "that all of these things we'd consider superstitions on the Mainland seem so real here?"

"Because so many people believe them," he told her. "Mass belief is a tangible psychic force. Notice the authenticated stories of persons who have violated Island beliefs and come to grief. Thousands of people have known of the violated *tabu*. Thousands of minds have believed some evil was going to befall the violator."

"Like hypnotism?" she asked.

"You might call it that."

"Here come Belle's mother and father," Della Street said. "I suppose they'll want to be introduced."

Mason turned to observe a slight, small-boned man of about fifty-five, with high forehead and piercing gray eyes. The woman at his side appeared much younger. She had retained a slender, graceful figure and walked with long, easy strides. Her dark brown eyes studied Mason's face with interest, then swung to Della Street. She bowed and smiled. The man, hatless, did not so much as shift his eyes.

Mason watched them as they walked past, the man

staring with preoccupation at the dark curtain of night beyond the ship, the woman frankly sizing up her fellow passengers.

"You've met her?" Mason asked.

"Yes. They were in the cabin for a few minutes."

Mason once more stared down at the couple on the lower deck. "Celinda Dail," he said, "had better hurry up and record her location notice or she'll find someone's jumped her claim—funny I can't place that girl. I've seen her before somewhere."

Della Street laughed. "You said that last night, Chief, and after you mentioned it I thought *I'd* seen her before. So I asked her about it tonight."

"Has she ever been in the office?" Mason asked. "Or, perhaps, on one of my juries?"

"No," Della Street told him. "It's simply a case of a remarkable resemblance to—"

"To Winnie Joyce, the picture actress!" Mason exclaimed.

Della Street nodded. "There's a natural resemblance," she said, "and Miss Newberry accentuates it by the way she does her hair. I think she more or less consciously imitates Winnie Joyce in her manner. She's a bit hypnotized by Hollywood."

"Everyone is," Mason grinned, "including Hollywood."

"Well," Della told him, "I'm going to hunt up a steward and have him put my *lei* in the refrigerator. See you in the morning, Chief."

She walked rapidly forward, leaving Mason standing at the rail, watching the intermittent flashing of signal lights, inhaling the scents of the warm tropical air. The decks became silent and deserted, as passengers, fatigued by a strenuous last day in the Islands, the night sailing, and the strain of farewells, sought their cabins.

Mason turned abruptly as a woman mentioned his name.

4

"I'm Mrs. Newberry, Mr. Mason," she said. "My daughter's sharing the cabin with your secretary, so I know all about you. I saw you standing at the rail as we walked past—I—I want to consult you."

"Professionally?" Mason asked.

She nodded.

Mason studied her with patient, appraising eyes. "What about?"

"About my daughter, Belle," she said.

Mason smiled. "I'm afraid you misunderstood, Mrs. Newberry. I don't handle a general law practice. I specialize in trial work, mostly murder cases. Surely Belle hasn't done anything which would require *my* services."

"Please don't refuse," she pleaded. "I feel certain you can help me. It wouldn't take much of your time and it might make all the difference in the world to Belle."

Mason noticed a hint of nervous hysteria in her voice and said, "Go ahead. Tell me about it. I'll at least listen. Perhaps I can make some suggestions. What's Belle been doing?"

"Nothing," she said. "It's my husband who's been doing things."

"Well, what's Belle's father—"

"He's not Belle's father," she interrupted to explain. "Belle is the child of a former marriage."

"She goes by the name of Newberry, however?" the lawyer asked, puzzled.

"No," the woman said, "*we* do."

"I don't understand."

"It's this way," she went on, speaking rapidly; "my husband's name is Moar. Up until two months ago I was Mrs. Moar. Overnight, my husband changed his name. He ceased to be C. Waker Moar, and became Carl W. Newberry. He simply walked out of his position as bookkeeper in the Products Refining Company. We hurriedly moved to another city, lived under the name of Newberry,

5

then went to Honolulu, and have been there for six weeks. My husband gave strict orders that under no circumstances were any of us ever to mention the name of Moar."

Mason's eyes showed his interest. "He left his job rather suddenly?"

"Yes, without even going back to the office."

."That," Mason said noncommittally, "is rather peculiar."

The woman came closer to him. Her hand rested on his wrist, and slowly the fingers tightened until the skin was white across her knuckles. "Belle," she said, "suspected nothing. She's a modern young woman, a strange mixture of sentiment and cynical acceptance of life. For more than a year she'd been wanting to take the name of Moar. She said that it was embarrassing to introduce her mother as Mrs. Moar and then explain that Carl was her stepfather. So when my husband said we'd take her name, she was overjoyed."

"She gets along well with your husband?" Mason asked.

"She's very, very fond of him," the woman said. "Sometimes I think she understands him better than I do. Carl has always been something of an enigma to me. He's undemonstrative and very self-contained. But he worships the ground Belle walks on. He never started complaining about any lack of opportunities in life until recently. Then he began to grumble. He couldn't get enough money to give Belle a chance to meet the right sort of people. She didn't have the clothes he thought she should have. She couldn't travel. . . ."

"You're traveling now," Mason observed with a smile.

"That's just the point," she said. "About two months ago we suddenly became affluent."

"And that was when he changed his name?"

"Yes."

"How affluent?" Mason asked.

"I don't know. He carries his money with him in a money belt. I've never seen the inside of that money belt, but occasionally he goes to a bank and gets a thousand-dollar bill changed."

She continued to clutch at the lawyer's wrist, and now her hand was trembling with nervousness. "Naturally," she went on rapidly, "I'm not a fool. I haven't lived thirty-nine years for nothing."

"Did you ever ask him any specific questions about the reasons for his actions, about where the money was coming from?" Mason asked.

"Yes, of course."

"What did he say?"

"He told me he'd won a sweepstakes—some lottery. . . . But I don't think he had. The newspapers publish the names of the winners, don't they?"

Mason nodded. "Only sometimes persons buy tickets under fictitious names."

"Well, he told me he'd won one of the sweepstakes. He said that environment had made our friendships, rather than natural selection. He said he wanted to begin life all over, take a new name, travel and have Belle meet people of the right sort."

"You didn't believe what he told you about winning the lottery?" Mason asked.

"I believed him at the time. Recently I've started to doubt him. Over in Honolulu someone from Los Angeles mentioned in my hearing that the Products Refining Company had employed auditors to go over its books. I'm worried . . . I feel certain . . . And then Belle . . ."

"All right," Mason said gently, "tell me about Belle."

"She took to this life like a duck takes to water. She's naturally happy, vivacious, impulsive, and a good mixer. It gave her a great thrill to be thrown in contact with wealthy tourists, the people she calls ritzy. A few days ago she met Roy Hungerford at the Royal Hawaiian. He's the son of Peter Coleman Hungerford, the oil millionaire. It seems that he's been dancing constant attendance on a Miss Dail, but since he's met Belle he's been putting in more and more time with *her*."

"What does Miss Dail have to say to that?" Mason asked.

"She doesn't *say* anything," Mrs. Newberry said. "She's far too clever for that. She's apparently taken quite an interest in Belle—you know, some women do that. They become very friendly with their rivals."

"And you think she considers your daughter a rival?" Mason asked.

"Yes, I think she does, Mr. Mason."

"And," Mason went on, "I suppose Miss Dail has been asking your daughter something about her background, where she has lived, and something about her father's occupation?"

Mrs. Newberry said, "Yes. So far, Belle's been clever enough to laugh it off. She says she's only a Cinderella, playing at the party until midnight, and then she'll disappear."

"That might get by with young Hungerford," Mason said, "but I presume it's merely made Miss Dail more curious."

"It has," Mrs. Newberry assured him.

"How does your husband feel about that, now that his background and occupation have attracted so much interest?"

"My husband," she said, "has almost gone into hiding. I had an awful time dragging him out for a single turn around the deck. He's gone back to his cabin now and is staying there."

Mason said, "Now let's get this straight. You suspect that your husband has embezzled money from the Products Refining Company?"

"Yes."

"Does your daughter have any suspicions?"

8

"No, of course not."

"Where does she think the money came from?"

"She thinks my husband won it in a lottery, but that she must never mention that fact because the lottery was illegal and it might make trouble for him. She's been too busy having a good time to do very much thinking about financial matters."

"And," Mason said, "I presume that nothing would suit Miss Dail better than to do a little amateur detective work and expose Belle as the daughter of an embezzler."

Mrs. Newberry started to cry.

Mason placed a reassuring hand on her arm. "Take it easy," he said. "Tears won't help. After all, nothing's apt to happen while you're on shipboard. Why not let this matter wait until you reach the Mainland? By that time your daughter will have had an opportunity to become better acquainted with young Hungerford and . . ."

"I'm afraid," she said, "it's too late for that."

"What do you mean?"

"Someone stole Belle's picture."

Mason raised his eyebrows in silent interrogation.

"Someone stole her picture from my husband's suitcase sometime after three o'clock this afternoon and before ten o'clock tonight."

"Well," Mason said, "what if they did? I don't see what your daughter's picture—"

"Can't you see?" she interrupted. "The Clipper leaves Honolulu at daylight tomorrow morning. Someone could have stolen my daughter's picture, sent it to the Mainland by air mail, and had detectives trace her, and find out everything about her."

"But surely," Mason said, "you don't think Miss Dail would resort to any such tactics?"

"I don't know what tactics she'd restort to," Mrs. Newberry said. "She's selfish, spoiled, rich, and ruthless."

"Why, she's just a kid," Mason exclaimed.

"She's twenty-five," Mrs. Newberry pointed out, "and she's done lots of living. She's a good polo player, holds an aviator's license, has a yacht of her own, shoots par golf and . . . Well, a young woman of twenty-five these days is quite apt to have done a lot of living. I'd consider her capable of almost anything."

"Tell me some more about the theft of the picture," Mason said.

"We packed early," she said. "I packed my husband's suitcase. Belle had given him a picture inscribed, *'To Daddy, With Love from Belle.'* I don't know, Mr. Mason, whether you've noticed that my daughter resembles Winnie Joyce, the actress, but—"

"I'd already noticed and commented on the resemblance," Mason said. "I believe she tries to accentuate that resemblance, doesn't she?"

"Of course she does," Mrs Newberry agreed promptly. "People comment about it and it tickles her pink. She sent to the studio for a fan-mail photograph of Winne Joyce. Then she had a photographer take *her* picture in the same pose and with the same lighting effects. It was one of those pictures she inscribed and gave to my husband. It was in an oval desk frame. I personally packed that picture in his bag a little before three o'clock this afternoon. After the bag was packed, he locked it. It wasn't unlocked again until ten o'clock tonight, half an hour before the ship sailed. I was unpacking the baggage in the stateroom and he took the keys from his pocket and unlocked it."

"And the frame was gone?" Mason asked.

"No," she said. "Belle's picture had been taken from the frame and a picture of Miss Joyce substituted."

She opened her purse, took out an oval desk frame and handed it to Mason. Mason held it so that the light from one of the deck lamps showed the photograph. "Notice the inscription," Mrs. Newberry said.

Mason deciphered, "Sincerely yours. Winnie Joyce."

"Perhaps the photograph had been substituted before you packed," Mason suggested.

"No. I noticed particularly. You see, my daughter's happiness has been on my mind ever since I heard this about the Products Refining Company. I looked at her picture when I packed it and hoped that she'd always be happy and smiling as she was in that picture."

"Well," Mason said, "there's no use beating around the bush. Go to your husband. Call for a show-down. After all, Mrs. Newberry, you may be alarming yourself needlessly. He *may* have won the money in a lottery."

"But I *have* talked with him. It doesn't get me anywhere. He simply says he won some money in a lottery. That's all I can get out of him."

"Did you ever accuse him of embezzling money from the Products Refining Company?" Mason asked.

"Not in so many words, but I intimated that I thought he might have."

"And what did he say?"

"Told me I was crazy, that he'd won a lottery."

"You don't know what lottery?"

"He said something about a sweepstakes once, and the other times he said lottery."

"Well, call for a show-down," Mason said impatiently. "Ask him just what lottery it was. After all, you're his wife. You're entitled to know."

She shook her head emphatically. "It would never do any good to talk with Carl that way. He'd lie out of it and it would simply make matters worse. When I have another talk with him, I want to have all the cards in my hand so I can play them. I want to know."

"What do you want to know?" Mason asked.

"I want to be absolutely certain," she said, "that he did embezzle that money. That's where I want your help."

"What did you want me to do?" Mason asked.

"Get in communication with your office," she said.

"Have your associates make a quiet investigation and find out whether Carl really embezzled the money."

"And if he did, then what?"

"Then," she said, "I'm going to take steps to protect Belle and safeguard her happiness as much as I can."

"How?" Mason asked.

She started to say something, then checked herself. After a moment, she said, "I don't know—yet. I'd want your advice."

Mason leaned over the rail and looked down at the deck below. The figures of Belle Newberry and Roy Hungerford had moved close together until they appeared as one dark silhouette.

"Very well," Mason promised. "I'll see what I can find out," and cut short her thanks to go to the wireless room.

Using his confidential code, Mason sent a wireless to Paul Drake, of the Drake Detective Agency in Los Angeles, asking him to investigate a C.W. Moar who had worked for the Products Refining Company; to investigate the winners of all sweepstakes within the past four months, and find out if any might have been C.W. Moar, using either his own or a fictitious name, and added as an afterthought a request to ascertain if Winnie Joyce, the picture actress, had a sister.

Chapter 2

Sun sparkled from the crested tops of restless waves as Perry Mason paced the deck, enjoying the fresh air and the morning sun. His hands were thrust deep in the pockets of a double-breasted coat, his rubber-soled shoes trod lightly along the teakwood deck. The warm breeze ruffled his wavy hair. He had circled the deck for the third time when the heavy door from the forward social hall was pushed open an inch or two. Della Street shouldered it open, to stand with wind-whipped skirts while Belle Newberry stepped across the high threshold.

As they released the door and the wind pushed it against the automatic door check, Mason, walking up behind them, called "Ship Ahoy!" and, as they turned, said to Della Street, "The other side is less windy."

Della nodded, the warm wind blowing tendrils of hair across her face. "Belle," she said, "this is the boss. Chief, I'd like to have you meet Belle Newberry, my roommate. We're working up an appetite for breakfast."

"Let's go," Mason suggested.

With a girl on each arm, he started forward along the deck. Rounding the bow, the wind pushed them on down the sloping incline, into the lee of the deck. Belle Newberry put her hair back into place, laughed, and said, "That's what's known as a wind-blown bob. I've been hearing a lot about you, Mr. Mason."

"If it's bad," Mason told her, "you can believe it; if it's good, it's slander."

She faced him with laughing, dark eyes, full red lips,

13

parted to reveal teeth which glinted like whitecaps in the sun. The silk blouse, open at the neck, disclosed the sweep of her throat, the rounded curve of her firm breasts. "I saw you and Moms talking last night," she said. "I'll bet Moms told you all about the family mystery."

"Mystery?" Mason asked.

"Uh huh," she said. "Don't stand there and act innocent."

Della Street flashed Mason a quick glance. "What's the family mystery, Belle?" she asked.

"The disappearing portrait," she said. "Mother packed my autographed picture in Dad's bag and locked the bag. When they unpacked, my picture was gone from the frame, and someone had inserted one of Winnie Joyce, my double. Now, what do you know about that?"

"I," Della Street said, glancing reproachfully at Perry Mason, "know nothing about it. What does your mother think about it?"

"She's making it darkly mysterious," Belle said. "Don't deprive her of her thrill. If she tells you about it, look frightened."

"You don't take it seriously, then?" Mason inquired.

"Me?" she told him, raising her chin and laughing up into his face. "I don't take anything seriously—life, liberty, or the pursuit of love. I'm the flippant younger generation, Mr. Mason—born without reverence—yet reared without guile, thank Heaven."

"And how about your father?" Mason inquired. "How does he take it?"

"Oh, Dad takes it right in his stride," she said. "Pops is a Thinker, carries the world on his shoulders. Only occasionally can I get him to set it down long enough to play with me."

"That," Mason said, "doesn't answer my question."

"Ooh, the Big Bad Lawyer!" she laughed. "I forgot I

was being cross-examined. What shall we call this, Mr. Mason—'The Case of the Purloined Picture'?"

"It wasn't purloined," he said, "so much as substituted."

"All right, then. 'The Case of the Substitute Face.' How will that do?"

"All right," he said, "at least temporarily. What does your father say about it—and, incidentally, what are *your* theories?"

She shook her head. "I don't have theories. I'm too young. . . . You don't mind being kidded a bit, do you, Mr. Mason? Because if you do, you only have to say so and I get worse. . . . No, seriously speaking, Dad and I both think it's just a joke someone in the hotel played. You know Moms. She swears that it was my picture in the frame when she was doing the packing, but Moms gets excited when we travel. You see, Miss Joyce and I look alike, even if Miss Joyce wouldn't admit it. Ever since I started traveling, people in restaurants and night clubs have been staring at me, nudging each other and whispering."

"You might capitalize on it," Mason said. "A stand-in or something."

"That's what *I* claim," Belle Newberry said, the banter instantly leaving her eyes, and her voice slightly wistful. "I think it would be a swell chance for me to go to Hollywood and look around, but Dad says nothing doing, that I stay with him until after I'm twenty-three, and that'll be six months. My Lord! It seems as though I've been twenty-two forever . . . there I go, telling my age!"

Mason laughed. "You liked Honolulu?"

"Crazy about it," she said. "Lord, how I hated to leave! I'd never even dreamt of such a glamorous, thrilling experience. I suppose I shouldn't indulge in all those enthusiasms, but should be more like the society bud at the hotel who raised her eyebrows and made her face look like a stifled yawn whenever anyone asked her how she enjoyed the Islands. Then, after just the right interval, she'd say, 'Oh, they're *quite* nice, thank you.' You know, that world-weary sophistication which comes to us blasé twenty-year-olds."

"Yes," Mason laughed, "I've encountered it."

"I've wallowed in it," she said. "It surrounded me all through college."

"Your first ocean voyage?" Mason inquired.

"Going to the Islands was not only my first ocean voyage," she told him, "but positively and absolutely the first time I've ever been . . . well now, wait a minute, I hadn't better make any confessions. After all, there's nothing so disillusioning as a woman with a drab past, and you know, I . . ."

She broke off as the door on the lee side opened, and Roy Hungerford, attired in white flannels, stepped out to the deck and looked eagerly to the right and left. He caught sight of them, smiled, and came swiftly toward them. Belle Newberry hooked her arm through his and performed introductions.

Della Street said, "You two go walk up that appetite. I see that I have to go into a huddle with the boss. He has a businesslike look on his face. You shouldn't have mentioned mysteries, Belle. Now you've reminded him that he's returning to the office."

Belle Newberry flashed her a grateful glance, and nodded to Roy Hungerford. They pushed forward into the wind, and Della Street looked up at the tall lawyer and said, "Okay, Chief, spill it."

"Spill what?" Mason asked.

She laughed and said, "Go on, don't pull that stuff on me. Tell me all about the family mystery—The Case of the Substitute Face."

"You know about all there is to know about it," Mason told her. "The photographs were switched."

"Who did the switching, and why?" Dellas asked.

"I don't know," Mason admitted. "There are complicating factors. Come on up on the boat deck and I'll tell you about them."

They climbed the stairway, walked past the gymnasium, across the deck tennis court, and found a sheltered spot in the lee of the rooms used as ship's hospital. Mason told Della Street of his conversation with Mrs. Newberry. "So," she said when he had finished, "you sent a radiogram to Paul Drake."

He nodded.

She laughed. "Well, that'll be a good preliminary training for Paul. He's had a rest while you were batting around the Orient. I'll bet he missed the wild scramble of your work. How about breakfast?"

He nodded. "In a minute. What do you think of her?"

"Of whom?"

"Of your cabin-mate."

"Oh, she's a kick. She's an observing kid, and chuck full of life. She's modern, impatient of all sham and pretense, and isn't too affected to show enthusiasm. She's as full of bounce as a rubber ball."

"Did she say anything about young Hungerford?"

"No. It's really deep and serious with her. She treats the world in that light, flippant manner, but this is something she won't treat that way. Come on, Chief, let's eat. I'm starved."

They were half through breakfast when Drake's first radiogram was received. It read simply:

PRODUCTS REFINING COMPANY ASSETS SHORT TWENTY-FIVE GRAND. PRIVATE DETECTIVES MAKING QUIET SEARCH FOR MOAR VANISHED EMPLOYEE. NO COMPLAINT FILED AS YET. APPARENTLY NIGGER SOMEWHERE IN WOODPILE AND AUDITORS LACK SUFFICIENT PROOF TO MAKE DEFINITE ACCUSATIONS.

17

Della, taking the cablegram from Mason, said, "That's fast work, Chief."

"Uh huh. But remember, it's later there than it is here. He's been on the job for two or three hours."

They were strolling the promenade deck, snapping colored photographs with Mason's miniature camera, when Drake's second message came. It read:

NO SWEEPSTAKE OR LOTTERY WINNERS NAMED MOAR. WINNERS LAST FOUR MONTHS ALL ACCOUNTED FOR.

And his third radiogram was received about noon:

WINNIE JOYCE HAS NO SISTERS. BETTER FORGET ROMANCE PERRY AND STICK TO BUSINESS. COME HOME. ALL IS FORGIVEN.

Mason, folding the message, said, "Damn him, I'll get even with him for that."

"Here comes Mrs. Newberry," Della Street said.

Mason returned Mrs. Newberry's good-morning, and said, "I have some information for you."

"Can you tell me now?" she asked, glancing dubiously at Della Street.

Mason said, "I have no secrets from Della. Do you want me to beat around the bush, or do you want it straight from the shoulder."

"Straight from the shoulder."

"All right. The Products Refining Company is about twenty-five thousand dollars short. Private detectives are looking for your husband. He didn't win any sweepstakes."

She kept her profile turned toward them, her eyes staring far out over the ocean. Weariness was stamped on her features. "It's what I expected," she said.

Mason said, "I think you'd better have a talk with your husband, Mrs. Newberry."

"It won't do any good," she said.

"Perhaps," he suggested, "if I sat in on the conference it would help."

"Help what?" she asked.

"Help to make him tell the truth."

"Well," she said dejectedly, "suppose he tells the truth. What then?"

Mason was silent for several seconds. Then he said, "Look here, Mrs. Newberry, I won't represent your husband in this business."

"I don't want you to."

"You're certain of that?"

"Yes."

"Then," Mason went on, "we may be able to reach an understanding. I *would* try to protect Belle if it were definitely understood I wasn't representing your husband."

She faced him then, her eyes showing a glint of hope.

"Your husband," Mason pointed out, "has sailed under the name of Newberry. No one on board this ship knows him except as Newberry. On the other hand, he embezzled money from the Products Refining Company under the name of Moar. No one in the Products Refining Company knows him except as Moar. I might be able to capitalize on that. Now then, *if* I were representing your husband, and tried to patch matters up with the Products Refining Company, someone might claim I was trying to compound a felony. But if I had nothing to do with your husband and was representing you on behalf of Belle, I might be able to work out a deal by which he could make restitution of whatever money he has left and receive in return some concessions. In other words, the company might be willing to co-operate with us, perhaps to the extent of joining in an application for probation, and they would probably agree to keep you and your daughter free from any publicity. If we could do that, do you think your husband would be willing to surrender, confess and make what restitution he could?"

19

"He'd do anything to help Belle," she said. "That's the only reason he took the money in the first place."

Mason said, "If I'm going to handle it that way, I want it distinctly understood I'm not representing your husband. I'm representing you, and you alone. Do you understand that?"

She nodded.

"And until I've brought matters to a head, I don't want your husband to even know that I'm working on the case. I don't want to talk with him. I don't want him to try to talk with me."

"That would be all right," she said.

"Have you any idea how much money he has left?"

"No. He carries it all in a money belt."

"Assuming that the original embezzlement was twenty-five thousand dollars, how much do you suppose you've spent?"

"In the last two months we've spent more than five thousand dollars," she said. "I know that for a fact."

"We could do a lot of trading with twenty thousand dollars," Mason observed, staring out at the blue horizon.

Mrs. Newberry said, "There's one other element of danger, Mr. Mason, something you've got to guard against."

"What's that?" Mason asked.

"Have you noticed the man with the broken neck?" she asked.

"No," he said. "What about him?"

"It isn't him," she said. "It's his nurse. Carl knows her."

"Well?" Mason asked.

"Don't you see what that means? He knew her before he married me. She knows him as Carl Moar. If she should see him and recognize him, she'd be sure to call him by the name of Moar."

"Just what do you know about her?" Mason asked.

20

"Her name's Evelyn Whiting. She's . . . here she comes now."

A young, attractive nurse, in a stiffly starched uniform, pushed a wheel chair along the promenade deck. A man lay in the wheel chair, his head cradled in a padded steel harness which was strapped to his shoulders. His eyes were protected from the sun by a huge pair of dark goggles.

Mrs. Newberry's lowered voice was sympathetic. "Poor chap, he was in an automoblie wreck. His neck's broken. He may have to wear that harness for two or three years. He can't turn his head, isn't even supposed to talk. She asks him a question and then puts her hand in his. He squeezes once for yes and twice for no. He can't use his legs. Think of not being able to even turn your head to avoid the glare of the sun."

Mason studied the nurse. She was in the early thirties, attractive, well-figured, auburn-haired. She felt his gaze and turned eyes to his which showed a frank interest before they shifted solicitously back to her patient. She stopped the chair and said, "Is it a little too sunny for you here, Mr. Cartman? Would you like to go around on the other side of the deck?"

She pushed her hand under the light blanket which covered the thin figure, and Mason saw the blanket move as the man squeezed her hand once. She turned the wheel chair and sought the shady side of the deck.

"How does your husband expect to avoid her?" Mason asked.

"I don't know," Mrs. Newberry confessed. "He'll only come on deck when she's in the cabin. The fact that she's nursing that man makes it easier for Carl."

"Couldn't he go to her and explain that he was using another name and—"

"I'm afraid not," Mrs. Newberry said. "He tells me that he handled some money for her once on an investment. The investment didn't turn out well and he thinks she might feel

21

a little bitter about it—particulary if she saw that he seemed to have plenty of money now."

Mason turned to Della Street. "Encode a wireless to my office, Della. Tell Jackson to find out what concessions the Products Refining Company would be willing to make if Moar should surrender and return intact approximately twenty thousand dollars of the embezzled money. Tell Jackson to have it definitely understood that he's merely asking questions on behalf of an interested party, is not representing Moar, does not know where Moar is, and is at present only asking for information. Tell him to handle it diplomatically and report progress."

Mrs. Newberry gripped his hand in thanks. After a moment she said, "I'll go now. It'll be better if I'm not seen with you too frequently. If you're not going to have any contact with Carl . . . Well, I wouldn't want Belle to suspect that I was consulting you professionally."

Mason said, "It'll probably take my office two or three days to get anything definite. In the meantime, you sit tight and don't worry."

He left her, to circle the deck. Celinda Dail, clad in a sun suit which showed her long, sun-browned limbs to advantage, was playing ping-pong wiht Roy Hungerford.

Chapter 3

The ship was scheduled to arrive in San Francisco late Sunday night, docking early Monday morning. On Saturday, Mason received a wireless from his office lawyer which read:

> C. DENTON ROONEY HEAD AUDITOR OF PRODUCTS REFINING COMPANY IN CHARGE OF LOS ANGELES OFFICE HAS AGREED TO CABLE PRESIDENT NOW IN HONOLULU. ROONEY TEN DEGREES COLDER THAN FREEZING. OUTLOOK DISTINCTLY UNFAVORABLE. WILL KEEP YOU POSTED.

"Isn't that rather an unusual attitude, Chief?" Della Street asked, when Mason had finished reading the message.

"I'll say it is," Mason said. "It's the first time I ever knew a corporation to snub twenty thousand dollars."

"But still, Chief, there's the question of ethics. Perhaps they don't want to establish a precedent——"

Mason laughed. "Don't worry, Della. They usually hook the embezzler in the long run. But when he offers to make restitution they unhesitatingly make glittering promises. Even the police do it. Let them arrest an embezzler who has a few thousand dollars cached away and they'll promise him probation, or a light sentence, or a chance to escape, or even that he's properly repentant by disclosing the hiding place of the money. Then, after they once get their hands on the money, they sing a different tune. It seems that the officer

23

the crook was talking with had no authority to make the promises, or the judge refuses to co-operate, or something of that sort."

"Then why did you give the Products Refining Company a chance to trap Moar that way?" Della Street asked.

"Because," Mason said, "after they once make promises in this case, I'm going to see these promises are kept."

"How?" she asked.

"You'd be surprised. I have a few tricks up my sleeve I can always use on chiselers."

"Is that why you didn't want to represent Moar?"

"That's partially it," he told her. "The other reason is that I don't like to represent persons who are guilty. Of course, every person is entitled to a fair trial. That means he's entitled to a lawyer. But I'd prefer that chaps like Moar would get some other lawyer. Of course, I can't *always* pick innocent ones. For one thing, I have to reach snap judgments. I'm like a baseball umpire who has to call the plays as he sees them."

"So what are you going to do now?" she asked.

"Right now," he said, "you can encode another wire to Jackson, reading as follows:

"'HAVE DRAKE DETECTIVE AGENCY PUT OPERATIVE ON ROONEY. DIG UP SOME DIRT WHICH WILL ENABLE ME TO BRING PRESSURE TO BEAR. QUIT PULLING YOUR PUNCHES AND GET RESULTS.'"

Mason grinned and said, "That'll make Jackson hopping mad."

"After all," Della Street pointed out, "you can't blame him. He's doing the best he can."

Mason shook his head. "Jackson's a rotten fighter. He's tagging along, taking what Rooney hands out. That's not the way to get anywhere. A good scrapper keeps the other man on the defensive, trumps the first ace he plays, and after that never lets him get a chance to lead with the others."

"I'm afraid," she told him, tucking her shorthand

notebook back in her purse, "that you're simply spoiling for a fight."

"I am," he admitted, "but with bigger game than Rooney."

"It's too bad you didn't know the president was in Honolulu."

Mason said, "*That's* a thought. However, he'll undoubtedly tell Rooney to go ahead and make any promises necessary to get the twenty thousand. Rooney is probably an officious nincompoop who wanted to put Jackson in his place—How's the romance going, Della?"

"Well," Della said, "outwardly it seems to be pretty much of a draw. He divides his time about evenly between Celinda Dail and Belle Newberry, but if you ask me, I think he has a lot better time with Belle than with Celinda. Celinda's more of a duty. She's in his social set. They have a lot of friends in common, and, above all, he doesn't want to appear to be dropping Celinda simply because he met some girl for whom he cares more."

"You're biased," Mason told her.

"Probably I am," she admitted.

"How does Celinda Dail treat you, Della?"

Della Street smiled. "At first she didn't know I was alive. Then when she found out I was Belle's cabin-mate, she became very cordial. Whenever I'm with her, she tells me how much she likes Belle and what a fascinating girl she is, and then takes occasion to add it's funny she's never met her and wants to know if Belle doesn't care for polo or yachting."

"Trying to pump you about her background?" Mason asked.

Della nodded.

"Okay," Mason told her, "put that message in code and send it to Jackson. We'll have Paul Drake start work on Rooney. However, I don't think we'll have to exert much pressure. My best guess is the president will fall all over himself promising anything we want. Then, after he gets his hands on the twenty thousand he'll step out of the picture and Rooney will gloatingly march into court and ask the judge to give Moar the limit."

Mason was reclining in his stateroom reading a book when Della Street brought him Jackson's reply late that afternoon:

ROONEY ADVISES CORPORATION WILL NOT MAKE TERMS WITH CROOK STOP INSISTS WILL PROSECUTE MOAR TO LIMIT WITHOUT ACCEPTING OR OFFERING ANY CONCESSIONS STOP CLAIMS HAS TAKEN MATTER UP WITH PRESIDENT BUT I THINK HE IS LYING STOP ROONEY ARROGANT SELF-IMPORTANT DETESTED BY ENTIRE FORCE HOLDS POSITION BECAUSE OF RELATIONSHIP BY MARRIAGE TO PRESIDENT OF COMPANY STOP PRESIDENT NOW ON VACATION IN HONOLULU NAME CHARLES WHITMORE DAIL ADDRESS ROYAL HAWAIIAN HOTEL SHALL I GET IN TOUCH WITH HIM THERE STOP HAD PAUL DRAKE PUT OPERATIVES TO WORK ON ROONEY SO FAR NO SUCCESS STOP WIRE INSTRUCTIONS

Mason finished reading the message, to reach for his telephone. "Get me Charles Whitmore Dail," he said to the operator. "He has a suite on A deck."

While Mason held the line, waiting for the call to be completed, Della Street said, "Chief, have you stopped to consider that Celinda Dail *may* have found out Moar's aboard and been in touch with Rooney?"

He nodded and said, "I'm calling for a show-down, Della—Hello—is this Mr. Dail? This is Mr. Perry Mason, Mr. Dail. I want to see you on a matter of business . . . sometime at your early convenience . . . I would prefer an earlier appointment if possible . . . Very well, at six o'clock then . . . In your stateroom. Thank you, Mr. Dail."

Mason dropped the receiver into place, grinned at Della Street and said, "You never get anywhere postponing a fight, Della."

"You mean if he knows all about Carl Moar and has found out who Belle really is you're still going to try and help Moar?"

"Not Moar," Mason said. "Belle."

"Is there anything you can do, Chief?"

"I don't know," he told her. "One thing's certain, I can smoke them out into the open."

Della Street said dubiously, "I'm not certain that you can, Chief. Celinda Dail is nobody's fool, if she was the one who got possession of Belle's picture and sent it to Rooney, and they know about . . ."

"Why to Rooney?" Mason asked.

"Because Jackson's wire says Rooney is related to the president by marriage. That means Celinda would have confidence in him and he'd probably be the one to whom she'd appeal. That would explain why Rooney is so set against allowing Moar to obtain any concessions by making a partial restitution."

Mason grinned and said, "Well, we'll find out within a couple of hours. Wireless Jackson that Dail's aboard and that I'll handle it from this end. Tell him to have Paul Drake keep a couple of operatives on Rooney and let me know if they uncover anything interesting."

Charles Whitmore Dail, looking ponderously dignified in his tuxedo and stiffly starched shirt, said, "Come in and sit down, Mr. Mason. I believe you have met my daughter?"

Celinda Dail wore a dark evening dress, which revealed the long, slender lines of her athletic figure. The black coral bracelets which circled her right wrist emphasized the creamy smoothness of her skin. She smiled at the lawyer with her lips. Her eyes were blue, wary and watchful.

Mason bowed, said, "I've had that pleasure. Good evening, Miss Dail," and dropped into a chair. He had not as yet dressed for dinner, and his double-breasted suit of tropical worsted, opposed to the formality of the other's attire, served as a reminder that his call was a business one, made his approach seem direct and aggressive.

27

He glanced casually about him at the furnishings of the palatial suite, stretched out his legs in front of him, crossed his ankles and said, "You're the president of the Products Refining Company."

Dail nodded.

"You have a man in your employ by the name of C. Waker Moar," Mason went on.

Dail's face became an expressionless mask. "I'm not familiar with all of the employees of the Products Refining Company," he said.

Mason regarded him with steady, patient eyes. "I didn't ask you that," he said. "I have reason to believe that the name of C. Waker Moar may have impressed itself upon your mind during the last few weeks."

Dail gave no faint flicker of expression. "What was it you wished to see me about?" he asked.

Mason glanced at Celinda Dail. "If you were planning to go in for cocktails," he said, "and it's not convenient to discuss the matter now, I can see you some time after dinner."

"That's all right," Dail said. "You can trust to my daughter's discretion. What did you wish to say?"

"I understand," Mason said, "there's a substantial cash shortage in your company, Mr. Dail, a matter of some twenty-five thousand dollars, and this shortage was, well, shall we say coincident with the departure of Mr. Moar from your employ?"

"Go on," Dail said. "I'm listening."

"I have reason to believe," Mason went on, "that it *might* be possible for your company to get back some twenty thousand dollars of the missing money."

"You're representing Moar?" Dail asked.

"No."

"Whom are you representing?"

"Interested parties," Mason said.

"Would you mind telling me just who they are?"

"Would it," Mason inquired, "make any difference in your attitude in the matter?"

"It might," Dail said.

"May I ask in what way?"

Dail hesitated a moment, then said, "I wouldn't bargain with a crook. Neither would I bargain with anyone who was representing a crook."

Mason said, "I take it your company would welcome the return of twenty thousand dollars?"

"It might."

Mason turned to Celinda, asked, "Mind if I smoke?" and took a cigarette from his pocket.

"Not at all," she said. "I'll have one with you, Mr. Mason."

Mason lit her cigarette, lit his own. Charles Whitmore Dail regarded him appraisingly. "You haven't told me, Mr. Mason, whom you're representing."

"I've told you I'm not representing Mr. Moar," Mason said.

"How can you guarantee the return of any money if you're not representing him or some confederate?"

"I'm not representing him. I'm not representing any confederate. I'm not guaranteeing the return of any money. I'm asking questions."

"Specifically, what is your question?"

"Would your company be willing to make some concessions in order to get back approximately twenty thousand dollars of the embezzled money?"

"I feel that my company would naturally like to have the spending of its own money," Dail said. "I feel quite certain that we would be willing to make some substantial concessions."

"How substantial?" Mason asked.

"What do you want?"

"For one thing," Mason said, "I want it definitely understood that no attempt whatever will be made to arrest Moar until he has surrendered of his own accord. That he will be permitted to plead guilty under any name he may choose, and be sentenced under that name."

"Do I understand," Dail asked, "that you want us to

guarantee we won't take any steps to apprehend Moar merely on your suggestion that the money may be paid?"

Mason shook his head. "You'd have my word in return for yours. I'd have approximately twenty thousand dollars paid into my bank. When that money was in my hands, I'd ask you to agree to hold off any attempt to apprehend Moar for a definite period, say two weeks."

"I think that could be arranged," Dail said, slowly.

"I understand there is as yet no warrant issued for Moar?" Mason asked.

"I'm not qualified to give you a definite answer on that," Dail replied cautiously.

"But you *could* give me your definite assurance as to what you would be willing to do in order to get this money?"

"Yes," Dail said, "we'd be willing to grant your request. We'd go farther. We'd do everything in our power to see that Moar received probation, with the understanding, of course, that he would repay the rest of the money. By the way, Mr. Mason, why do you say *approximately* twenty thousand dollars?"

"Because I don't know just how much money remains in Moar's possession."

Suspicion showed in Dail's eyes. "Your offer was predicated on twenty thousand dollars."

"It wasn't an offer, it was a question, and I said approximately twenty thousand dollars," Mason corrected.

"Well, I would take approximately to mean within a thousand dollars of that sum."

"I'm not making any definite proposition," Mason said. "I'm merely asking a question. The proposition will come later. At that time I'll know exactly what I have to offer. At the present time my understanding is there is approximately twenty thousand dollars available."

"Very well," Dail said, "you know my attitude, Mr. Mason."

Celinda Dail said, "It seems strange that you've been on

board ship with us for four days, Mr. Mason, and have just come to Father with this proposition."

Mason shifted his eyes to her. "I didn't know your father was president of the Products Refining Company."

"Are we to understand that the clients whom you represent are aboard the ship?" Celinda asked innocently.

"I think," Mason said, smiling, "that so far I have carefully avoided answering any questions about my client, other than to state that I am *not* representing Mr. Moar."

"Then your client *isn't* aboard," Celinda Dail asked.

Mason said, "You really should have been an attorney."

Dail said, "That doesn't answer my daughter's question, Mr. Mason."

Mason stared at him with amused eyes. "No," he said, "it doesn't, does it?"

There were several seconds of silence. Then Dail got to his feet. "Very well, Mr. Mason, you understand my attitude."

Mason stood looking down at the other man. "All right," he said, "now let's not misunderstand each other. Don't make any promises to me on behalf of your company which your company won't carry out to the letter. If we go through with this thing, I'll shoot square with you and I'll want your company to shoot square with me."

"Just what do you mean, Mr. Mason?" Dail asked coldy.

"I mean," Mason said, "that your auditor, C. Denton Rooney, doesn't seem to have the interests of the corporation as much at heart as you have. If we reach an agreement I wouldn't want to have him misunderstand the terms of that agreement. In fact, I would take steps to see that he didn't."

"Don't worry," Dail said. "Rooney married my wife's sister. He owes his position to that relationship and to me."

"I want to make certain there won't be any misunderstanding with Rooney," Mason insisted.

"There won't be," Dail assured him.

As Mason reached for the knob of the door, Celinda Dail said, "Don't you think, Father, it would be well to have some time limit with Mr. Mason? Some time within which he'd make you a definite offer?"

"Yes," Dail said instantly. "Let's put a time limit on this, Mason."

"Unfortunately," Mason assured him, smiling at Celinda Dail, "that is impossible. I will have to both send and receive wireless messages before I'm in a position to make any definite offer."

"But you think you can do so before the ship docks?" Dail asked.

"I hope to be able to do so before the ship docks," Mason said, opening the door.

Mason dressed for dinner, strolled into the cocktail lounge and found Mrs. Moar seated at a corner table.

"Well," he said, raising his voice for the benefit of any passenger who might be listening, "while you're waiting for your family may I invite you to join me in a cocktail?"

She nodded.

Mason dropped into the chair at her side.

"What's new?" she asked, in a low voice.

"Della told you about Dail being the president of the Products Refining Company?"

"Yes. She said you were going to see him. I've been waiting here, hoping you'd show up."

"Dail," Mason said, "wants to get his hands on the money. He's willing to promise anything. After he gets the money he'll pass the buck to the board of directors and let them assume responsibility for the double-cross."

"How can we prevent that?" she asked.

Mason said, "Let me get my hands on the money and I'll handle it in such a way there won't be any double-cross. Since I'm not representing your husband I'll have more latitude than I otherwise would."

"Was Celinda present when you talked with her father?"

"Yes, Celinda was there."

"I don't like that," Mrs. Moar said. "I don't like that girl. She's nursing a deadly hatred for Belle."

"All right," Mason told her. "The thing to do now is to get some quick action. Find out how much money your husband has left, and get it in my hands. You can tell your husband what's being done, but don't tell him who's representing you."

"You won't want him to talk with you?"

"No, I want to have no connection with him whatsoever. My connection is with you."

"And how'll you get the money?"

"He'll give it to you and you'll give it to me. And when I get it, I don't want to know that it's embezzled money. It'll simply be money which you have given me to pay over to the Products Refining Company under certain conditions. It must be your money, as between you and me. Do you understand that? I don't want it to come from your husband. I don't want it to be money which was embezzled from the Products Refining Company. I want it to be your money which you are giving to me to accomplish a certain specific thing. Do you understand?"

"I think so," she said. "Look, Mr. Mason, there's Celinda Dail watching us."

Mason laughed heartily, picked up his cocktail glass, tilted the brim slightly toward Mrs. Moar as though proposing a toast and said in a low voice, "All right, don't look so businesslike, and above all, don't look apprehensive. Laugh and act as though we were having a casual cocktail."

Mrs. Moar raised her glass. Her smile was patently forced.

"Have you," Mason asked, "discussed this any further with your husband?"

"No."

"Does your husband realize that Dail is president of the Products Refining Company?"

"Apparently not. Carl has made no attempt to avoid him. We've walked right past Mr. Dail and Celinda several times when we've been promenading the deck. But Carl's taken every precaution to avoid that nurse. I think he has someone paid to watch her and let him know whenever she's coming on deck because he always goes into hiding somewhere and doesn't come out until after she's gone."

"Well," Mason said, "the Products Refining Company is a big concern. It's not surprising that the president of that company wouldn't know a bookkeeper, but you'd think Carl would have seen his picture, or heard his name mentioned often enough to know who he was."

"Perhaps he does," she said, "but feels safe because he knows Dail doesn't know him except by name, whereas that nurse knows his real name is Moar, and would probably blurt it out if he met her."

"Don't look so businesslike," Mason warned. "Celinda's watching you. Laugh. Look around the room, and, pretty quick, look at your wrist watch, jump up and leave the table. Here, turn around so you're not prompted to look over at her.

"Now here's something else. It would be particularly unfortunate if Carl should be recognized now. Until I've reached an agreement with Dail *his* hands aren't tied. If he found out the man he's looking for was aboard this ship and had funds in his possession, Dail would have him arrested and laugh at me when I tried to get any concessions."

"Then it would be better if Carl didn't have the money in his possession?" she asked.

"Much better," Mason said.

She glanced at her wrist watch, jumped to her feet and said, "Oh, I must be going."

Mason arose, bowed, and said, in a low tone, "Laugh."

Mrs. Moar gave a feeble attempt at laughter, turned and swept from the room.

Mason sat down at the table, twisted the stem of his cocktail glass in his fingers, glanced up at the door where Celinda Dail had been standing. She was no longer visible.

Chapter 4

Sunday afternoon, a wind, howling up from the south and west, caught the ship on the quarter, sent smoke from the funnels streaking down the sky, and kicked up a sea which made for a nasty roll. The weather deck was lashed by torrents of rain, while oily smoke and hot gas from the funnels made the deck untenable.

Mason, threading his way down the creaking corridor of C deck, confronted Belle Newberry as she swayed along the passageway, bracing herself from time to time with her hands.

"Hello," she said. "I've been looking for you."

"Long?" the lawyer asked.

"All day."

"I've been in my cabin, reading. Why didn't you give me a buzz?"

She laughed, and said, "I wanted the meeting to appear casual."

"And so you start out by telling me you've been looking for me?" he inquired, smiling.

She made a little grimace. "It's my candid nature. It's always betraying me. I hate sham and hypocrisy. Come on into the social hall, I want to talk to you."

Mason turned, took her arm, and, together, they swayed toward the stern of the ship. "Nasty weather for the captain's dinner tonight," Mason said.

"I think it's fun," she told him. "I get an awful bang out of it. If you go on deck and stand in a sheltered place, you can hear the wind howling around the masks. I thought it was only in windjammers you heard that sound."

Mason said, "There's quite a bit of rigging on a steamer these days. Did it frighten you?"

"No, I think it's wonderful! There's something fascinating and awe-inspiring about it. It's a long-drawn-out, steady, hollow sound. You can't describe it."

"I know the sound," Mason said, "and never tire of listening to it. I like storms."

Belle Newberry's eyes sparkled. "You *would*," she said.

Mason said, "I think that's a compliment, Belle. But you didn't search me out to talk about storms, did you?"

"No. It's about Mother."

"What about her?" Mason asked.

"What's she been telling you about Dad?"

"What makes you think that she's told me anything about your father?" Mason asked.

She waited for an advantageous roll of the ship, then pushed him into a deep-cushioned chair. "Sit down," she said, "and like it. I see this is going to be one of those interviews where I'll ask you questions and you'll answer with questions."

"After all," Mason told her, "if you want information, you *could* ask your mother."

"I could," she said, "but I'm not doing it."

"Why not?"

"Because she . . . Wait a minute, I almost gave you a straight answer. I shouldn't do it. I'll have to think up a question. . . . *Why* should I ask my mother?"

"Who else is there to ask?" he inquired.

"Would you tell me if you knew?"

"Is there any reason why I shouldn't?"

She laughed and said, "That's fine. No one's said anything yet. How long do you suppose we can keep this up?"

"All afternoon," Mason told her, his lips unsmiling, but his eyes twinkling.

"That's what I was afraid of. Tell me, Mr. Mason, did Mother tell you about Dad's giving up his job and never going back to the office?"

"What gave you that impression?" Mason asked.

"Well, you see," she said, "Moms is nice, but rather naïve, as so many of the older generation are. The last few days, whenever she's been standing by the rail and talking to you, there's been a sudden silence when I come along. Now, that's poor technique. As one of the precocious younger generation, I know you're discussing something you don't want me to hear, and I think it concerns Dad and our sudden influx of wealth."

"Will you kindly tell me what has put *that* idea in your head?" Mason asked.

She sighed and said, "Yes, I guess you can keep it up all afternoon. I'm trying to question you, Mr. Perry Mason, but so far you're asking all the questions in response to my questions, and I'm giving all the information in response to your questions."

"But," Mason protested, "I don't see why you came to me in the first place. Was there something? . . ."

"No," she interrupted, "please don't ask me any more questions. I see that I'd better handle the interview myself if I'm going to get anywhere. Now, I'll say, 'Is Mother trying to keep something from me, Mr. Mason?' and you'll say, 'What do you think there is to conceal from you, Belle?' and I'll say, 'Something about Dad,' and you'll say, 'But what could there be about your father which should be concealed from you?' and I'll say, 'Well, after all, Mr. Mason, he *has* done some rather peculiar things during the last two months. That is, they look peculiar if you don't know Dad,' and you'll say 'What things?' and I'd say, 'Hasn't Mother told you?' and you'd . . . No, don't interrupt me now, Mr. Mason, because I'm driving you into a corner by relentless cross-examination. And you'd say, 'Don't you think you should ask your mother rather than me?' and then that, Mr. Perry Mason, would give me just the opening I'm looking for and I'd say, 'Mr. Mason, don't *you* think that, in justice to all concerned, *you* should hear Dad's side of the story?' and before you could ask me another question I'd say, 'Well, *I* do, and I'm going to arrange for you to have a talk with Dad. Personally, I think Moms is all wet. Dad is peculiar and he's eccentric, but he's done nothing to be ashamed of, and there's no need of Moms getting herself all worked up thinking that he has.' So, Mr. Perry Mason, I'm going to ask you to talk with Dad and hear his side of it before you form any opinion or agree to do anything for Mother."

"Don't you think your father might be rather prejudiced against me?" Mason asked.

"Absolutely not," she said. "He has about the sanest perspective of any man I've ever known. He knows you've been talking a lot with Mom and . . ."

"And your father," Mason interrupted, "has rather studiously avoided me. I've gathered from what your mother has said that he's prejudiced against lawyers."

"Now that shows all Mom knows about it," Belle exclaimed indignantly. "Dad used to be prejudiced against what he called criminal lawyers, but that was before he served as a juror when a man was being tried for murder. The man was innocent, Dad says, but his lawyer, a man named Van Densie, seemed to have sold him out. But they couldn't fool Dad. Dad held out for an acquittal, even when the other eleven were against him. And Dad finally managed to convince those other eleven jurors that the man really was innocent. It made quite an impression on Dad. He said anyone might be accused of crime and circumstantial evidence might look black against him. He said the lawyers who defended men should be more able. He thought Van Densie was incompetent, as well as being a crook. Dad was all worked up about it. He said some day *he* might be accused of crime, and he'd want a good lawyer to represent him."

Mason said, "Apparently your father has a mind of his own."

"Then you'll see him," she asked, "and hear what he has to say?"

Mason said, "Look here, Belle, I'm going to be frank with you. I don't want to see your father and don't want to talk with him."

"Why?"

"I can't explain."

Her eyes searched his. "Does it," she asked, "have anything to do with my happiness?"

"I think," Mason told her, "since you've gone so far, I'd prefer to have you talk with your mother."

"Look here, Mr. Mason," she said, "I'm not a child. I know something's in the wind. I have an idea it affects me. Now, Dad won some money in a lottery. If that was an illegal thing to do, then he has to give back the money. But I'd prefer—very much prefer—not to have anything said or done until after the ship docks. I think you know why."

"I do," Mason told her, "and I want you to understand that your mother has your best interests at heart."

Her eyes swam with tears. "I wish," she said, "things had been different. I wouldn't have missed knowing Roy for anything. But you know what it means, Mr. Mason. He's out of my class. I've had my little masquerade and that masquerade is about over. I've realized all along the price I was going to have to pay, but I know it has to be paid. Now then, I'm afraid that Carl, or Moms, or both, are planning to carry on, thinking they can give me a chance. They can't. I'm not in Roy's world and he's not in mine. We could pretend while we're on shipboard, or while we were in Honolulu, but as soon as we hit the Mainland it's different. . . . Tell me, Mr. Mason, is Moms planning to sue Carl for divorce?"

"That isn't what we've been talking about," Mason said kindly.

Belle Newberry scraped back her chair. The roll of the boat threw her off balance. Mason jumped to her side, steadied her with his hand on her elbow.

"Please," she said, "don't let Mom make any useless sacrifices for me. She doesn't see the thing as clearly as I do. Tomorrow morning after we land it will be over."

"Don't you think Roy will try to keep in touch with you?" Mason asked.

"I won't let him," she retorted. "I'll walk out of his life and slam the door behind me. We can't keep up with his set. I've been able to put on an act just because Dad was fortunate enough to win some money in a lottery. If it hadn't been for that, I'd have been living a drab existence with perhaps a two weeks' vacation with Moms at some beach city, where we'd have a cheap furnished cottage, or maybe a motor trip where we could spend the nights in auto camps. . . . *Please*, Mr. Mason, don't let Moms try to do something to give me a chance I could never use."

Mason walked with her to the door. "You," he said, "talk like a quitter. If you want him, why don't you fight for him? If he loves you, he won't care whether your father was a bookkeeper or . . ."

"You don't understand," she interrupted. "It isn't as though Roy had met me as the daughter of a bookkeeper. Pops gave me a chance to crash into the ritzy tourist crowd. You know how it is on the Islands. I played I was one of them. I let Roy take my position in life for granted. You see, I . . . I didn't know he was going to mean so darn much to me.

"Now I can't back it up. If I'd met him so he knew all about me, he *could* go to his set and say, 'Meet Belle Newberry. She's not in our set, but I like her.' That would have been one thing. But to have Celinda Dail know all about . . . Oh, I can't explain. You'd have to know Roy to understand . . . He doesn't like sham. He hates girls who try to make a play for him. He'd never understand I was just having a little game of makebelieve with myself. He'd think I'd deliberately planned . . ."

She broke off abruptly, her voice choking.

Mason said, "I see your angle, Belle. It's your hand. You play it. Personally, I'd shove all my chips into the center of the table. Go talk with your mother, Belle. You can explain . . ."

The eyes which she turned up to him were laughing through tears. "No," she said, "*you* do it. This is my last night of happiness. I'm leaving it up to you, Perry Mason, to do the dirty work."

She turned and walked rapidly down the swaying corridor, steadying herself from time to time with an outstretched hand, Mason stood watching her with sympathetic eyes.

Chapter 5

There were many vacant chairs at the captain's dinner. Sheeted rain lashed against the portholes. Those passengers who made merry with colored paper cups, balloons and pasteboard horns lacked spontaneity. Their merriment seemed merely a forced attempt to comply with maritime conventions. Waiters felt their way, a few steps at a time, half-filled dishes carried in deep serving trays.

Mason, dining with Della Street, looked across to where Carl Newberry and his wife and daughter were entertaining Roy Hungerford.

"Isn't it about time you were getting something definite from them?" Della Street asked.

"Yes," Mason said, "I've warned Mrs. Newberry I must know where I stand before ten o'clock tonight. She told me to be in her cabin at nine-thirty and she'd have the money for me. Then I can go to Dail and make my proposition."

"Moar—or I guess I should remember to call him Newberry—doesn't seem particularly concerned," Della Street said.

"No," Mason admitted. "He seems to be having a good time. It's fortunate for him that Evelyn Whiting has all of her meals in the stateroom with her patient."

"Chief," she said, "I have an idea Newberry's reached an understanding with that woman."

"What makes you think so?"

"I saw him coming out of her stateroom yesterday afternoon, and he was smiling."

"You're certain it was Newberry?"

She nodded.

42

"Perhaps," Mason said, "that's why he's acting so carefree now. I've been wondering how he was going to manage it when the passengers went through customs and quarantine tomorrow. He's almost certain to meet her face to face."

"I think he's figured that all out. After all, all he needed to do was   go to her, make some explanation and ask her to keep quiet."

"The only trouble with that," Mason pointed out, "is that she might indulge in gossip with some shipboard acquaintance and let the cat out of the bag. If Celinda Dail had any idea Evelyn Whiting knew anything about Belle's father, she'd certainly move heaven and earth to find out what it was."

Della Street said, "Belle, poor kid, realizes she could never fit into Roy's life."

"Don't you think he'll try to keep in touch with her just the same?" Mason asked.

"He won't have the chance, Chief. She's going to tell him she'll meet him at the Santa Anita Race Track next Tuesday. She told him her folks have a box there. She'll never see him after she gets off the boat."

Mason said, "If she's in love with him I don't see . . ."

"I understand *exactly* how she feels," Della Street interrupted. "Taking things in her stride, mingling with him on terms of equality, she's been able to interest him. But the minute he realizes she's not in his set, the minute his friends start patronizing her, he'll begin to lose interest in her. She and the Dail girl have been running neck and neck. Give Celinda Dail the handicap of being able to patronize Belle, and Belle will be entirely out of the running."

"I'm not so certain," Mason said.

"Well, I am," Della Street told him. "That Dail girl is clever. She won't rub it in. Instead, she'll try and drag Belle out to all sorts of affairs where Belle will be among strangers but everyone else will know each other with that intimacy which comes of years of rubbing elbows and

43

taking each other for granted. Belle will be completely out of place."

"Well," Mason said, "I think Belle should tell her mother exactly what she plans to do."

"Why?"

"Because," he said, "if Belle's going to step out of Roy's life, there's no reason why I should go to a lot of trouble trying to fix things up with the Products Refining Company."

"Oh, yes, there is," Della told him. "It would be the greatest tragedy of Belle's life if detectives should meet her father at the gangplank tomorrow and snap handcuffs on his wrists. And particularly if he had embezzled money from a company operated by Celinda Dail's father. Chief, you *must* stop that, no matter what happens. Can't you see? She wants Roy to remember her as a woman of mystery, not pity her. And she could never bear to have Celinda Dail gloating in triumph over her."

"Well," Mason said, "I'll meet Mrs. Newberry at nine-thirty. She'll have a definite answer by that time. I'm going to take a turn on deck. How'd you like to go out and get a lungful of storm?"

"No," she told him, "I'm going over and join the Newberrys for a minute. I promised Belle I would. It's eight-thirty-five now. I'll hunt you up around nine o'clock. That'll give us time for a *liqueur* and then you can meet Mrs. Newberry at nine-thirty."

Mason nodded, crossed over to pull back her chair, gave her arm a squeeze and said, "I'll be over on the lee side, probably on the promenade deck."

Mason went to his stateroom, put on a top coat, wound a light silk scarf around his collar, and went on deck.

Doors on the weather side were locked. On the lee deck, rain lashed down in torrents, spurting up into little geysers, where the big drops hit the planking. Electric lights, burning in glass-enclosed cages, shed reddish rays which reflected upward from the wet deck, and were swallowed in the enveloping maw of wind-swept darkness. The roar of troubled waters furnished a steady, ominous undertone of sound.

Mason found the promenade deck a little too exposed, so went to the deck below. He walked slowly, skirting a pile of deck chairs which had been folded back and lashed securely. Water soaked up through the thin soles of his dress shoes. Spray from the beating rain moistened his face and beaded his hair. He squared his shoulders, inhaled the driving freshness of the ocean gale, listened to the roar of the waves, the shrieking of the wind—and was content.

The ship's bells clanged twice—nine o'clock. The wind whipped the sound and dispersed it, just as it snatched the smoke from the stacks of the steamer, tore it into black ribbons, and dissolved them into the night. On the port beam, a lighthouse winked intermittently.

The ship, rolling heavily, swung far over to port, paused, then, instead of righting itself, rolled still farther, until Mason, clinging to a stanchion for support, could look down the slanting deck to the dark, tossing waves.

He heard a faint scream, then an explosive sound. He stood still, listening. The scream was repeated. It seemed to come from two decks above him.

As the ship slowly righted, Mason ran to the rail, leaned over, and tried to peer upward. The rain flooded his eyes, beat down upon his coat, trickled in rivulets along his neck and down the angle of his jaw. He could see nothing.

The ship sluggishly swung over to starboard. The waves, as though concentrating in a surprise attack, crashed against her quivering hull. Mason heard the faint jangling of a bell somewhere, then the whistle blew five short, quick blasts. The ship heeled far over and was filled with thumping jars, as though it had been an automobile running on a flat tire.

Mason realized one screw had been reversed, while the other was going full speed ahead, swinging the ship in a quick turn.

Feet pounded along the boat deck. Mason saw a circular life buoy whirl out into the darkness. It struck the water, and almost immediately the inky darkness was dispelled by a bright flare of light which drifted back and to one side as the ship turned.

The big seas now struck on the beam. The ship rolled in the troughs. Mason held to a stanchion, then fought his way back to the door, which suddenly burst open. A uniformed officer shouted, "Get back inside!"

"What's the matter?" Mason asked.

"Man overboard!" the officer yelled, and ran forward, clinging to a hand rail to keep from slipping on the wet, slanting deck.

Mason stamped water from his soggy shoes, ran to the stairway and started down it.

He made straight for Mrs. Newberry's stateroom. The ship had turned enough to catch the huge seas on her bow, making the craft pitch and plunge.

Mason pounded on the door of the stateroom. There was no answer. He tried the knob. The door was locked. He banged with his fist, then, when there was no response, kicked with the toe of his shoe.

After a moment, he heard Mrs. Newberry's voice. "Who is it?"

"Mason," he said.

"Just a minute," she told him. "I'll let you in."

Mason rattled the doorknob. "Open the door now," he ordered.

She unlocked and opened the door, said, "Oh, well, come in if it's *that* important."

She was clad in stockings and peach-colored underwear. As Mason closed and locked the door, she slipped a dress over her head. "What is it?" she asked.

"Where's your husband?"

She wiggled the dress down from her shoulders, smoothed it across her hips, frowned at the lawyer, and said, "He had to see a man. He promised he'd be back in five minutes. What's the matter with your watch? It's not nine-thirty yet."

"How long since you've seen him?"

"Five minutes ago. Our party broke up when my husband received a note. He said he had to see a man on some business."

"And what did you do?"

"Came to my stateroom. I slipped my gown off, because I'd spilled some wine on it. Carl and I are going to have a show-down. He'll be back any minute— What's all the commotion about? The ship's jumping around so I can hardly stand up. We haven't run into anything have we? Look, there's a light over there on the water! And look at the searchlights!"

Mason nodded, watched her while she hooked up her dress, and said, "I'm particularly interested in finding out about where your husband went and what he did."

"Look here, Mr. Mason," she said, facing him, "I've been married twice. I'm not exactly a prude. But I'm not accustomed to having men burst into my room while I'm dressing. I let you in because your voice indicated you wanted to talk with me on a matter of the greatest importance. Now, if you'll please explain . . ."

Mason said, "I heard the sound of a shot. An officer tells me there's a man overboard. Does that mean anything to you?"

For a moment she stared at him with wide, frightened eyes, then she crossed to the drawer of a dresser, jerked it open and stood looking down at the empty interior.

"What is it?" Mason asked.

"Carl's gun," she said. "It's gone."

"Now let's get this straight," Mason said. "You and Carl were going to have a show-down?"

"Yes."

"Did you tell him what you wanted to talk with him about?"

"I told him that I wasn't going to stand for a lot of vague generalities any longer; that I wanted to know exactly where he obtained that money, and that I wanted him to turn it over to me."

"What did he say?"

"He said we'd talk it over later."

"He wouldn't discuss it then?"

"No. You see, just as we were finishing dinner, a bellboy handed him a note. Carl said he had to see a man on some business. That broke up our little dinner party. Carl and I came to the stateroom. I told him I was going to have things out with him, that for Belle's sake I wanted that money. He said he'd be back within five minutes, but he simply had to see someone on a matter of the greatest importance."

"There was a gun in that drawer?"

"Yes."

"When did you see it last?"

"This afternoon."

"It was Carl's gun?"

"Yes."

"How long has he had it?"

"About two months. When he started carrying large sums of money with him, he thought he needed a gun for protection."

Mason said, "I happen to know that your husband has been in touch with Evelyn Whiting, the nurse. I think he's tried to reach some agreement with her so she wouldn't disclose his real identity. I don't know what *she* told *him*. It's a fine situation for blackmail—if she's that type. Do you suppose he could have gone to meet her—and taken a gun with him?"

"I don't know."

Her hand clutched his arm. "Mr. Mason," she said, "I want you to promise me that you'll stand by me, will you? Please, for Belle's sake."

Mason hesitated a moment, then said, "Okay, I'll see you through. Now, let me ask you some more questions before Carl gets here. Just how much have you told him?"

"I told him that Mr. Dail, the president of the Products Refining Company, was aboard. It seems that wasn't any news to him. I told him Mr. Dail was willing to make some concessions if Carl made restitution. He told me I was absolutely crazy. He said that if I ever approached Dail with any proposition like that, he'd kill me. He said he hadn't taken a cent from the Products Refining Company. So then I told him that Celinda Dail was looking for an opportunity to expose Belle . . . and that made him furious."

"What else?" Mason asked.

"That's all," she said. "That's all I had time to tell him."

"Was that after he received this note, or before?"

Afterwards. We had left the others and entered the stateroom. I talked to him for just a minute or two. Then I stepped into the closet to get out another dress and I heard him slam the door."

"And he told you he had to see a man?"

"Yes. He said he'd be back in five minutes and have it out with me."

Mason said, "I think we'd better go on deck and find out what's happened. You're certain Carl took the gun?"

"Yes. I heard him slam the drawer in the dresser. I didn't realize what it meant at the time. If . . . if somebody's overboard, can they find him—her?"

"It's a pretty slim gamble," Mason told her. "There's a heavy sea running. They *might* swing the ship broadside to the wind and launch boats in the lee, but I don't think they'll do it until they have something definite to go on. They'll play searchlights on the water, throw flares overboard, and keep a sharp lookout. They certainly won't risk men's lives in an open boat unless there's some indication the person's still alive—and don't forget that a shot was fired."

"Do you suppose it could be Mr. Dail?" she asked. "Oh, Heavens! Carl wouldn't have done that!"

"There's no use speculating," Mason told her. "Let's get on deck. I want to find Carl."

"And you'll stand by me?" she asked.

"I'll stand by you for Belle's sake. But I'm *not* going to represent your husband."

She nodded. "Come on, let's go."

As they were opening the door, Mrs. Newberry suddenly gave a gasp of dismay.

Mason turned to her. "What is it?" he asked.

"I just thought of something," she said, in a voice which was hardly above a whisper.

"Go ahead," Mason told her, "talk fast. What is it?"

"Carl," she said. "Carl knew we were having a show-down. He knew he couldn't keep up the pretense any longer, and he knew that Belle's happiness depended . . . Oh, Mr. Mason, you don't suppose he went up on deck and . . . and . . ."

"Committed suicide?" Mason asked.

She nodded.

"What do *you* think?" Mason asked.

"I don't know," she said. "I'm afraid . . . That would leave Belle in the clear, wouldn't it?"

"What do you mean?"

"They couldn't do anything about that embezzlement, could they?"

"They can't arrest a dead man, if that's what you mean."

"Well, that's what I meant."

"If Carl left any money, they could go after that."

"How about the insurance? Could they touch it?"

"How much insurance?"

"Fifty thousand."

"In whose favor?"

"Mine."

"Taken out when?"

"Two months ago."

Mason said, "Look here, Mrs. Newberry, if it should appear your husband had embezzled money, would you want to make reimbursement to the company out of the insurance?"

"No, not unless I had to."

"I asked the question," Mason said drily, "to get your viewpoint. The policy doubtless contains a clause making it void if suicide takes place within one year from the date of the policy."

There was dismay in her eyes. "You're sure?"

"Yes."

"Come on, Mr. Mason, let's go up on deck. *Please* stay with me."

Mason opened the stateroom door. They started down the corridor and were nearing the stairs when Della Street swung around the corner and almost ran into them. A cloak over her shoulders dripped rivulets of water. Beneath the edge of a beret, tendrils of hair were plastered to the sides of her head.

"I've been looking all over for you, Chief," she said.

"I was up on deck," he told her, "but a man fell overboard and I came . . ."

"I know," she interrupted. "Good Lord, I was frightened! You said you'd be up on the promenade deck, and I couldn't find you. I suppose you dashed down to Mrs. Newberry?"

"Yes," he said.

She raised her eyes to his significantly. "I wanted to see you *first*, Chief."

An officer came running along the corridor. "Will the passengers kindly go to their cabins at once," he called out, "and stay there until you're summoned. A man's overboard. We're doing everything that can be done. Passengers will simply be in the way. The purser is making a roll call, to find out who's missing."

Mason took Mrs. Newberry's arm and turned her back toward the cabin. "After all," he said, "that's probably the best thing to do."

"But I can't stand this suspense," she told him. "I can't simply wait in the cabin."

Mason lowered his voice and said, "You don't want Belle to be known as the daughter of an embezzler, do you?"

"No. Of course not."

"How would you like it," Mason asked, "if she were the daughter of a murderer?"

"But I don't understand . . ."

"Can't you see?" Mason interrupted. "You don't dare do

anything which would attract attention to Carl. So far as you're concerned, you're going to act just like any other passenger."

She hesitated a moment, then turned and started back toward the cabin. Della Street crowded close to Perry Mason. "Are you going to represent her?" she asked. "If she's mixed up in what happened on deck?"

Mason nodded. "*She* isn't mixed up in anything. I won't represent her husband, but I'll see her through."

"I wish you hadn't told her that," Della said.

Mrs. Newberry paused at the sound of their whispered voices. "Is there," she asked, turning toward them anxiously, "anything I should know? Anything you're keeping from me?"

Della Street smiled reassuringly and said, "No."

Mason held the cabin door open and was about to go in the room after them, when he heard running steps, and Belle Newberry, holding the skirt of her evening dress up over her arm, came running into the corridor, staggered, swayed, was flung against the wall as the ship rolled, pushed herself upright, and came running once more.

"Oh, Mr. Mason!" she called. "Is Mother in there?"

Mason nodded, held the door open for her, and, when she had entered, closed it. "Oh, Moms," Belle said, "someone's overboard! I was so frightened. I thought perhaps . . . Where's Pops, Mumsy? . . . I'm sopping wet, I ran out looking for him and couldn't find him!"

"Oh, he'll be along in a minute," Mrs. Newberry said. "Where is he *now?*"

"He went up to see someone—at the bar probably."

"But, Mumsy, someone's overboard. He went upstairs, and I've dashed madly all over the ship, out on deck, and . . ."

Mrs. Newberry said, "Now, don't be a foolish little girl, Belle. You know your father wouldn't go out on deck in this weather, and, if he did, he'd be far too careful to fall overboard. It's probably someone from the second class or the steerage, someone who'd been drinking too much."

"Well, where *is* Pops? He should be here. They're sending all passengers back to their staterooms."

"Exactly," Mrs. Newberry remarked, taking a carved ivory cigarette case from her purse. "And Carl is lost in the jam of people on the stairways. You know perfectly well he's not one to elbow his way. No, thank you, Mr. Mason, I have a match. Don't bother."

She scratched a match with a deft motion and held it to the cigarette. Her hand trembled slightly.

Belle Newberry, standing in the doorway, said, "I wish Pops would come . . . *Good Lord, where's Roy?*"

"In his stateroom, probably," Mason said.

"I'll be back," she told them, and dashed out into the corridor.

Mrs. Newberry came over to join Mason and Della Street in front of the porthole. Searchlights sent beams crisscrossing out over the water. Floating flares tossed up and down on the angry waves. Mrs. Newberry put her hand on Mason's shoulder. "I can't bear to think of any human being out in that awful ocean. I . . ." She broke off, choked back a sob and walked away.

Mason continued to stand at the porthole, staring moodily out at the tossing water. His legs, spread wide apart, braced his body against the motion of the ship.

With the slowing engines, sounds had been intensified, the creak of the ship, the rush of waves against the sides, the pound of feet running along the decks.

Della Street walked across the stateroom, to look down the corridor, and said, "The captain and the purser are coming this way, Chief. . . . Here's Belle. . . . Was he all right, Belle?"

Belle Newberry nodded breathlessly. ". . . Lord, what a scare! . . . Yes. . . . He's sitting in his stateroom. . . . *Where's Dad, Moms?*"

Her mother said, "He'll be along any minute, Belle."

The captain and the purser pushed past Della Street and into the cabin.

53

"I'm sorry," the captain said, "I'm performing an unpleasant duty. You people know why we've turned around, don't you?"

"We'd heard there was a man overboard," Mrs. Newberry said.

"Yes," the captain said. "When did you last see your husband, Mrs. Newberry?"

"Why, I left him right after dinner."

"Where?"

"He came to the stateroom with me, then left almost immediately. Why, Captain? Tell me, you don't . . . Have you . . . That is . . ."

The captain said grimly, "We think your husband's missing. Do you know anything about it?"

"Why, what do you mean?"

The captain glanced at the purser. "Mrs. Newberry, are you *absolutely* certain you haven't seen your husband since he left this stateroom?"

"Why, yes, of course."

"And you came directly here to your stateroom after you left the dining saloon?"

"That's right."

"Do you know where your husband went?"

"I think . . . I think he went up to the bar to see a man. I don't know."

"You didn't go with him?"

"No."

"You didn't go up on deck with him?"

"Certainly not."

Once more, the captain exchanged glances with the purser. "I remember when your party left the table, Mrs. Newberry. It was about eight-fifty, wasn't it?"

"A little later than that, I would say," she said. "About eight-fifty-five."

"I think I can help you there, Captain," Della Street interposed. "Mr. Mason left the dining room at eight-thirty-five. I then went over to the Newberry table. I was there for fifteen minutes. When the party broke up, I glanced at my watch, and it was eight-fifty-two."

"Any particular reason for looking at your watch?" the captain asked.

"Yes. Mr. Mason was on deck, and I was to join him at nine o'clock."

"Did you leave the dining saloon with the Newberrys?"

"No," Della said, "I chatted with them for a while, then Mr. Newberry received a note from a bellboy. He said he had to see a man on a business matter. The party broke up then. I went to my stateroom."

"What did *you* do?" the captain asked.

Her eyes showed surprise. "Why," she said, "I put on a rain coat and beret, and went up to try and find Mr. Mason."

"And *he* was on deck?"

"Yes."

The captain regarded Mason thoughtfully for a few moments, then turned back to Mrs. Newberry. "I notice you've changed your dress, Mrs. Newberry."

Her eyes flashed indignation. "Will you kindly tell me," she demanded, "what business that is of yours, and if you know anything about my husband please say so."

The captain said doggedly, "I want to know why you changed your dress."

"I shall report you for impertinence," she said coldly.

The captain hesitated for a moment, then blurted, "I'm going to inspect your closet, Mrs. Newberry—with your permission."

"Well," she snapped, "of all the nerve! I most certainly *won't* give you permission."

"I'm sorry," the captain said, "because I'm going to search it anyway."

Mason stepped toward the closet door, regarding the captain with puzzled eyes. "Just a minute, Captain. I think we're entitled to know exactly what it is you're looking for.

After all, the law makes a person's property safe from unreasonable search."

The captain said shortly, "I don't care to hear any law, Mr. Mason. This is my ship. On board it *I'm* the law. I'm responsible for what I do. I'm going to look in that closet. Get back out of the way."

For a moment Mason and the captain locked eyes, the captain's weatherbeaten countenance showed dogged determination, Mason's granite-hard features devoid of expression. Then Mason stepped to one side and said, "You're taking the responsibility for this, Captain."

"I'm taking the responsibility."

Mrs. Newberry flung herself toward the closet. "You can't do it! It's an outrage! Mr. Mason, why don't you stop him?"

The lawyer, trained from years of courtroom experience to make lightning-fast appraisals of character, said simply, "I can't stop him, Mrs. Newberry. He's going to search that closet."

She stood with her back against the closet door, her arms outspread. "Well," she said, "*I* can stop him!"

The lawyer stared at her intently until her defiant eyes shifted to his.

"If anything significant should be in that closet, you're not helping things any," he warned.

"I don't know what he's looking for, and I don't care," she blazed. "It's the principle of the thing. The captain should be out on deck, saving the man who's fallen overboard, instead of snooping through my things!"

The captain said, "I'm going to search that closet." He moved forward. "Will you get away from that door, Madam?"

Mason said, "Captain, will you please tell us *what* you expect to find in that closet?"

The captain shook his head. "It's something I'm not going to discuss until I've seen if it's in there."

"Let's get it over with," Mason advised Mrs. Newberry.

Slowly, and reluctantly, she moved away from the door, and came to stand at Mason's side, her right hand resting on his arm. Mason, watching the captain, could feel her hand tremble. "He'd have done it anyway," Mason said in an undertone. "It looks better this way. What's the matter?"

"Nothing," she said defiantly. "I hate to be shoved around, that's all."

The captain opened the closet door, fumbled around for a moment, then dropped to his knees to look on the floor. A moment later he backed out of the closet, straightened, and held up a wet black lace evening gown in one hand, a pair of wet black satin shoes in the other.

"This is the gown you wore at dinner, Mrs. Newberry?" he asked. "And these are your shoes?"

She hesitated a moment, then said, "Yes."

"And since you didn't go out on deck, how did these articles get wet?"

Mason stepped forward and said, "You'll pardon me, Captain, but here's where I take a hand. What difference does it make whether she went up on deck or whether she went to her stateroom? As I see it, there's no reason why she should be called upon to account for *her* actions."

"I'm sorry, Mr. Mason," the captain said, his eyes never shifting from Mrs. Newberry's countenance, "but there are things about this you don't know about."

"Would it," Mason inquired, "be asking too much if I asked you to tell me what they are?"

"Yes," the captain said, "it would. Will you kindly explain, Mrs. Newberry, how it happened that your dress became soaking wet?"

Mason said, "All right, Captain, you were supreme in your field; I'm supreme in mine. As master of this ship, you took the responsibility of searching that closet. Now then, as Mrs. Newberry's attorney, I'm taking the responsibility of telling you this has gone far enough. If you want Mrs. Newberry to co-operate with you, you'll tell her exactly what you're after and why you're after it."

"I've asked a question," the captain said, his eyes fixed on Mrs. Newberry, "I'm going to have an answer."

Mrs. Newberry, standing very erect, said, "I haven't the slightest intention of answering."

The captain nodded to the purser. "We'll look the place over, Mr. Buchanan."

"I take it," Mason observed, "that means you're going to make a further search."

"It does," the captain said shortly.

Mason circled Mrs. Newberry with his arm, the fingers gripping her wrist. Her flesh was cold to his touch. "Take it easy," he cautioned.

Belle Newberry said, "Well, *I'm* not going to take it easy! I think this is an outrage and an insult to Mother and to me. I demand an explanation! And I want to know what you know about my father and why you think he's missing."

"I'm sorry," the captain said, facing her, "this thing may not have been an accident. Now do you understand?"

"You mean . . . that . . ."

Mason said, "Let's get this straight, Captain. Are you insinuating that Mr. Newberry may have committed suicide?"

The captain's eyes met those of Perry Mason. "I mean," he said, "that we have information leading us to believe Carl Newberry was murdered."

Mrs. Newberry stifled a half scream. Belle moved to her mother's side.

Mason said, "Wouldn't it be better, Captain, if you were to concentrate your efforts on trying to find the man who has gone overboard and postpone making this unwarranted search until later?"

"I'm doing everything in my power," the captain said. "A man doesn't stand much chance in this sea. I have a boat in readiness, with a volunteer crew at their stations. I'm not going to risk lives needlessly. We're going back over our course. We've thrown out flares and life buoys. I don't think there's one chance in a thousand. I've told the first officer what to do, and he's doing it. This investigation I'm making here is something I have to do myself. If you people will co-operate, it'll be easier. If you won't co-operate, I'm going ahead anyway, Now, if you will stand over there near the porthole, I'm going to search this cabin."

He herded them into the corner by the porthole.

Methodically, carefully, the captain and the purser opened drawers, checked the contents, looked in bags and trunks. The purser raised the mattress of one of the twin beds. The captain said, "Wait a minute, Mr. Buchanan," thrust his arm under the mattress, and dragged out a chamois-skin money belt. It, too, was wet. The contents bulged in the closed pockets.

"Can you tell us what this is, Mrs. Newberry?"

"Certainly," she said, "it's a money belt."

"Can you tell us what's in it?"

"It's none of your business."

"Can you tell us how it got wet?"

"I can, but I won't."

The captain said, "I'm going to find out what's in this money belt. Would you like to help me count the money, Mrs. Newberry?"

She stood defiantly silent.

The captain shifted his eyes to Perry Mason. "You are her lawyer?"

"Yes."

"Will you help me count this?"

Mason said tersely, "It's your party, Captain."

The captain nodded to the purser. "Very well, Mr. Buchanan, we'll count the money."

They opened the pockets of the money belt. The captain placed the contents of each pocket on the bed, where it was in plain sight of the people in the room. Somewhat clumsily, his sturdy, competent fingers separated the bills of large denomination. He and the purser added the total. "Eighteen thousand, seven hundred and fifty dollars," the captain announced.

"This money is yours, Mrs. Newberry?" the captain asked.

Mason said, "Does it make any difference whether it belongs to her or to her husband, Captain?"

"It may," the captain said. "I want her to answer that question."

She said, "It's . . ."

"You don't have to answer any question you don't want to," Mason warned.

"It's my money," she declared vehemently.

"Where did you get it?" the captain asked.

"That," she said, "is something else which is none of your business."

The captain frowningly regarded the money belt which he held in his hand. "How did this belt become wet?"

She remained silent.

"Can you tell me how long it's been under that mattress?"

Again she made no answer.

The captain raised the mattress. "You'll notice that the mattress isn't wet, except for a spot or two where the belt touched it."

Mrs. Newberry remained defiantly silent.

The captain lowered the mattress. "I'm sorry this was necessary, Mrs. Newberry. I'm taking over the custody of this money. The purser will give you a receipt for it and keep it in the ship's safe."

The purser took a notebook from his pocket, scribbled a receipt, signed it, and handed it to Mrs. Newberry. She snatched it from his fingers, tore it across, dropped the pieces to the floor, and stamped on them.

"You—!" she began, but Mason's palm slid across her lips.

"Shut up," the lawyer said.

For a moment they stood motionless, the woman's body rigid. Then Mrs. Newberry clutched her fingers about Mason's wrist, pulled his hand away from her mouth. Mason said, "Shut up."

She controlled herself by an effort.

The captain said, "Come, Mr. Buchanan," and led the way from the stateroom. He paused in the door, to turn and say to Mrs. Newberry, "I'm doing everything humanly possible to find your husband."

He stepped into the corridor and pulled the door shut after him. Belle put her arms around her mother. "Mumsy," she pleaded, "what does this mean! What is it?"

Her mother shook her head. Her lips quivered. Mason guided her to the bed. She sat down, suddenly whirled, buried her face in the pillow, and started to sob. Belle knelt by her side, her hands stroking her mother's hair. "Mumsy, Mumsy," she pleaded. "Can't you tell me?"

Mason nodded to Della Street. Together, they slipped from the stateroom.

Outside in the corridor, Della Street turned to Perry Mason. The ship, with the propellers turning only fast enough to give her steerage-way, rode slowly up the waves, then slid down to the troughs creaking with protest.

"Why didn't you want me to help her?" Mason asked.

She hesitated for a moment, then raised her eyes to his. "Chief," she said, "I don't want you mixed up with that woman! Helping Belle was all right. I hate to see you mixed up with the mother."

Mason laughed. "Good Lord, Della! Don't let the captain's attitude prejudice you. Frankly, I don't know just *what* he's trying to get at, but if he had an idea she carried her husband up to the deck and tossed him overboard, he's having a pipe dream."

She smiled. "Okay, Chief, let's go to your stateroom and you can buy a drink."

"Sold," he told her, "and you'll get over this silly prejudice against Mrs. Newberry."

"As a client," Della said, "I'm simply crazy about her. But . . . if she hadn't been a client . . . Oh, well, skip it."

Chapter 6

Monday morning found the ship slowly throbbing its way toward the docks, while representatives of the sheriff's office held mysterious conferences with the ship's officers.

The passengers, hushed by the tragedy, whispering bits of gossip which were magnified and distorted with each surreptitious repetition, stood huddled in groups about the deck.

Roy Hungerford sought out Perry Mason.

"Look here, Mr. Mason," he said, "I don't pretend to know what this is all about. But I want you to know where *I* stand."

"All right. Where *do* you stand?" Mason asked.

"Mrs. Newberry impresses me as being a fine woman," Hungerford said. "She's absolutely incapable of having murdered her husband. And Belle's one girl in a million."

Mason nodded.

"Don't you suppose," Hungerford asked, "that you could get the captain to drop this silly business and—"

"No," Mason interrupted, "not as matters stand. I hear there's a witness who claims to have seen Mr. and Mrs. Newberry on deck together shortly before nine o'clock. The officers are being particularly secretive about it. Apparently they don't want me to know who this witness is, or—"

"I can tell you who the witness is, if that'll be any help," Hungerford said eagerly.

"It'll help a lot," Mason told him. "They're keeping her under cover."

Hungerford said, "She's Aileen Fell."

"You mean the spectacled schoolteacher?"

"Yes, the one from Santa Barbito who's on a six months' leave of absence—nervous breakdown or something."

"How do you know?" Mason asked.

"I talked with the girl who shares her cabin. She said Miss Fell had hysterics and the doctor had to give her an opiate. The doctor advised her not to talk with anything about what she saw, but she talked to her roommate before the doctor came. She's pretty nervous. Personally, I think she's crazy."

Mason said musingly, "Let's see: She's about thirty-four or five, has funny eyes and a muddy skin. That the one?"

"She gives her age as twenty-nine," Hungerford said. "She's peculiar, you know—always walking around deck by herself."

Mason said, "Yes, I've seen her a number of times. She wears flat-heeled shoes, a short walking skirt, and forges determinedly around the deck every night after dinner."

"That's right—always walking by herself. They say she walks two miles every night."

Mason said musingly, "I know the type, finds out how many laps to the mile, religiously counts every lap. . . . Did she really see Mrs. Newberry on deck?"

"She swears she did. She was standing just below the boat deck, huddled up in a dark rain coat. The door opened, and Mr. and Mrs. Newberry came out. They walked past her without seeing her. She was within three or four feet of them and heard Newberry say something about it being necessary to handle things his way. He told Mrs. Newberry to keep her fingers out of his affairs, and started for the boat deck. Mrs. Newberry followed, and he kicked at her and yelled, 'Keep back!' but she went on up behind him.

"After a little while Aileen Fell heard a scuffle on the deck above. She climbed the stairs to the boat deck. She told her roommate she heard a pistol shot as she was climbing the stairs. When she got on deck, she claims she saw Mrs. Newberry leaning over Newberry's body, and then saw Mrs. Newberry drag the body toward the rail. Just about that time, the ship gave a big lurch to port, and Aileen Fell took a spill. She thought she was going overboard. Somewhere in there she heard a second shot. She started to scream and kept on screaming. After she got to her feet, she saw Mrs. Newberry running along the deck. Newberry had disappeared."

"So she kept right on screaming?" Mason asked.

"That's right."

"It must have been dark up there on the boat deck," Mason said. "She couldn't . . ."

"Now, that's the funny thing," Hungerford told him. "Aileen Fell swears there was a light in the hospital and the hospital door was open. You know, the hospital's really a penthouse. It's up there forward of the gymnasium, and just aft of the officers' quarters."

"And there was a light on in the hospital?" Mason asked, frowning.

"That's what Aileen Fell says. Of course, I got it second hand. She was hysterical when she told her roommate. Personally, I don't put one bit of faith in what she says she saw. But it started the captain searching Mrs. Newberry's cabin and it's going to put Belle's mother in an awful spot."

"Did the captain search the hospital?" Mason asked.

"Not then, I don't think," Hungerford said. "I heard he did later on."

Mason frowned. "You know, Hungerford, this thing, just doesn't make sense."

"Of course it doesn't," Hungerford declared. "Miss Fell is crazy. Ida Johnson, her roommate, will do anything she can to help Belle. She doesn't like Aileen Fell, and is crazy about Belle. She says Miss Fell is one of those opinionated people who make all sorts of positive statements, and then lie to back them up if necessary."

"Did you get her address?" Mason asked.

Hungerford nodded, passed over a slip of paper. "She wrote it down for me. She said she'd prefer to talk with you some time after we dock. She'll do everything she can."

Mason took the slip of paper, said, "I'm going in now to talk with Mrs. Newberry."

"I wanted to, but they wouldn't let *me* see her," Hungerford said. "Would you mind telling her . . . well . . . where I stand, Mr. Mason?"

"I'll tell her," Mason said, gripping Roy Hungerford's arm, "and I wish you luck, Roy."

A guard was standing in front of Mrs. Newberry's cabin. He nodded to Mason. "I want to see my client," Mason said.

The guard stood to one side. Mason knocked on the door.

"Who is it?" Mrs. Newberry asked.

"Mason," he said.

She opened the door. Her eyes showed that she'd had a sleepless night. "Come in," she said, and dropped dejectedly into a chair as the lawyer shut the door.

Mason sat down beside her. "We'll be docking within half an hour," he said. "Are you prepared for it?"

"As much as I'll ever be."

"Police will push you around. Newspaper men will give you the works. They'll question you and keep questioning you."

"Of course," she said listlessly. "I guess I can take it."

"Are you going to talk?" Mason asked.

"Should I?"

"No."

"Very well, then, I won't."

"It's going to take considerable will power."

She raised her voice nervously. "I said I wouldn't talk—*I won't talk!*"

Mason studied her for a few seconds, then said, "Do you want to hear something?"

"Good news or bad?"

"Bad."

"All right. Let's hear it."

Mason said, "Aileen Fell, that schoolteacher from Santa Barbito, claims she saw you and your husband go up to the boat deck. You'd been having an argument about something. After a few minutes she followed you up there. She heard a pistol shot as she was on the stairs. Then she saw you bending over your husband's body and dragging it toward the rail. Then she heard a second shot."

"She's a liar!" Mrs. Newberry said.

Mason said tonelessly, "I thought perhaps you might want to change the story you told me."

She said indignantly, "Well, I don't. That girl's a liar. She's crazy anyway. I'm telling you the truth. I went up on deck with my husband. I wanted to talk with him and he was trying to avoid me. I told him I could save Belle's happiness if he'd give me the money and let me handle things my own way. He said to go back to the cabin and wait for him."

"How about the money belt?" Mason asked.

"He gave it to me.

"When?"

"After I went up on the boat deck. He said, 'Here's the money, but don't do anything with it until I get back. I want Belle to have it all for her own. You remember—it's Belle's'—I can't remember his exact words. I tried to get him to come back to the cabin with me. He tried to strike me. That was too much. I ran downstairs, went to my cabin and started changing my clothes."

"How did you leave the boat deck?" Mason asked.

"By the forward stairway on the starboard side."

"Did anyone see you?"

"No."

"Did you meet anyone while you were going to your cabin?"

"I don't remember."

"Why did you tell the captain you hadn't been on deck?"

"Because I felt certain that Carl had jumped overboard and I didn't want to be mixed up in it."

"Do you mean that when you left him, you thought he was going to . . . ?"

"Don't be silly," she interrupted. "I'm not a fool, and please don't mistake me for one. After I went to the cabin and heard the five short blasts of the whistle, I knew someone had gone overboard. Naturally, I guessed who that someone must have been. There I was, standing with my wet clothes on the floor and my husband's money belt in my hand. I knew what it was going to look like as well as you did. So I decided to change my clothes and hide the money belt."

"Where was your husband when you left him?"

"On the boat deck."

"You know where the hospital is up there?"

"There's the little cluster of rooms in a cabin off by itself, with . . . ?"

"That's the place," Mason said.

"Yes, I know where it is."

"Was there a light in the hospital?"

"No," she said, "I don't think so. It was dark up there."

"Did you see anyone else on the boat deck?"

"No."

"And you're sure there wasn't a light in the hospital?"

"Quite certain."

Mason said, "Look up at me. I want to impress something on you."

"Go ahead," she said, avoiding his eyes.

"No, look up here."

She raised sullen, defiant eyes.

Mason said, "I want you to listen carefully to everything I say."

"Go on and say it," she said impatiently, "and don't beat around the bush."

Mason said, "You told the captain you didn't go on deck. You insisted that you'd left the dining saloon, gone to your stateroom, and your husband had left you there. Now then, you're going to have to change that story. Public sentiment is a funny thing. You can change your story once and get away with it, if you have some good explanation as to why you didn't tell the truth the first time. But you can never change your story *twice*. The next time you talk, you're going to have to tell the truth, and you're going to need some mighty good explanation of why you didn't tell the truth the first time. Now then, don't make any other statement until you're prepared to go the whole way. I want the truth and the whole truth. . . . Where did you get that money?"

"My husband gave it to me."

"When?"

"After I'd gone up to the boat deck."

"*Why* did he give it to you?"

"Because I told him I had to have it to protect Belle's interests."

"Did he intimate that he was going to commit suicide?" Mason asked.

"Certainly not."

"You didn't have any idea he was going to jump overboard?"

"No, not then."

"He didn't try to jump overboard while you were with him?"

"Absolutely not."

"Did you have a revolver?"

"No, of course not. That woman's a liar."

Mason said, "Look here, Mrs. Newberry. Suppose your husband told you he was going to commit suicide. Suppose you tried to stop him. Suppose he produced a revolver and shot himself, despite anything you could do. Suppose you tried to drag him to the stairs so you could get help, and

68

suppose the ship, at that time, took a heavy roll to port which sent you sliding down against the port rail, still holding on to your husband's body. You knew you were going to have to summon help. Would you, under those circumstances, have decided it would be better to remove his money belt before you gave the alarm?"

"Probably," she said, "but that isn't what happened."

"And if you had, and your husband had recovered consciousness while you were doing it, started to struggle and gone overboard, then what would you have done?"

"I don't know," she said.

Mason said, "Wouldn't you have given the alarm of 'Man overboard'?"

"I might have."

"Well," Mason said, "*I* think you *did* give the alarm."

She shifted her eyes and said, "Well, I didn't."

Mason said, "The Fell woman was up there on the boat deck, screaming. She was frightened and hysterical. Her screams could never have been heard on the bridge, but the telephone operator says some woman called from the social hall and said to report to the bridge there was a man overboard, and then hung up the telephone without giving any particulars. She seemed to be in a hurry to go some place or do something. Now, were you that woman?"

"No."

Mason, staring thoughtfully at her said, "I think you were."

"What makes you think that?" she asked, avoiding his eyes.

"You're the only woman on the ship who could have put through that call and who wouldn't have come forward and admitted it."

"Well, I didn't do it."

Mason said, "You have two defenses. One of them is that you had an argument with your husband on the boat deck. He tried to strike you. You went below to your cabin. After you left, some other person stepped out of the hospital and shot him. You could have used that as a defense if it hadn't been for lying to the captain and trying to conceal that money belt. Your other defense is that your husband shot himself and plunged overboard after giving you the money belt. You can't make that defense stick unless you can break down the testimony of Aileen Fell."

"So what?" she asked.

"So," Mason said slowly, "I'm not going to let you commit yourself until I know two things."

"What are the two things?"

"One of them," Mason said, "is whether Aileen Fell's story will stand the test of cross-examination. The other one is why you're lying about putting in that call from the social hall."

"You don't trust me?" she asked.

Mason said, "I'm afraid to trust you. There's too much at stake. I'm afraid to let you tell your story until I *know* you're telling the truth. You lied once because you thought you could get away with it. You'll do it again if you think you can get away with it. And don't overlook the fact that you can't tell your story to the officers without telling them why you wanted the money. You can't do that without disclosing that your husband was Carl Moar and that you thought the money had been embezzled."

"That's going to come out anyway," she said in a dull, hopeless voice.

"It's going to come out that he's Carl Moar," Mason said, "but it isn't going to come out for a few hours. And during those few hours, I'm going to get busy with the Products Refining Company. There's something queer about that embezzlement. Rooney, the head auditor, holds his job because he's related to the president. I have an idea he may be incompetent and the books may be in such shape he can't show definitely who took the money. Now, if that's the case and he knows Moar's dead, he'll make a flat accusation and perhaps doctor up the records to make that accusation stick. That will save his own face. But if there's some legitimate reason why the Products Refining Company has been afraid to get out a felony warrant for Carl Moar, I'm going to find out what that is and spike their guns before they realize he's dead."

"Then you mean the embezzlement would never come out?"

He nodded.

"That would mean everything to Belle," she said.

"Yes," Mason said. "*If* I can find some weakness in their auditing system and capitalize on that weakness before they know it's Carl Moar who's dead. But that means I'll have to dash out just as soon as we dock. It means I'll have to leave you to the mercy of the police officers and the newspaper men."

"All right," she said, her chin coming up, "I can take it. You do what's necessary to help Belle."

"You see," Mason told her, "I've arranged for a detective to meet me at the dock. We'll fly to Los Angeles and get busy. When I fight, I don't stand up and block the other man's punches. I try to find his weak point and hit him there. Now, in order to build up a good case against you, the district attorney will claim you wanted to get that money from Carl so you could get immunity for your husband, thereby saving Belle the unhappiness incident to exposure. It'll take the district attorney a little while to get all that motivation pieced together. By the time he does, I want to have brought enough pressure to bear on the Products Refining Company so they won't dare to make the embezzlement charge."

Mason moved toward the door. She came to his side. There was animation in her eyes. "You can depend on me, Mr. Mason," she said. "I'll sit tight. They can't drag a word out of me."

"All right," Mason told her. "Don't answer any questions about your past. Don't give them any clue which will enable them to link your husband with Carl Moar. Every minute you can delay them will give me that much more time within which to work. And," he said grimly, as he opened the door, "I'll need it."

Mason found Belle Newberry in her stateroom with Della Street.

"How goes it, Belle?" he asked.

"Okay so far," she told him. "They questioned me up one side and down the other."

"What did you tell them?"

"I told them they weren't officers of justice," she said, "but persecutors. I refused to answer any of their questions. I said that anyone who would accuse my mother of a crime like that was a monster."

Mason's eyes were sympathetic. "I'm sorry I had to tell you to play it that way, Belle," he said, "but for certain reasons it was the only thing to do."

"You mean that if I told them Carl's real name, they'd find out about that lottery and—"

"Something like that," Mason said. "In order to build up a defense, I want a few hours during which no one will even suspect that Carl Newberry was really Carl Moar."

"Will a few hours be enough?" she asked.

"I don't know," Mason told her. "I'll do my best."

"Celinda Dail has been trying to see her," Della Street said. "She's full of sympathy and—"

"Keep Belle away from Celinda," Mason said. "Tell everybody that Belle's upset and isn't to be questioned; that you're sorry, but she can see no one."

"That's what I've done," Della Street said. "Of course, the officers insisted on coming in."

"Tell me, Mr. Mason," Belle asked. "How about Moms? Is she holding up?"

"She's holding up," Mason said.

"What's this about some witness having seen her on deck?"

Mason made a gesture of dismissal. "Pay no attention to it, Belle. You can hear all sorts of stories." He turned to Della Street. "Della, I want to find out who sent that note to Carl Newberry. The bellboy says he got it from the purser. The purser says he was doing some book work and when he looked up the note was lying on the glass shelf in front of his window. On the envelope had been written, *'Please deliver immediately to Carl Newberry.'* The purser called a bellboy and told him to deliverr the note."

Belle said, "I think I know what was in that note, Mr. Mason."

"What?" he asked.

"There was just three words scribbled on a piece of paper with a lead pencil. It said simply, 'Promenade Port Okay,' and there was no signature."

"Could you tell if it was a man's writing?"

"No. It was scribbled in pencil. I got the impression it was a woman's writing. That's why I didn't say anything at the time. I knew Carl wouldn't carry on an affair, but I thought perhaps Moms might get jealous."

Mason said, "It wouldn't do any harm for you to give that information to the officers, Belle, but be absolutely certain not to tell them anything about your past, where you went to school, where you've been living, or anything about it. And, incidentally, do your hair differently. You look too much like Winnie Joyce with your hair done that way. The officers may trace you through that resemblance."

Della Street reached for a comb. "I'll fix that," she said.

Chapter 7

Paul Drake, head of the Drake Detective Agency, was waiting at the dock. His long legs lifted his face, with its filmy, expressionless eyes, and droll grin, over the heads of the crowd which pushed against the customs barrier.

Mason winked surreptitiously at the detective, rushed his baggage through customs, parried questions from a group of reporters, and pushed Della Street into a taxicab.

Paul Drake, loitering at the curb, apparently an innocent bystander, popped into the cab just before the driver slammed the door.

"Make time to the airport," Mason ordered.

Drake said, "I have a chartered plane waiting, Perry. . . . My gosh, you two had better take a vacation every six months. It's taken years from you both. Della looks positively immature."

Mason grinned and said, "No go, Paul. She's been kidded by experts since you've seen her. Spill the dope, and spill it fast."

"What's this about the murder?" Drake asked.

"I'll tell you about that after you tell me about the Products Refining Company."

Drake pulled a notebook from his pocket. "There's a shortage of twenty-five grand. It was discovered by C. Denton Rooney, the head auditor, a couple of days after Carl Moar failed to show up. Rooney accused Moar of embezzlement and wanted the company to have a warrant issued immediately, but the lawyer who handles things for the corporation is a conservative chap. There's a nigger in the woodpile somewhere. I don't know what it is. They've engaged outside accountants to make an audit of the books and hired a firm of private detectives to pick up Moar's trail. So far, as nearly as I can understand, the detectives have drawn a blank.

"I haven't met Rooney myself. I talked with Jackson, who had a talk with Rooney and got no place. Jackson hates him, says he's a pompous little bantam rooster; that he's absolutely incompetent and holds down a four hundred and sixty dollar a month job because he married the sister of the president's wife."

"She's dead, isn't she?" Mason asked.

"You mean Dail's wife?"

"Yes."

"Yes, she's dead. Rooney's wife is very much alive. She rules Rooney with an iron hand. At home he's nothing but a doormat. At the office he's a dictator. You know the type."

"Yes," Mason said. "What have you got on him, anything?"

"He's buying flowers for a blonde," Drake said dejectedly. "That's everything we can find out about him."

"Who's the blonde?"

"A Margie Trenton, who lives in apartment 14B, at 3618 Pinerow Drive. Does that mean anything to you?"

"Not a thing," Mason said. "She doesn't fit into the picture anywhere, so far as I know."

"Well, I put a man to work on her," Drake said, "and got nowhere. Here's a picture snapped with a candid camera."

Mason looked at the enlargement printed on glossy paper, which the detective handed him, grinned and said, "I'll say it's candid! Where was this taken?"

"While she was sun-bathing at the beach."

"She looks expensive," Mason observed, and, after a moment, added, "and interesting."

Della Street, studying the picture with that skeptical appraisal which one woman gives to another, said, "She spends money on herself, and she wasn't wearing that suit to attract sunshine so much as attention. Notice that wrist watch?"

Mason studied the wrist watch. "Any dope on it, Paul?" he asked.

"I can probably get some," Drake said. "Why?"

Mason said, "We're going to make a play on that wrist watch, Paul, and we're going to have to work fast."

"What sort of a play?" Drake asked.

"I don't know yet," Mason told him, "but we're going to get Rooney in some sort of a jam. The only way he can get himself out is by giving us the low-down on that embezzlement and, using that as ammunition, we'll scare the Products Refining Company into keeping its mouth shut."

Drake said, "I can tell you what I *think* is the joker, Perry. The Products Refining Company, and a couple of other companies, have an interlocking directorate and a holding company. There are a lot of accounts payable and accounts receivable. Some of the subsidiary companies pay in money and others borrow that money and give notes for the indebtedness. Then they gradually retire the notes, and that money is borrowed by another company, and everybody gets dizzy."

"You mean they're dodging income tax?" Mason asked.

"Sure. The holding company juggles cash around. The Products Refining Company is in on that. I think there's a lawyer back of the whole business somewhere, but he isn't coming forward to claim any laurel wreaths, if you get me."

"I get you," Mason said with a grin. "Now, then, if Charles Whitmore Dail tries to double-cross me, I'll bring the income tax people down on him like a ton of bricks."

"You've got to have a lot of dope before you can do that," Drake said.

"And we'll get the dope from Rooney," Mason assured him. "We'll pin something on Rooney."

"What do you mean by 'something'?" Drake asked.

"Hell, Paul, we haven't time to be particular. We'll frame him. We'll begin with the wrist watch and smoke him out into the open."

"Now wait a minute, Perry," Drake remonstrated. "This chap, Rooney, is a respectable, influential citizen. If he's playing around with a blonde, that's his business. If you're going to jail all the married men who buy flowers for girl friends, there won't be enough citizens outside the jails to pay the taxes."

"There aren't anyway," Mason said, grinning.

"Now listen, Perry, you're going off half-cocked. That girl may have had that wrist watch from a mother or a sweetheart. Rooney may be just a casual acquaintance. . . . Hell, I've given you a button and you've sewed a vest on it. I tell you you're playing with dynamite."

"Well," Mason told him, "if engineers didn't play with dynamite, they'd never build railroads, and, after all, it's just as true to say that the vest is on the button as that the button is on the vest."

"There's no use arguing with him, Paul," Della Street said. "His mental system is deficient in mystery vitamins, and fighting calories, and he's out to balance his diet all at once."

Mason looked at his wrist watch and said to the cab driver, "Squeeze a little more speed out of it, buddy."

Drake said dejectedly, "This is a hell of a time to try a murder case in San Francisco, Perry. Baldwin Van Densie had a hung jury the other day which looked suspicious to the district attorney. He started men working on a couple of chaps who held out for acquittal, and it looks as though he's going to get enough evidence to hook Van Densie on jury bribing. It's thrown a scare into jurors and you can't get a juryman to vote not guilty now, even on a tentative first ballot. He's afraid someone will think he's been bribed. The district attorney is rushing all of his important cases to trial and getting convictions in one-two-three order."

"That'll blow over in a week or so," Mason said. "It always does."

"Not this time it won't," Drake said. "The Bar Association is after Van Densie. They're having a clean-up on all criminal lawyers. They're investigating Van Densie's hung juries and—"

"They can investigate my juries as much as they damn please," Mason said. "If I can't get a client acquitted by using my wits, I'll let him rot in jail."

"Van Densie hasn't any wits to use," Drake said.

"Has anyone said anything about me?" Mason asked.

"Well," Drake said, "the district attorney has made some remarks about spectacular methods used by an attorney with a statewide reputation which have turned the administration of justice into a burlesque."

Mason grinned and said, "In other words, Paul, you're trying to talk me out of making a fast play on that wrist watch."

"Well," Drake said, "I'd hate to see you go to jail as soon as you get off the ship."

Mason said, "We're fighting a combination that stacks the cards against us, Paul. Newberry, who was murdered on that ship, is really Carl Moar. His stepdaughter is in love with the son of a millionaire. And in addition to that, she's a darn nice kid. The newspapers will be on the street with her picture this afternoon. By night, the district attorney will know that her stepfather was C. Waker Moar instead of Carl Newberry. When Rooney finds that out, he's going to cover up his bookkeeping mistakes by heaping disgrace on a dead man. And if there's been any juggling of funds in order to avoid income tax they'll push a lot more dirty linen in Moar's coffin. I'm going to beat them to the punch."

Della Street smiled across at the detective. "It's no use, Paul, unless that chartered airplane falls down and goes boom, Margie Trenton is going to have a disagreeable afternoon."

Drake groaned and said, "And to think that fifteen minutes ago I was actually glad to see you."

Chapter 8

Drake slid his car to a stop, regarded the imposing façade of the apartment house and said, "This is the place—3618 Pinerow Drive."

"It costs something to keep up these apartments," Mason observed. "What have you found out about her past, Paul?"

"Not a darn thing," Drake says. "She passes for twenty-five, is probably around thirty, wears her clothes well and has plenty of clothes to wear. Somewhere she had some sort of a past, but so far we can't find it. She popped up here as Marjory Trenton."

"Jewelry?"

"Quite a bit."

"And you're sure about the wrist watch?"

"Yes. My man reports she's had it just about six weeks."

"You haven't been able to find out where it was purchased?"

Drake said, "Hell, no, Perry. You had me telephone my office from the San Francisco airport. That wasn't over three hours ago. A private detective can't do the things the police can. In the first place, he hasn't the organization. In the second place, he hasn't the authority. In the third place . . ."

Mason opened the car door and said, "Keep your shirt on, Paul. I know what you're up against. That's the problem we have to lick. A person is accused of crime, and immediately the whole law-enforcement machinery gets busy unearthing evidence to prove he's guilty. When he tries to get evidence to prove he's innocent, he runs up against a brick wall. The authorities are sullen, indifferent or down-right hostile. He has to hire his investigators, and naturally he can't hire a whole police force, no matter how rich he is. That's why I have to resort to what it has pleased the district attorney to refer to as 'spectacular practices which have made a burlesque of justice.'"

Drake said, "As far as that's concerned, I'm not too happy about going through with these amateur theatricals. You're certain we're not going to wind up in jail?"

"Reasonably certain," Mason replied.

"Well, you know the law," Drake remarked dubiously.

"It isn't the law," Mason told him, "it's human nature. As far as the law's concerned, we're coming out on top. There's a legal risk, but no practical risk."

"That's what you think," Drake said.

Mason said, "The thing I want to be dead certain of is that we haven't mistaken the type of girl we're dealing with."

"Well," Drake assured him, as they crossed the curb to the apartment house, "times have changed a bit since a girl could take only flowers, candy and books from a boy friend, but this girl knows which side of the bread has the butter."

Mason pushed open the door of the lobby. "She's in, Paul?"

"Sure," the detective said, "I've had a man covering her ever since she got in this morning, about three-thirty, to be exact. That's the chap in the roadster across the street. He gave me the 'go ahead' sign."

Mason approached the desk. "Will you ring Miss Trenton, please," he inquired of a bored clerk, "and tell her that a Mr. Drake is very anxious to see her at once upon an important business matter?"

The clerk plugged in a line, and, after a moment, said, "Two gentlemen in the lobby to see you, Miss Trenton. One of them is named Drake. . . . What? . . . A business matter. . . . Just a moment." He turned from the mouthpiece to ask Mason, "Exactly what sort of business did you want to see her about?"

"About some jewelry," Mason said.

The clerk was supercilious. "You'll have to be more definite," he said.

Mason, raising his voice, so that it would be audible to the party at the other end of the line, said, "Tell her we want to see her about some jewelry; that it's private and a personal matter; that if she wants to have it spread all over the apartment house, that's her business. I'm giving her a chance to keep her private affairs to herself."

The effect was instantaneous. The receiver made squawking noises, and the clerk said, "Very well, Miss Trenton," jerked the plug out and said, "Go on up, apartment 14B, on the fifth floor."

Mason and Drake crossed to the elevator. Mason said to the colored boy at the controls, "Five. Make it snappy." The cage shot upward. Mason led the way down the corridor and pounded with peremptory knuckles on the door of 14B. The door promptly opened a crack, to disclose two appraising blue eyes, a head of blonde hair, a full-lipped, rosebud mouth, and a slender, white hand which clutched the negligee about the throat of the wearer. "I don't know you," Marjory Trenton said in a tone which implied the barrier was not insurmountable.

Mason nodded. "That's right, you don't."

"Well, what is it you want?"

"Want us to talk it over in the corridor?" Mason asked.

"I'm certain I don't intend to ask you in," she said acidly. "I'm dressing, and I haven't the faintest idea who you are nor what you want."

Mason raised his voice and said, "All right, we'll talk it over right here. This is Mr. Paul Drake. His wife had a platinum wrist watch. That watch was stolen. You have that watch in your possession. We want to talk it over. Do you want to get tough or do you want to avoid publicity?"

Her eyes grew apprehensive. "Why," she said, "I . . .
I . . . come in, please."

She held the door open. Mason pushed his way into the
room, followed by Paul Drake.

"Are you detectives?" she asked, closing the door.

Mason said, "Never mind who we are. Let's take a look
at the wrist watch."

Sudden suspicion flared in her eyes. "You'll do nothing
of the sort!" she said. "Don't think for a minute you're
going to come in here with some trumped-up story, and talk
me out of a wrist watch. Say, what kind of a racket is this,
anyway?"

Mason motioned to the telephone and said, "It's okay
with me. Call police headquarters. I thought we could
handle it just among ourselves, but if you want to have it
done formally, we can do it formally."

"You can't touch me, even if it *is* the same wrist watch,"
she said.

"That's what you say," Mason told her. "Let's concede
that someone gave you the wrist watch and you didn't know
it was stolen. You know it's stolen now. What are you going
to do about it?"

"You can't prove it's the same wrist watch," she said.

Mason said, "A platinum oval wrist watch, rimmed with
diamonds, with four emeralds on the top, bottom, and each
side."

"There's some mistake . . ." she said. "I . . . I have
such a wrist watch, but that doesn't mean anything. How do
I know it belongs to you?"

Drake said, "I think she's right, Perry. You can't expect
her to give up the wrist watch just on *our* say-so."

Mason said, without sympathy, "Okay, let's call headquarters and get them to send a man from the burglary detail
out here. They can take the girl down to headquarters, your
wife can make the identification and back it up with an
identification from the jewelry company. I thought your
wife didn't want her picture in the papers."

"She doesn't," Drake said. "We'd much prefer . . ."

"Wait a minute," Marjory Trenton said as Mason strode toward the telephone. *"I* certainly don't want *my* picture in the papers."

Mason hesitated, one hand on the telephone.

"The watch I have was given to me," Marjory Trenton said, her eyes puckered in thought. "Wait a minute and let me make a telephone call. I think perhaps we can straighten this all out."

"Whom are you going to call?" Mason asked.

"The man who gave me the wrist watch," she said.

Mason pushed the telephone away from her and said, "Oh, no, you're not."

"Why not? That's the way to settle this."

Mason said, "He may be the chap who lifted the wrist watch. Now, you look like a lady. We're willing to give you all the breaks, but you're not going to tip off the bird who gave you the wrist watch and give him a chance to skip out. Come on, sister, we'll go down to headquarters and they can handle it from there."

"But I'm absolutely, positively certain," she said, "that a mistake has been made. *If* this is a stolen wrist watch the thief sold it to some reputable jewelry store, which sold it to the man who gave it to me. That man has plenty of money. He's an executive in a big company and would no more steal a wrist watch than . . ."

"Tell you what we'll do," Mason interrupted. "You can ring him up and tell him to come over here right away on a matter of the greatest importance, but don't tell him what it is, and don't tell him anyone else is here. Now, is that understood?"

She nodded.

"All right," Mason said, moving away from the telephone, "go ahead. But remember, no funny stuff or I'll have the burglary detail on the job within ten seconds after you make the first phoney move."

She dialed a number, said, "Let me speak to Mr. Rooney, please," and then, after a moment, "Hello, Custer, this is Margie. Listen, Big Boy, I want you to come over here right away. . . . It's something I have to see you about. . . . I can't tell you what it is over the phone. . . . No . . . no, it's not that. . . . I can't tell you, but it's important. Please come. . . . How soon? . . . All right, just as fast as you can. . . . Of course I do, sweetheart, you know that. . . . All right, precious."

She hung up the telephone and said, "It'll be just a few minutes."

Mason dropped into a chair, crossed his long legs in front of him. Drake perched on the edge of a table. Marjory Trenton crossed to a chair, pulled her negligee together above her crossed knees, and said, "Well, it looks as though we have to wait."

"Do you want to dress?" Mason asked.

She shook her head. "I'm not going to leave you men alone in this room, and I'm not going to have you standing in the bedroom while *I* dress. So we'll wait just the way we are."

Drake said, "How about a drink?"

"I think you men are detectives," the girl charged.

"That's no reason why you shouldn't buy a drink, is it?" Mason asked.

"Okay," she said, "come on in the kitchenette, and help get out the ice cubes."

Mason laughed. "Come on, Paul, it's a two-man job. She won't leave you alone here in the room."

"Do you blame me?" she asked.

Mason said, "You're a smart kid."

"You'd be smart, too, if you'd been through what I have," she told him, as Mason opened the ice box, took out a tray of cubes and held them under the tap in the sink.

"That bad?" Mason asked.

"Listen," she told him, "I'm not going to bust out and tell you the story of my life."

"Well, we have to talk about *something*," Mason pointed out.

She laughed nervously.

"How long have you had the wrist watch?" Mason asked casually.

"How long since it was stolen from Mrs. Drake?" she countered.

"About three months," Mason said.

"Well, it certainly looked new when *I* got it."

"I'll take Scotch in mine," Drake remarked. "Let's forget the wrist watch until her boy friend gets here."

"I didn't say he was my boy friend!" she blazed.

"Sure not," Mason agreed, dropping ice cubes into the glass, "probably just a chap who knocked at the door with an armful of magazines. He was working his way through college and you wanted to help him out, so you subscribed to a club of half a dozen magazines, and got this wrist watch as a premium."

She held a bottle of Scotch over the glasses and said, "A little more of that sarcasm, and you won't get any drink."

"Under those circumstances," Mason assured her, smiling, "we'll discontinue the sarcasm."

Her hand held the whiskey bottle tilted over the glass as she studied him. "You," she announced, "are putting on this hard-boiled act. You're not really like that. Why don't you snap out of it and be natural? What are you trying to do, frighten me?"

For a moment Mason was disconcerted, then he laughed and said, "Thanks for the compliment. I'm not trying to act hard-boiled. I'm trying to act like a gentleman."

"Baloney!" she said, and poured the whiskey.

"Make mine light," Mason warned.

She continued pouring, until she had a good two fingers of whiskey in the bottom of the tumbler.

"Okay," Drake said, "just make them all alike."

She carefully measured the liquor into the three glasses. The detective squirted in charged water and said, "That's fine. Do we drink here or do we go back to the other room?"

"We go back to the other room."

When they had seated themselves, Drake looked around and said, "Nice apartment."

"I like it."

"Been here long?"

"Three months."

"This place," the detective remarked, "runs into money."

"If," she told him, "you're interested in the rents, you might talk with the management."

Mason laughed. She shifted her eyes to his and said, "Why don't you snap out of it? You and I could be friends."

"Thanks," Mason said.

Her eyes made an interested survey of his features. She nodded slowly, sipped her drink, and said, "You put on that hard-boiled act to frighten me, didn't you? Now, why did you want to scare me?"

"We want to find out about that wrist watch," Mason said.

"What about it?"

Drake interposed hastily. "Take it easy, now, Perry. She's handing you a little soft soap. Personally, I don't want to prosecute her on the charge of receiving stolen property, because I don't think she knew it was stolen, but that's just what *I* think. You know what'll happen if we let her out of this and it turns out she's a fence. We'll be guilty of compounding a felony."

She shifted her eyes to Drake's and said, "The more I see of this, the more fishy it sounds to me. Mr. Rooney is a busy man. If you're trying to pull something, you'd better beat it while the beating's good. Otherwise, you're going to find yourselves in a lot of trouble."

"Trouble's our middle name," Mason grinned, clinking the ice in the glass. "What does Rooney do?"

"He's an executive."

"Where?"

"In a big company."

"What sort of a company?"

She smiled sweetly at him, and said, "After all, it was the wrist watch that was stolen, wasn't it? Mr. Rooney wasn't stolen, was he?"

"I don't know," Mason countered. "Was he?"

"Not that I ever heard of."

"He isn't married, is he?"

"Poof!"

"No kidding, is he?"

"Of course not."

"Are you engaged to him?"

"I think we were talking about wrist watches, weren't we?"

"I'm trying to get a line on him," Mason told her, "because if he bought this watch in good faith, that's one thing; if he bought it from a crook, knowing it was stolen, that's another thing. This wrist watch is worth fifteen hundred dollars. If he picked it up for a hundred or two, it's a pretty good sign he knew it was stolen."

"Well," she said emphatically, "he didn't pick it up for a hundred or two. Mr. Rooney is a sport and a spender."

"We'll talk with him when he comes," Mason said. "What's your opinion of the European situation?"

"I haven't any."

There followed several seconds of silence, then Marjory Trenton said, "Suppose you tell me about you?"

"What about me?" Mason asked.

"You're a lawyer?"

"Yes."

"Why did you want to frighten me?"

"Take it easy, Perry," Drake warned.

She moved her chair a few inches nearer Mason's. The negligee slid back along the silk of her stockings. "Is this," she asked, "a game of some kind? Because if it is, you might just as well come out in the open and be frank."

"All I want is that wrist watch," Drake interposed hastily.

"I think this is a racket. I don't think your wife ever had a wrist watch."

A latchkey clicked back the lock of the outer door. Marjory Trenton frowned at the sound, started to get to her feet, then sank back in the chair. Drake grinned at her discomfiture. She flashed him a disdainful glance, drew her negligee around her. The door opened, and a man in the late forties, with a dark mustache, very black eyes, and hair which had turned gray at the temples, recoiled as he saw the two men.

"Come in, Rooney," Mason invited, "and close the door behind you."

Rooney indignantly kicked the door shut. "What's the idea?" he demanded of Marjory Trenton. "Why didn't you tell me these men were here? Who are they, and what the hell . . . ?"

"Take it easy," Drake cautioned. "We're doing this to give *you* a break. We're trying to save you a lot of publicity."

Rooney's face became cold and cautious. "What do you mean, publicity?" he asked.

"Simply this," Drake said. "The wrist watch you gave this little lady was stolen from my wife. Now then, what I want to know is how it happens you were dealing in stolen property."

"You're crazy," Rooney said.

"Not so you can notice it," Drake rejoined.

Rooney turned to Marjory Trenton. "This is a skin game. These men are trying to shake you down for something. They're blackmailers. I suggest you call the police."

"Suits me," Mason said.

She flashed him a warning glance. "That was what *they* wanted to do all along. I thought it would be better to keep it out of the papers."

Rooney sat down. "Look here, there's been some mistake. I bought that watch."

Mason said, "If you'll tell us which pawnshop . . ."

"It wasn't a pawnshop. What sort of a man do you think I am? I bought it at a reputable jeweler's."

Mason's smile was patronizing. "I understand how you feel," he said. "You want to put up a good front with your girl friend. But this sort of thing isn't going to help you any. You're in a spot, and she's in a spot, and the only way you can get out is to come clean."

Marjory Trenton said, "Go ahead, Custer, tell him the truth. I've had that trick played on me before. A man gets a bargain at a pawnshop, picks up a box from a first-class jeweler and . . ."

"I tell you I didn't do any such thing!" Rooney exclaimed hotly. "I got that watch at Coontz & Cutter, and paid thirteen hundred and fifty dollars for it!"

Mason yawned.

Marjory Trenton became impatient. "Listen," she said, "are you going to keep stalling around, trying to save your face and get us all in hot water? I don't want to have to go up before the D.A. and explain how I happened to come by that watch. I'll have my pictures in the paper and it'll look like hell."

"Maybe you think *I* want *my* picture in the paper!" Rooney shouted.

"Well," Mason said, "I'm going to put the whole thing up to the police. God knows, *I've* tried to give you a break. You insist on playing ring-around-the-rosy. So I'm all finished."

"Wait a minute," Rooney said. "How the devil do we know that this is *your* watch? Did they identify it, Margie?"

"They described it, all right."

"Give any numbers or anything of that sort?"

She shook her head.

Rooney became belligerent. "You two heels!" he said. "What are you trying to pull? I know damn well where that watch came from. I tell you, I bought it from Coontz & Cutter. You've probably seen Margie wearing that watch someplace and tried to pull a fast one!"

Mason said wearily, "Okay, brother, we go to police headquarters."

"No, we don't go to police headquarters!" Rooney said. "You two guys get out of here, and get out fast."

"Or else?" Mason inquired.

Rooney tried to think of an alternative, and the thought took some of the color from his face.

"There's one thing we *can* do," Drake suggested, his manner that of an impartial conciliator. "We can go down to Coontz & Cutter's and take the watch along. You can't tell. Maybe the thief was slick enough to put up some stall that Coontz & Cutter fell for. After all, these big jewelry stores are always willing to pick up a little dough if the deal looks right."

"I don't think I like that idea too much," Rooney said. "After all, you folks are prying into a lot of my private affairs."

"I didn't think you'd like the idea," Mason said pointedly.

"So you *did* get it at a pawnshop!" Marjory accused.

Rooney reached for his hat and said, "Get your clothes on, Margie."

"You watch these two," she said.

"Don't worry," Rooney said grimly. "I'll watch them."

"It won't take me over three minutes," she told him, dashing for the bedroom, her negligee trailing out behind her.

Rooney nervously consulted his watch. "I'm a busy

man," he said "I'll have to get back to the office before five o'clock."

"I'm busy, myself," Mason told him. "And Drake is busy, too."

Rooney sat in stiff, awkward silence, his eyes shifting apprehensively to the bedroom door. After a few minutes, Marjory Trenton, attired in a light blue tailored suit, opened the door and said, "Okay, let's go."

In the taxicab, the girl tried to make conversation, but Rooney was moody and preoccupied, so she lapsed into a silence, which she broke only when the cab swung in at the curb. "Okay, Big Boy," she said to Perry Mason, "it's your party. You pay for the cab."

Mason grinned and handed the cab driver a bill. "You win," he told her. "Let's go."

They found Arthur P. Cutter in his office. He spoke with effusive cordiality to Rooney, eyed Marjory Trenton with the approval of one who has learned to appreciate beautiful things, nodded to Drake and Perry Mason.

Mason said, "What we want is to find out whether Mr. Rooney bought a wrist watch from your store."

Cutter said cautiously, "He has made several purchases. Perhaps . . ."

"Show him the wrist watch, Margie," Rooney commanded.

She produced the wrist watch. Cutter looked at it, then glanced at Rooney. "You wish me to answer that question?" he asked.

Rooney nodded.

"Mr. Rooney bought that wrist watch from this store," Cutter said. "He bought it approximately six weeks ago."

"What did I pay for it?" Rooney asked.

"I'd have to look it up on our books to tell the exact price," Cutter said. "I don't remember those things. I remember the watch and remember the transaction. I think it was between twelve and thirteen hundred dollars."

Rooney said, "These two men insisted that the watch had been stolen. What have you to say to that?"

Cutter's eyes fastened in cold appraisal on the lawyer and the detective, then he reached for the telephone and said, "I'll show you what I have to say to that! Get me police headquarters."

Rooney grabbed Cutter's arm. "We don't want any publicity," he said.

"There won't be," Cutter told him grimly. "I have an understanding with the bunco department on men of this type. I've seen this man's picture somewhere—probably in a circular sent out. . . . Hello, this is Cutter, of Coontz & Cutter. I have a couple here for questioning. Rush a radio car over right away, will you? . . . Thanks. . . . Yes, looks like a skin game of some sort. I haven't figured it out yet. You can do the questioning."

He dropped the receiver back on the hook and said to Mason, "Now you two sit down and stay put. Don't try to leave the store. Otherwise, our private detective, who's a regularly deputized officer, will take you into custody."

Mason dropped into a chair and said to Drake, "May as well sit down, Paul."

"I'm sorry you've been annoyed about this," Cutter apologized to Rooney, and once more his eyes swept approvingly over Marjory Trenton's figure.

Marjory Trenton said uneasily, "I knew he was putting on some sort of an act. He tried to be tough and hard-boiled, but it was an act, you could tell it. What I can't figure is what they thought they were going to gain. You certainly don't think they were dumb enough to suppose I'd turn over a thirteen-hundred-dollar wrist watch to them on their say-so, do you?"

"You can't tell," Cutter said. "Some people are very credulous and some are easily intimidated, particularly under . . . under certain circumstances."

"Say, wait a minute," Rooney said apprehensively. "There isn't going to be any publicity . . ."

"You may leave that entirely in my hands," Cutter assured him. "The police department co-operates with us, and we co-operate with it. The only thing that will be in the paper will be a paragraph to the effect that two men were picked up by the bunco detail, trying to victimize a prominent jewelry company. You people will be kept out of it. This man claimed the watch had been stolen from his wife?"

"That's right," Marjory Trenton said.

"That's all I want to know," Cutter snapped, "and that's all the police will want to know."

He looked out through the glass window in his private office, which commanded a view of the store below, and said, "Here come officers from a radio car now."

Heavy feet climbed the stairs, and pounded down the corridor. The door pushed open, and two uniformed officers, holstered weapons prominently displayed, crossed over to Cutter's desk and asked, "What is it?"

Cutter motioned toward Mason and Drake. "These two."

The officers whirled. One of them, taking a step toward Mason, suddenly stopped. "Wait a minute, this is Perry Mason."

Mason nodded and said, "Good afternoon, gentlemen."

The officer turned to Cutter, puzzled. "You've heard of Perry Mason, the lawyer?" he asked.

Cutter's face was cold. "I don't give a damn who he is, he tried to run a flim-flam on a client of mine."

The officer appeared dubious. "Are you," he asked, "going to prefer charges?"

"I don't see why not," Cutter said. "He claimed that a watch purchased here by Mr. Rooney had been stolen."

The officer said, "I don't suppose it would make the chief bust out crying if you actually had something on him, but I'd go pretty easy, Mr. Cutter. He's the lawyer who defended that woman in the lame canary case, and tried that case where there was a murder about a howling dog."

Cutter looked at Mason and frowned. "Perhaps, Mr. Mason," he said, "you'll be good enough to explain."

Mason said, "As I understand the situation, it hinges entirely on the identification of a watch. Now, suppose we go at this thing in a businesslike manner and definitely identify that watch."

"It's been identified," Cutter said.

"Only by your recollection of the appearance of the watch. Suppose you identify it by numbers. You may save yourself a lawsuit."

Cutter hesitated a moment, then pressed a button. A young woman opened the door from an adjoining office. The clack of typewriters and the clatter of adding machines poured sound into the room. "Get me the account of Custer D. Rooney," Cutter said.

The girl nodded, vanished, came back in a few moments with a card. Cutter laid the card on the desk, pried back the cover on the wrist watch, adjusted a magnifying glass to his eye, and nodded his head. "This," he said, "is the same watch."

Mason said, "I think there's been a mistake somewhere," and leaned across the desk, but didn't pick up the wrist watch. Instead, he picked up the card. He studied it a moment, then turned to Marjory Trenton and said, "Did you know he was married, Margie?"

Rooney jumped to his feet and said, "Look here, I don't see what the hell . . ."

"And," Mason said, fixing him with a cold eye, "you've purchased four thousand, six hundred and fifty-two dollars and twenty-five cents' worth of jewelry within the last two months at this place alone. Now, then, Mr. C. Denton Rooney, would you mind telling us where you secured the money with which to pay for these purchases?"

Cutter sent his chair crashing backward. He lunged forward and grabbed at the card which Mason held. Mason jerked the card back from Cutter's grasp, and Cutter shouted to the officers, "Arrest that man! I don't give a damn who he is!"

One of the officers moved forward. Mason stepped backward, his outstretched left arm holding the officer back, his right hand keeping the card behind his back. "Don't be a fool," he said to the officer. "Look at Rooney."

Rooney collapsed into a chair, as though his knees had suddenly become unhinged. His face was gray and pasty.

Mason said, "You're head auditor at the Products Refining Company, Rooney. You draw a salary of four hundred and sixty dollars a month. Between two and three months ago, Carl Moar, who worked under you as a bookkeeper, mysteriously disappeared. You immediately called the attention of the directors to the fact that there was a shortage in the books. You knew that shortage would be discovered anyway, because they'd insist on a complete audit, with a bookkeeper vanishing as Moar did. Now then, perhaps you'll be kind enough to explain to these gentlemen how *you* managed to save enough money to buy almost five thousand dollars' worth of jewelry out of a salary of four hundred and sixty a month."

Rooney made a deprecatory gesture with his hands, and said, "All right, you've got me."

"How long," Mason asked, "has this embezzlement been going on?"

Arthur Cutter slowly seated himself in his big swivel chair.

"By God," he said, "I don't like this."

"No one asked you to," Mason told him. Then, turning to Rooney, "How long has this been going on, Rooney?"

Rooney said, "Look here. We can fix this thing up. No one needs to know anything about it except us. I'm related to Charles Whitmore Dail, the president of the company. He'll give me hell, but he'll put up the money rather than have the scandal."

One of the officers moved forward. Mason motioned him back and said, "But there has to be someone for a fall-guy, Rooney."

Rooney's eyes, sullen and defiant, met Mason's. "Moar could be the fall-guy."

"And what do you suppose Moar would have to say to that?" Mason inquired.

"He won't say anything," Rooney said, "he's dead. He was killed last night coming on the steamship to San Francisco from Honolulu."

"Are you sure?" Mason asked.

Rooney said, "Of course I'm sure. Mr. Dail and his daughter were on the same ship. Celinda became suspicious of Carl Moar's stepdaughter. She sent me a wireless asking me to find out all about a Belle Newberry who had graduated from the University of Southern California. I found out her mother was Ann Newberry, who had married Carl Moar."

"And notified Celinda?" Mason asked.

"Yes," Rooney said. "And then this morning Celinda telephoned me to tell me what had happened. Mrs. Moar murdered her husband last night. Now, we can fix this thing all up so there won't be any publicity."

Mason grinned. "No, we can't, Rooney. And when you see Mr. Charles Whitmore Dail, you might tell him that Perry Mason asked you to remind him that chickens have a habit of coming home to roost. Come on, Paul, we have work to do."

Chapter 9

Standing on the curb in front of Coontz & Cutter's office, Drake mopped his forehead with a handkerchief, looked reproachfully at the lawyer and said, "Perry, you told me you were only going to carry on the act until she flushed Rooney from cover."

Mason said, "Well, I changed my mind."

"I don't suppose it makes any difference to you that you damn near scared me to death," Drake said. "How did *you* know he'd done embezzling?"

"I didn't," Mason confessed. "It was just a hunch. When he latchkeyed the door of that apartment I figured it would be a good time to see it through."

A cruising cab saw Mason's signal, swung into the curb.

"What would have happened if we hadn't been able to make it stick?" Drake asked.

Mason grinned. "You'd probably have had your supper in jail, Paul."

"Good Lord, Perry, you take awful chances," Drake said, as he climbed into the cab.

"I like to gamble," Mason told him.

"I'll say you do!"

It lacked twenty minutes to five when Mason opened the door of his private office and ushered Paul Drake into the room.

Della Street, seated at a private switchboard, with an ear phone clamped over her head, and covering her right ear, looked up as they entered, snapped a plug and said, "What's new, Chief?"

"The embezzlement business is out," Mason said.

"You threw a scare into Rooney?" she asked.

"Did more than that," he told her. "Rooney confessed. He's the embezzler. What's new at this end?"

Della Street consulted a notebook. "They're holding Belle Newberry in San Francisco without charges. They're holding the mother on suspicion of murder. They found a thirty-eight caliber revolver on the boat deck. Two chambers had been fired. They've identified Mrs. Newberry as Mrs. Moar and one of the San Francisco papers has run a story about the embezzlement. Roy Hungerford's waiting in the reception room."

"I thought we'd head off that embezzlement," Mason said, dropping into the big swivel chair back of his desk and looking at his wrist watch. "Seconds were precious. I guess we missed it by a matter of minutes. What does Hungerford want?"

"I don't know. I've been too busy to see him. I've engaged a suite of rooms in San Francisco and have a plane chartered and waiting."

Mason said, "Get me the district attorney's office in San Francisco. Find out who's in charge of this case and get him on the line."

"Donaldson P. Scudder is in charge," she said. "Just a minute, I'll get him on the line."

She moved a mouthpiece up to her lips, snapped a switch and put through a call.

Mason said, "Wait here, Paul. I'm going to see Hungerford."

"Want me to get out," Drake asked, "and let you have the office?"

Mason said, "No. I'll see him in the law library." He walked through the law library to the reception room, opened the door and said, "Come in, Hungerford."

Hungerford jumped to his feet and shook hands with

Mason as the lawyer closed the door of the library and motioned toward a seat. "Well?" Mason asked.

Hungerford dropped into a chair, as Mason seated himself on the other side of a long, mahogany table.

"I wanted to talk with you about Belle," Hungerford said.

"What about her?" Mason asked.

"I came down on a plane," Hungerford said. "I was talking with San Francisco a half hour ago on long distance. I understand the newspapers are carrying a story that Carl Newberry, posing as a well-to-do tourist, was C. Waker Moar, an absconding employee of the Products Refining Company. He'd been working on a salary of a hundred and eighty-five dollars a month."

"So what?" Mason asked.

"And the San Francisco newspapers carry an interview by Charles Whitmore Dail in which he says that Moar absconded with twenty-five thousand dollars of the company's funds; that had he lived, detectives would have met him at the gangplank and jailed him on a charge of embezzlement; that he has every reason to believe the money which Moar had in the money belt was part of the funds embezzled from the Products Refining Company."

Mason lit a cigarette and said, "Go on."

"I want to know what you know about it," Hungerford said.

"Have you talked with Belle?"

"No. I can't. They're holding her in San Francisco."

Mason met Hungerford's anxious eyes. "All right," he said. "Newberry was Moar. He was employed by the Products Refining Company."

"Where did he get the money on which he was traveling?" Hungerford asked. "Do you know that?"

"He says he won it in a lottery," Mason said.

"And was there a twenty-five thousand dollar shortage in the Products Refining Company?"

"Yes," Mason said. "I believe that's correct."

For several seconds Hungerford was silent. His eyes focused on the shelves of leather-backed law books. Then he once more met Mason's eyes. "She told me," he said, "that she'd see me at the Santa Anita Race Track. Apparently she intended to keep right on—well, traveling in my set."

Mason watched him thoughtfully. "Let's see if I get you straight, Hungerford. You come to me with all this dirt, hoping I'll be able to contradict it, hoping I can tell you something good about her, is that right?"

"No," Hungerford said.

"The hell it isn't!" Mason told him. "You're interested in Belle, but you don't know how much. You're so wrapped up in conventions that you can't separate her from her parental environment. When you come right down to it, it's not Belle you're uncertain of, but yourself."

Hungerford flushed, started to make an angry retort, then, under the steady stare of the lawyer's eyes, lost his anger. After a moment, he said, "I guess you're right, Mr. Mason. I hadn't stopped to analyze my own feelings . . . but I can tell you now that this little talk has helped me understand myself. I know how I feel *now*."

Mason watched him with sympathetic eyes.

"Now then," he said, "I'll tell you something. Belle didn't intend to keep right on traveling in your set, as you've expressed it, because she never intended to see you again."

Hungerford's face showed surprise.

"Get this," Mason said, "and get it straight. If there was anything illegal about the manner in which Carl Moar acquired that money, Belle didn't know it. He told his family he'd won it playing a lottery. That's what Belle thought. Moar had been working and saving on a small salary. He'd been a bachelor much of his life. He wasn't Belle's father. Belle's father abandoned her and her mother when she was three years old. They've never seen or heard from him since. Mrs. Newberry had a little money, enough to get by on. She put Belle through college. Then she married Carl Moar. Naturally, Belle had but little sympathy for her natural father. She became very much attached to Carl Moar. He was the only real father she'd ever known. Then the family had this windfall. She had a chance to travel. She met you. You were inclined to accept her as one of your crowd. You found her interesting, and because her father and mother *seemed* to be well-to-do tourists, you acted on the assumption they were.

"That's the only ground on which Belle could have met you and enjoyed your companionship. Otherwise you'd have patronized her, or ignored her, or pitied her. She was smart enough to know she could never be received on that basis after you returned to your friends on the Mainland. Therefore, she intended to walk off the ship and never see you again. The memory of a few days of pleasant companionship would be something which she'd always cherish. It never entered her head that her stepfather was an embezzler. If she had thought there had been anything illegal in the manner in which he acquired his money, she'd never have touched a cent of it."

Hungerford said simply, "I care for her—a lot."

Mason said, "*I* don't know where Moar got the money. I do know that he wasn't Belle's father, and I do know that Belle believed he won it in a lottery."

"Who's taking care of your fees?" Hungerford asked abruptly.

"Mrs. Moar will," Mason said. "I haven't discussed fees with her as yet."

Hungerford said, "Look here, Mr. Mason. I want to help."

"Why?"

"Because I care for Belle—a lot more than I ever realized."

"You're not hypnotizing yourself into believing you care for her because she's in a jam, are you?" Mason asked.

Hungerford said, "Mason, I don't know as I'd ever have known exactly how I felt toward Belle if it hadn't been for what has happened. I've known lots of girls. I suppose I'm considered a good matrimonial catch. The girls themselves have been pretty decent. But mothers have dangled their daughters in front of my eyes until I feel that I've seen them all. Belle is different. I've met lots of girls who were flippant and full of wisecracks. It's the attitude they cultivate, for the purpose of appearing modern. Belle's different. She's naturally buoyant. She's eager to live. She wants to wade right out and meet life halfway."

"Go ahead," Mason told him, "you're doing fine."

Hungerford stared steadily at Mason. "I want to marry her."

"A Hungerford," Mason asked, "marrying the daughter of a criminal?"

"Stepdaughter," Hungerford corrected.

"What will your father say?" Mason asked.

"I hope he'll say the right thing," Hungerford said, "because if he doesn't, it's going to mean we'll be estranged from each other. I'm telling you this, Mr. Mason, because I want you to understand why I'm asking to be allowed to contribute toward your fees. Naturally, I'll ask you to consider what I've told you as a sacred confidence. I . . . well, I naturally want to . . ."

"Naturally you want to ask Belle yourself?" the lawyer asked with a smile.

"Something like that," Hungerford said. "I hope she cares for me. I think she does."

Mason said, "All right, after you've asked her, and heard what she has to say, we'll talk about letting you contribute something toward my fees. In the meantime, we'll carry on the way we are. One thing, however, may be of interest to you. Carl Moar didn't embezzle any money from the Products Refining Company."

"He didn't?"

Mason shook his head.

"You can prove that?" Hungerford asked eagerly.

"I wouldn't make the statement unless I could prove it," Mason said, "and"—with a dry smile—"for your own personal information, I think that some of the funds for Mrs. Moar's defense will be contributed by your friend, Charles Whitmore Dail—that is if he has released an interview to the newspapers in which he accuses Moar of embezzlement."

"Then Moar did win the money in a lottery?" Hungerford asked.

"I don't know," Mason said. "I'm afraid not."

"Where did he get it?"

"That remains to be seen. Of course, we don't know that the money which was found in a money belt under the mattress of Moar's bed belonged to him. It *may* have belonged to Mrs. Moar."

"What does she say about it?" Hungerford asked.

"She doesn't say," Mason said drily.

For a moment Hungerford was silent.

Mason said, in a kindly tone, "I want you to know these things, Hungerford, before you burn any bridges."

"My bridges are burnt, as far as that's concerned," Hungerford told him simply. "There's only one person in the world who can make me happy and that's Belle. I want her."

Mason said, "One other thing you don't want to overlook is that at present her mother is accused of murder. Circumstantial evidence against her looks rather black."

"Her mother didn't do it," Hungerford said. "Belle's mother simply couldn't have done anything like that."

"Well, opinions differ in those matters. The San Francisco district attorney seems to think otherwise."

Hungerford said, "That reminds me, Mr. Mason, I've uncovered something I want to tell you about. In fact, a couple of things."

"Go ahead."

Della Street opened the door, smiled at Hungerford and said, "Mr. Scudder, the deputy district attorney in San Francisco, is on the line."

Mason picked up the phone on the law library table and said, "Put him on here, Della."

Della closed the door and Hungerford said, "The message which Mr. Newberry—I mean Mr. Moar—received just before he left the table was sent by a Miss Evelyn Whiting, a nurse who was accompanying a man with a broken neck."

Mason heard a click on the line and a man's voice saying, "Yes. . . . Hello. This is Mr. Scudder."

"Mason talking, Mr. Scudder," Mason said. "I want a preliminary hearing in that Newberry case."

"You can have it any time," Scudder told him. "However, I deem it only fair to advise you, Mr. Mason, of what you may not know at this time. The San Francisco papers are carrying a story to the effect that Mr. Moar had embezzled twenty-five thousand dollars from the Products Refining Company. The money in the money belt which was recovered by the captain was undoubtedly a part of that embezzled money which Mrs. Moar had removed from Moar's body before pushing him overboard. It, therefore, can't even be used by Mrs. Moar to defray any legal expenses."

"That doesn't change my position in the least," Mason said. "I want an immediate hearing, and you're holding Belle Newberry. I want her released."

"I'm afraid," Scudder said, "that will be impossible."

"All right," Mason told him, "I'm getting out an application for a writ of *habeas corpus* and flying to San

Francisco with it tonight. Either put a charge against her or release her."

He snapped the receiver back into position, looked up at Hungerford and said, "How do you know?"

"About Miss Whiting?"

"Yes."

"One of the room stewards saw Miss Whiting slip a note on the glass-covered shelf in front of the purser's window. He feels certain it was the same note that was delivered to Moar."

Mason frowned thoughtfully. "How was she dressed?" he asked. "Did the room steward say anything about that?"

"No," Hungerford said, "he didn't. He merely mentioned he saw her putting the envelope there. His name is Frank Bevins. I don't think he's said anything to the officers. In fact, I gathered from what he told me, he didn't want to have any contact with the officers. I think the man may be wanted himself. He told me he had some information he'd give me for fifty dollars."

"You paid him the fifty?" Mason asked.

Hungerford nodded. "You see," he said, "the stewards knew that I'd been with Belle quite a bit."

"And this man didn't want to be a witness?"

"I think," Hungerford said, "he was going to take the fifty dollars and skip out. He told me that he'd taken the job as room steward so that he could lie low for a while."

"Then it's just a tip," Mason said, "nothing I could use as evidence."

"That's right."

"Know anything else?" Mason asked.

"I understand the Fell girl is telling a different story now from what she did at first. She claims now she actually saw Mrs. Newberry shoot her husband and push him over the rail."

Mason said, "The thing grows with repetition, doesn't it?"

"It seems to."

Mason picked up the telephone and pushed the button which connected him with Della Street. "Della," he said, "tell Paul Drake to telephone his correspondents in Honolulu and have them find out everything they can about Evelyn Whiting, the nurse who came over on the ship with us. Have him send an operative to see Ida Johnson, Aileen Fell's cabin-mate, and get a written statement from her. The Johnson girl's friendly. And tell Paul to get a photograph of Aileen Fell in a dinner dress."

"Just a minute," Della Street said.

Mason held the phone and could hear her transmit the message to Drake, then she said into the telephone, "Drake says he can get a prompt report from Honolulu but he doesn't know how he's going to get a photograph of Aileen Fell in a dinner dress. He says the district attorney will have a couple of detectives guarding her and—"

"Get some politician to throw a party for the detectives," Mason interrupted. "Tell them it's formal and the dicks will show up in their tuxedos, then Drake's photographer can pose as a newspaper photographer and take a flashlight. No detective ever overlooked an opportunity to have his picture taken in a tuxedo. . . . My God, do I have to tell Drake how to run his detective agency?"

Della Street laughed and said, "Paul was just telling me his parents had made a mistake. He should have been quintuplets."

"You'd think he was from his expense accounts," Mason said. He hung up the receiver, reached across the table and shook hands with Hungerford. "Thanks a lot, Roy," he said. "If it becomes necessary to call on you for a financial contribution, I'll let you know. I don't think it will be. Would you like to fly up to San Francisco with us right after dinner?"

"No, thank you," Hungerford said. "I have my own plane. But I'll see you up there."

Mason escorted Hungerford to the door, stepped into the outer offices, shook hands with the office force, chatted for a few minutes about China and Bali, then piloted Jackson into the law library.

Jackson blinked studious eyes from behind tortoise shell glasses and said, "You're going to have a tough time with Rooney, Mr. Mason. I feel that I should warn you."

Mason grinned, "You don't seem to like him, Jackson."

Jackson said, "He's an arrogant, dictatorial, obstinate nincompoop."

"You really should take up profanity, Jackson. It's a lot more satisfying," Mason told him.

"You insinuated I wasn't fighting," Jackson went on in a hurt voice. "I want you to know I did everything humanly possible. I left no stone unturned, Mr. Mason. I told Mr. Rooney in no uncertain terms exactly what I wanted, and when he refused to accede to my request I openly accused him of betraying the best interests of the corporation."

Mason opened a drawer, took out a bottle of whiskey and two glasses. "Jackson," he said, "when you start fighting, never try to hit the other man where he's expecting the punch. And when you once start a fight, never give up until the other man's licked. If you can't do it by hook, do it by crook. By the way, I don't suppose you happen to know a Marjory Trenton?"

"No, sir."

Mason filled the whiskey glasses. "That's where you made your mistake, Jackson."

Chapter 10

Tuesday morning dawned with overcast skies and a cold, drizzling rain. Mason, a temporary office established in his hotel suite, finished dictating the application for a writ of *habeas corpus* and said to Della, "All right, Della, transcribe those records. We'll get these writs issued and served."

The telephone rang. Della picked up the receiver, smiled up at Mason and said, "Mr. Charles Whitmore Dail is in the lobby."

"Tell him to come on up," Mason said.

Drake, who had been in communication with his San Francisco branch office on another telephone, came in through a connecting door and said, "I have a report on Evelyn Whiting, Perry. She's a registered nurse. She's been married and divorced, resumed her maiden name, and has her own private opinion on husbands, taken by and large, as a class and as individuals."

"Like that, eh?" Mason asked, grinning.

"Exactly," Drake said.

"She didn't impress *me* as being a man-hater," Mason told him.

"I didn't say she was a man-hater," Drake said. "I said she was a husband-hater."

"So what?" Mason asked.

"So when Moar fell for her like a ton of bricks and wanted her to marry him, she said nothing doing, they'd be friends and that was all."

"Wasn't she a bit high-powered for a chap of Moar's type?" Mason asked.

"I don't know," Drake said. "You saw Moar, I didn't. But I gathered that Moar rated about one date a week and she was trotting out to night clubs in between times. In other words, her intentions weren't honorable or serious. Moar's were."

"Where did you get the dope?" Mason asked.

"She has a sister here in San Francisco, a Marian Whiting, who lives in the Wavecrest Apartments."

"Your men talked with the sister?"

"Yes."

"What else did they find out?"

"That's all that's shown in the report," Drake said.

"Was the sister suspicious or close-mouthed?"

"Apparently not," Drake told him. "She was excited because Mrs. Moar had been accused of murder, and she wondered what Evelyn would say to that."

Mason stared at Drake and said, "What's that, Paul?"

Drake raised his eyebrows. "She was wondering what her sister would say when she heard about it."

Mason said, "Wait a minute, Paul, that doesn't make sense. Her sister's here in San Francisco?"

"Well. . . . Oh, I see," Drake said, frowning into his notebook. "You may have something there, Perry. Want me to have my men make a further investigation? They can go see the sister and—"

"No," Mason interrupted. "I want to think it over. It's either unimportant, or it's important as the devil; I don't know which. If it's important, we won't trust anyone else with it. We'll handle it ourselves.

"Now here's something else that bothers me: Just before the ship left Honolulu, someone picked the lock on Moar's suitcase, took out a picture of Belle Newberry and substituted a picture of Winnie Joyce."

"What was the idea?" Drake asked.

"The idea of the substitution," Mason said, "was

evidently to keep the theft of Belle Newberry's picture from being discovered. Apparently there's rather a startling resemblance between Belle and the picture actress. The picture which was substituted was just about the same pose and lighting."

"How come?" Drake asked.

"Belle got a fanmailed photo of Winnie Joyce and then had one of her own taken in just the same pose and with the same lighting effect. Someone got hold of a Winnie Joyce publicity photograph and made the switch."

"You don't think Winnie Joyce is mixed up in it, do you?" Drake asked. "There's big money invested in her. If her name ever came into the investigation they'd . . ."

"No, I don't think so," Mason said.

"You could raise hell with the Prosecution by letting Winnie Joyce's studio get a hint that you were going to drag her name in, and . . ."

"No," Mason interrupted. "I don't play ball that way, Paul. From what I've seen of Winnie Joyce on the screen, she's a nice kid. There's a startling resemblance, though. Not only does Belle Newberry resemble her in face and figure, but in actions and temperament. They have high-powered personalities, if you know what I mean."

"And you think this substituted picture had something to do with the murder?" Drake asked.

"I don't know, Paul. So far, I've been acting on the assumption that Celinda Dail, who apparently has matrimonial designs on Roy Hungerford, stole the picture and sent it by air mail to Rooney for an investigation. But I'm not so certain that's correct. Rooney admitted he'd made an investigation for Celinda, but didn't say anything about the picture. He intimated Belle had let drop some remark which had given Celinda a clue she'd gratuated from U.S.C. I'd like to find out something about that picture. Have your men cover the Royal Hawaiian Hotel over in Honolulu and see if they can uncover anything. Perhaps some of the employees may have seen someone hanging around Moar's room—Remember, though, Paul, he was registered under the name of Newberry."

Drake said, "Okay, Perry, on my way," and dashed through the door into his room.

Someone knocked on the door of the sitting room. Mason said, "That's Dail. Let him in, Della."

Della Street opened the door and said, "Come in, Mr. Dail."

Charles Whitmore Dail seemed far from comfortable. "Good morning, Mr. Mason," he said. "Good morning, Miss Street. I seem to have placed myself in rather an unenviable position."

"Sit down," Mason invited.

"Thank you," Dail said. He glanced around him at the room with its dictating machines, protable typewriters, and law books.

"Field headquarters," Mason explained.

"You move around rather rapidly," Dail observed.

"I don't let any grass grow under my feet when I'm working on a murder case," Mason admitted.

"I'll say you don't," Dail said. "I suppose you know what I want to see you about, Mr. Mason. I must confess you stole a march on me."

"In what way?" Mason asked.

Dail laughed nervously. "You move too fast for me, Mr. Mason. I can't keep up with you."

"Did you," Mason asked, "intend to keep up with me?"

"Well," Dail said, "I think you'll agree that I had every reason to think Carl Moar was guilty of embezzlement."

Mason lit a cigarette. "*I* don't see that you had *any* reason to think so."

"Surely," Dail said, "when a man has been in your employ, suddenly leaves without a word of explanation, and there's a shortage of twenty-five-thousand dollars, it's at least a reasonable inference he's guilty of embezzlement."

111

"That's the weakest sort of circumstantial evidence," Mason retorted. "It might justify you in auditing the books. It certainly wouldn't justify you in making a bareface accusation."

"Well," Dail blurted, "consider the *other* circumstances. Here we were on a boat on the high seas. You're aboard the ship. Moar's aboard the ship, traveling under an assumed name. You come to me and offer to return twenty thousand dollars—"

"I beg your pardon," Mason interrupted. "I didn't make any offer. I said I was asking questions. I wanted that specifically understood."

"Well, it amounts to the same thing," Dail insisted.

Mason said, "Speaking as a lawyer, I beg to differ with you. But you're doing the talking."

"I didn't come here to argue," Dail said. "I appreciate I'm in an embarrassing predicament if Mrs. Moar cares to take advantage of it."

"She does," Mason told him conversationally.

"You mean she's going to sue me?"

"Exactly."

"Well," Dail said, "if you want to get technical about it, Mason, I didn't accuse *her* of anything, I accused her husband, who is now dead."

"You said, however, that the money which was found in her possession was money which had been embezzled from the Products Refining Company. It now appears that your relative was responsible for that embezzlement. Moar was innocent."

"Then why the devil did Moar leave in the way he did?" Dail asked.

Mason shrugged his shoulders.

"You're not making this particularly easy for me," Dail said.

"Did you expect that I would?" Mason inquired.

"I thought that you'd be reasonable."

112

"I always try to be reasonable."

"Look here," Dail blurted, "I don't want to have it publicly known that Rooney embezzled that money. Under the peculiar circumstances, it would hurt my prestige with the stockholders of the company. I have, therefore, arranged to cover the shortage."

"I'm glad to hear it," Mason said.

"The financial structure of the Products Refining Company is such that . . . Well, it's rather complicated."

"I understand."

"If Mrs. Newberry filed any action against me, and alleged in her complaint that there actually had been a embezzlement by the auditor . . . Well, Mason, I want to settle."

"On what basis?" Mason asked.

Dail said, "I don't think there's been any great damage done to Mrs. Moar's case, but if I should assume the responsibility of underwriting your fees, that should be more than a fair settlement."

Mason smiled. "My fees come high."

"I was afraid they would," Dail admitted.

"How high are you prepared to go?" Mason asked.

"Shall we say five thousand dollars?" Dail asked.

"I'll take the matter up with my client," Mason said.

"Can you give me a prompt answer?"

Mason said, "I feel quite certain my client's answer will be that she wouldn't consider a cent less than ten thousand dollars."

"As *your* fees?" Dail asked, raising his eyebrows.

Mason said, "Oh, say five thousand dollars for my fees, and five thousand to give her funds with which to cover additional expenses."

"She's not exactly impoverished," Dail pointed out.

"Thanks to the circumstances and to your newspaper interview, Dail, the Prosecution is holding all of her funds as evidence."

Dail abruptly arose and started toward the door. Half way there, he stopped and turned to Mason. "Ten thousand is too much," he said.

Mason said, "Evidently, Mr. Dail, you were aware of Moar's identity when I first approached you to ask about your attitude in the event of a restitution. I further understand, from a remark made by Mr. Rooney, that detectives would have met the ship and arrested Mr. Moar at the gangplank, under circumstances which would have been exceedingly humiliating both to Mrs. Moar and her daughter. Taking all that into consideration, I think ten thousand dollars is exceedingly reasonable. In case *you* consider it unreasonable, you might take into consideration how promptly any promise you could have made me would have been broken."

"That's the thing I can't understand," Dail said. "Why the devil did Moar offer to return twenty thousand dollars if he hadn't embezzled the money?"

"He made no such offer," Mason said.

Dail walked across to the door, opened it and paused on the threshold to say to Mason, "Understand this, Mr. Mason, when we were on the ship we were dealing at arm's length. I was under no obligation to you to disclose that I knew Newberry's real identity."

"Exactly," Mason said, "and at the present time, we are *still* dealing at arm's length."

Dail said, "All right, you have me. Fix up an agreement." He stepped out into the corridor and pulled the door shut behind him.

Della Street regarded Mason's grinning countenance with anxious eyes. "When you come right down to it, Chief, why *did* Moar want to return any money?"

"He didn't. Mrs, Moar did."

"Well, why did *she* want to?"

"She thought he'd embezzled it."

"Do you think she really thought that?"

Della turned to stare out of the window, her eyes focused on the gray, low-flung clouds which sent a drizzle of cold moisture trickling down the windowpanes. Abruptly, she turned back to Perry Mason. "Chief," she said, "you're clever when it comes to figuring evidence. You're usually good when you figure character. But there are some things about this woman I don't think you've taken into consideration."

"What?" Mason asked.

"She's attractive," Della Street said, "and you can see by the way she throws her personality around that she's been accustomed to rely on it. A woman who uses her charm to get the things she wants out of life becomes dangerous when she reaches the late thirties and early forties. I'm telling you, Chief, that woman is shrewd, clever and designing. She trapped Moar into marriage, not because she cared anything about him, but because she wanted a home for her daughter and a veneer of respectability for herself. Moar was sufficiently unsophisticated to be easy. You never did hear Moar's side of this thing. Now you never will. It's my opinion that if you'd ever heard Moar's story, you'd have an entirely different slant on the whole thing. I think Belle realized that when she wanted you to talk with her father, and I think Mrs. Moar realized it and was willing to do absolutely anything to keep you apart."

Mason, studying her patiently, said, "Go ahead, Della. Tell me the rest of it."

"You've now established that Moar didn't embezzle from the Products Refining Company," Della Street said.

"It still doesn't account for where he got the money," Mason pointed out.

"What makes you think he had any money?" she asked.

"Well," Mason said, "an assistant accountant doesn't suddenly give up a job and start traveling around the world without having something to use for cash, and a man who has eighteen thousand seven hundred and fifty dollars in cash in a chamois-skin money belt . . ."

"Wait a minute, Chief," she interrupted. "How do you know he had that?"

"Why . . ." Mason said, "the captain counted it in my presence. He . . ." He stopped abruptly, to stare at Della Street. "Go on," he said, "spill it."

"*I* haven't anything to spill," she said, "only I'm trying to point out that all the facts you have in this case came from Mrs. Moar. Suppose *she* was the one who had the sudden influx of wealth? Suppose *she* gave the money to her husband to finance the trip to Honolulu. Suppose *she* talked him into quitting his job. Suppose *she* was the one who suggested that it would make it much easier for Belle if they changed their names from Moar to Newberry."

"Wait a minute," Mason interrupted. "How about that money belt?"

"Can't you see," Della Street said, "she never intended to let her husband reach shore alive. She intended to make his death look like suicide. Until you told her differently, she didn't realize that the life insurance policy wouldn't pay on suicide. When she did realize it, it was too late. She had to go through with the plan. If her husband had apparently committed suicide, later on she could have "found" the money belt. The fact that he'd removed the money belt and placed it under the mattress would have been perfectly consistent with his going up on deck to commit suicide. All Mrs. Moar had to do was to swear she hadn't been on deck with him. She might have made it stick if it hadn't been for Miss Fell's testimony and the search the captain made of her stateroom closet."

"Has it occurred to you," Mason asked, "that this theory you're outlining presupposes, that Mrs. Moar had been deliberately planning her husband's death for some time?"

"Of course it has."

"It doesn't make sense," Mason said.

"Think it over," she told him. "It makes plenty of sense. It makes the facts all fit together. She knew that Evelyn

Whiting knew Carl Newberry was really Carl Moar. She had reason to believe Celinda Dail also knew. By setting the stage with you, she thoroughly convinced you Moar had been guilty of embezzlement. Under the circumstances, if he'd gone on deck, shot himself, and gone overboard, it would have looked like suicide."

"That," Mason said, "doesn't coincide with my idea of Mrs. Moar's character."

"I know it doesn't," Della Street said quietly, "but it coincides with mine."

"Look here," Mason told her, "has it ever occurred to you that if the testimony of Aileen Fell doesn't stand up, the Prosecution hasn't a leg to stand on?"

"There's the circumstantial evidence that Mrs. Moar had been on deck with her husband: her wet dress, wet shoes, and the money belt."

"All right, suppose she *did* go on deck with her husband. That doesn't mean she killed him."

Della Street stared thoughtfully at the carpet. "Chief, if you can break down Aileen Fell's testimony, can you get her off?"

Mason nodded. "With Aileen Fell's testimony out of the way, a jury will figure it was as apt to have been suicide as murder."

"What makes you think you can get Aileen Fell's testimony out of the way?"

"Because of the statement she made to her cabin-mate. It doesn't coincide with what she's saying now. Remember this, she's rather a morbid personality. She was on deck, standing by herself, thrilling to the storm. I noticed her earlier in the evening. She was seated by herself over at one of the tables, wearing a blue dinner gown, and attacking her food with grim efficiency."

"She'll be a hard woman to cross-examine," Della Street said.

"Why?" Mason asked.

"She won't have too much regard for the facts. She'll consider the cross-examination as a personal duel between herself and the attorney for the Defense. She'll get more and more positive as you seem to doubt her word. She's just that type."

Mason grinned and said, "Don't worry about her, Della. She's going to fold up on cross-examination."

"You seem to be certain, Chief."

"I am," he said, grinning—"that is, if Paul Drake gets that picture of her in her dinner dress."

"What's that got to do with it?"

Mason chuckled. "It's a secret."

The telephone rang.

Della Street picked up the receiver, received a message from the desk, and said, "Oscar's downstairs. He wants to see you."

"Oscar?" Mason asked.

She nodded. "Remember, the chap who waited on our table."

Mason said, "Oh, yes. Go on out and talk with him, Della. If he's broke and wants a loan, give him twenty-five bucks and my compliments. If he has some information, bring him in."

Della Street glided from the room. Mason started pacing the floor, his head bowed in thought, hands thrust deep in his trouser pockets.

After a few moments, he paused by the window, stared moodily at the rivulets of rain which made patterns down the windowpane. He turned as a door opened and Della Street escorted the table steward into the room.

"Hello, Oscar," Mason said.

Smiles wreathed the man's face. "Good morning, Mr. Mason. I don't want to take up much of your time. I just wanted to run in and speak to you for a minute. You were so nice to me on the ship that I thought . . . Well, I thought perhaps I could help *you*."

Mason glanced inquiringly at Della Street. She gave an almost imperceptible nod of the head. Mason said, "What is it, Oscar?"

The man stood somewhat ill at ease. "Well, Mr. Mason, I don't know as I'm doing right in this thing, but you see, we went through a bit of a blow coming into port, and then there was this business of all the commotion on the upper deck, and the boats being made ready to lower, and all that. Well, the next morning, come daylight, they sent us up to get the canvas covers back on the boats and get everything shipshape. One of the men found a gun up there and the first officer took charge of it."

"What sort of a gun?" Mason asked.

"A thirty-eight caliber blued-steel revolver. I couldn't see the make. It looked like a pretty good gun."

"Anything else?" Mason asked.

"Yes, sir."

The man fumbled in his pocket, produced a folded piece of paper and said, "I found this, sir. I asked the first officer if it was important and he said no, to pitch it overboard. You know, the first officer's in command, but I felt perhaps . . . Well, I thought I'd save it. And then when I heard you were Mrs. Moar's lawyer—I thought I'd bring it in and let *you* have a look at it."

He took from the paper a long, irregular piece of blue silk print. "I found this stuck on one of the cleats, sir."

Mason took the bit of cloth. "Looks like a piece torn out of a woman's dress."

Oscar nodded.

"Any idea where it came from?" Mason asked.

"No, sir, but it was on a cleat on the outside of the rail."

"On the *outside* of the rail!"

"Yes, sir."

"Port or starboard?"

"Port, sir, and a little aft of amidship."

Mason said, "Let's get this straight. You mean the cleat was on the outside of the rail. Is that right?"

"Yes, sir. And from the way it was caught, I'd say this part of the hem caught on the cleat and then the rest of it ripped loose, leaving this triangular piece."

"How much of it was wrapped around the cleat?" Mason asked.

"This hem part was wrapped around a couple of times, and about eight or ten inches up at this end was flapping in the breeze. Perhaps I should have reported it to the police, sir, but I was working under the first officer and he said to throw it overboard. So if I turn it in to the police and it *should* be important, the first offiver would have it in for me as long as I was on the run, so I'm handing it to you and asking that you'll just keep it confidential, sir."

Mason smiled and said, "Oscar, thanks a lot. That's appreciated. I'll keep quiet about it and you do the same. Now you've been to quite a bit of trouble, coming in here and I'm wondering if you wouldn't accept a . . ."

"No, sir," the man said hastily. "You were so nice to me on the ship that it's a pleasure to do something for you in return. I thought I'd bring this up to you, and hope it might be some help."

Mason shook hands with him, escorted him to the exit door and said, "Well, Oscar, perhaps some day I'll be able to do something for you."

"Yes, sir, thank you, sir. I hope you sail with me again, sir."

Mason closed the door, came back, looked at Della Street and asked, "Well?"

She shook her head. "I can't place it, Chief. And yet I remember having seen it. Some woman wore that dress, but for the life of me, I can't tell right now who she was. After all, there were a couple of hundred passengers in first class."

Mason took a small pair of scissors from his toilet case.

He was cutting the cloth into three pieces as Paul Drake opened the door from his room and said, "Going into the dressmaking business, Perry?"

Mason said, "Paul, here's something: A piece of cloth torn from a woman's dress. I want you to make a few quiet inquiries among the passengers and see if you can find out who had a dress of that description."

"Wouldn't you know?" Drake asked. "You were on the ship."

"Good Lord, no!" Mason said. "I see that they have clothes on and that's about all."

"I've seen it somewhere," Della Street said, "but I can't place it. It may come to me later."

Drake said, "I have a bunch of news, Perry."

"Good or bad?"

"Mostly bad," Drake said.

"Go ahead," Mason told him. "Spill it."

"There's another witness against your client, Perry."

"Who is it?"

"I don't know yet. The D.A. doesn't know, either, but he's hot on the trail. You see, the alarm of 'Man Overboard' wasn't given by the Fell woman. She screamed and let it go at that, but some woman telephoned the operator from the social hall and told her to notify the bridge. That woman must have seen the man go overboard because she said to tell the bridge a man had been *pushed* overboard. The telephone operator says she'll recognize the voice if she hears it again, and thinks she can place it. She's going over the passenger list."

Mason grinned and said, "I'm not particularly worried about *that* witness, Paul."

"Why not?"

Mason said, "I think it was Mrs. Moar who put in that call. That's just between you and me, Paul."

Drake said, "Well, the operator reported she said a man had been *pushed* overboard. Suppose she recognizes Mrs.

Moar's voice when she gets on the witness stand, and swears Mrs. Moar said a man had been pushed overboard?"

Mason frowned. "That isn't so hot," he admitted.

"They've identified the gun they found on the boat deck as being Carl Moar's gun. They've also found Mrs. Moar's fingerprints on the barrel."

"On the barrel?" Mason asked.

"Yes."

"None on the butt of the gun?"

"No."

"Anything else?" Mason asked.

"That's all the news. Evelyn Whiting's sister is in her apartment if you want to go up there. So far, my men haven't been able to locate either the nurse or the man with the broken neck. An ambulance was waiting for them at the dock and drove them away. We'll locate that ambulance within an hour or two. In the meantime, do you want to talk with the sister?"

"Might as well," Mason said.

Chapter 11

The drizzle had developed into a cold drenching rain when Mason and the detective emerged from a cab in front of the Wavecrest Apartments.

"Do you do the talking," Drake asked, "or do I?"

"I do," Mason said.

"Going to throw a scare into her or take it easy?" Drake inquired.

"Take it easy if she'll let me," Mason told him, his eyes exploring the index of tenants on the front of the building. He found the name MARIAN WHITING opposite Apartment 1329 and pressed the button. A moment later an electric buzzer released the catch on the door, and Drake said, "Well, there's a good index to her character. She's on the up-and-up. If she'd been two-timing anybody, she'd have made whistles up and down the speaking tube."

Mason nodded. They took the elevator to the thirteenth floor, found the apartment they wanted, and tapped on the door. The woman who opened it had alert brown eyes, dark chestnut hair, a slightly upturned nose and delicate lips. She was wearing black and orange lounging pajamas. Sandals on her feet showed red painted nails.

"Yes?" she asked. "What is it?"

"I want to talk with you," Mason said.

She eyed the two men a moment in silent appraisal, then stood to one side and said, "Come in."

When they were seated, Mason said, "It's about your sister."

"Oh, you mean Evelyn?"

"Yes."

"Are you newspapermen?"

"No," Mason said, "we're just gathering facts. I wanted to find out about your sister's friendship with Carl Moar."

"Why?" Marian Whiting asked, her eyes suddenly defiant.

Mason returned her stare, smiled and said, "You win. I'm Perry Mason. I'm a lawyer representing Mrs. Moar. I'm collecting facts."

"What does my sister have to do with it?"

"I don't know," Mason said. "Probably nothing. I'm simply investigating."

"What did you want to know?"

"How long ago did she first become acquainted with Carl Moar?"

"Oh, heavens, I don't know. It's been . . . Let's see . . . it must have been five or six years."

"How long did the friendship continue?"

"Up until two or three months before Carl was married."

"You're certain it didn't continue up until the time of marriage?"

"Of course I am," she said. "Sis saw him on the street in Los Angeles two or three months ago, but it was just a casual meeting."

"Was there any particular reason why your sister terminated her friendship with Carl Moar shortly before his marriage?" Mason asked. "In other words, did any other woman come between them?"

"Good heavens, no. If you want the truth, I think Carl gave Sis some bad financial advice. Of course Carl meant all right, but you know how those things are. Sis had about a thousand dollars she'd saved up and Carl told her he thought he could make her a hundred percent profit. She gave him the money and received interest on it for a while, and then lost everything."

"What was the nature of the investment?" Mason asked.

"I'm sure I couldn't tell you. It was something Carl was promoting. He lost all his own savings along with Evelyn's, but that didn't help Evelyn any. You know, when a man tells a girl he has a wonderful investment for her he can't be expected to guarantee she's going to make money on it, but when her savings are wiped out she naturally doesn't feel so cordial toward him. She's lost her respect for his judgment."

"Where is she now, by the way?" Mason asked.

"Why, in Honolulu."

Drake flashed a significant look at the lawyer, but Mason, taking a cigarette case from his pocket, said, "Mind if I smoke?"

"Not in the least," she said. "I'll have one with you."

She took a cigarette. Drake also took one. "Three on one match?" Mason asked.

She laughed heartily. "Good Lord, yes! Six on one match if you want to."

She leaned forward and accepted his light. Drake held back, looked sheepish for a moment and said, "Go ahead, Perry. I'll light my own."

Mason said to Marian Whiting, "He's a confirmed pessimist. No use trying to reform him. How long's your sister been in Honolulu, Miss Whiting?"

"Just two weeks."

"You're working?" Mason inquired. "Pardon me, I'm not trying to pry into your affairs, but . . ."

"It's quite all right, Mr. Mason," she told him. "No, I'm not working now. I'm looking for a secretarial position. I have two or three offers but they're not just what I want and I'm able to hold out for a while . . ."

"That isn't what I'm interested in," Mason said. "I was wondering if your time was your own."

"Yes. Why?"

"Did you," Mason inquired with an elaborately casual manner, "go down to the dock to see your sister off?"

125

She laughed. "I'll say I did. Four or five of her friends fixed up a stunt sailing basket for her. It had fruit and nuts on top and was all covered with cellophane and looked like a regular sailing basket, but down underneath we had all sorts of stuff for practical jokes."

"Did she get a kick out of it?" Mason asked.

"I'll say! You should have seen the letter she sent back on the *Clipper*."

Mason got to his feet and said, "Well, thanks a lot for the information. . . . Oh, by the way, do you know where your sister's staying at the present time in Honolulu?"

"Yes. Would you like her address?"

"If you don't mind," Mason said.

"It's somewhere on Alewa Drive," Marian Whiting told him. "I'm no good at remembering numbers. Just a minute and I'll get her last letter."

She left the room, and Drake said to Mason, "What is this, a run-around, Perry?"

Mason shook his head. "That girl's on the square, Paul. I'm not so certain about the sister. The sister's different from her—thicker lips, smoldering eyes, and hair of . . ." He broke off as Marian Whiting entered the room with some letters in her hand. "It's 1091 Alewa Drive," she said.

"Honolulu?" Mason asked.

"That's right."

Mason looked at the envelopes, laughed, and said, "I see you're not a stamp collector."

"Oh, but I am."

"You haven't removed the *Clipper* stamps."

"No," she said, "I'm saving the envelopes. That gives me the complete postmark."

Mason casually extended his hand, and she unhesitatingly passed over the envelopes. Mason looked at the stamps, studied the postmarks and said, "This one left Honolulu day before yesterday."

"Yes," she said, "I got it yesterday. It's the last letter I've received from Sis."

"Interesting handwriting," Mason said. "It shows a lot of character."

"Oh, do you read character from handwriting, Mr. Mason? I'm very much interested in it."

"Yes," Mason said, "it's a hobby of mine. Of course, you can't read character from just a few words, such as the address on the envelope, but if I had a page of handwriting, I'd be willing to bet I could tell you quite a good deal about your sister, what she looks like, where she's been recently, what she's been doing, and . . . oh, quite a lot of things about her."

"Can you really? I think that's wonderful."

Mason took a ten-dollar bill from his wallet and said, "I'd even be willing to bet you ten dollars against ten cents."

Laughing, Marian Whiting took ten cents from her purse, placed it on the lawyer's ten-dollar bill, and took the letter from the envelope. "There you are," she told him.

Mason opened the letter.

"Now, wait a minute," Marian Whiting said. "You can't read it, because she says lots of things in there about what she's been doing, things you were going to tell me from her writing."

"Oh, certainly," Mason conceded, "I merely want to glance at the handwriting. Here, I'll let Mr. Drake hold the letter while I tell you. In the first place, your sister is younger than you are. She's taller and has blonde hair. Her eyes are blue, with just a shade of green. Her lips are rather thin. She's . . ."

Marian Whiting interrupted him to say, "You'd better take another look at that handwriting, Mr. Mason. You're going to lose ten dollars."

Mason frowned. "Why, I'd swear I was right." He peered over Drake's shoulder at the letter for a moment, then raised his eyes to Marian Whiting and said positively, "That letter was written by a tall, thin woman with a nervous temperament. Your sister may have the external appearance of a jolly good fellow, who lives a happy-go-lucky existence, but secretly she worries a lot. She's quite a bit underweight. I hope the trip to the Islands does her good."

"You're wrong on that," Marian Whiting said. "You haven't described her at all. Now, what's she been doing?"

"Well," Mason said, "she's been nursing someone."

Marian Whiting perched herself on a corner of the table and said, "No cheating. You knew she was a nurse. That's simple. Go on now, and tell me something else from the handwriting, something intimate. What's she been doing over in Honolulu?"

"She's been on a special case, a case involving a man who was injured, perhaps in an automobile accident, a man who has some sort of a harness around his shoulders and on his neck. . . . Of course, Miss Whiting," Mason added, laughing, "you understand I'm more or less of an amateur at this psychic business. I don't see things too clearly."

"Well, you're not seeing this clearly," she said. "In fact, you're not seeing it at all, Mr. Mason."

"Hasn't there been someone like that whom she's been nursing?" Mason asked.

"No. She didn't do any work on the Islands at all. This wasn't a working trip."

Mason's expression indicated puzzled bewilderment. "Look here," he charged, "you're not trying to kid me out of ten bucks, are you?"

"Certainly not," she said indignantly.

"Well," Mason said, "either this isn't your sister's handwriting, or else . . ."

"Of course it's my sister's handwriting."

"It couldn't be a forgery?"

"Why, Mr. Mason, who would want to forge my sister's handwriting? Good heavens, no! That letter's filled with little intimate details. I know absolutely it's from Sis."

"You share this apartment?" Mason asked.

"Yes."

"And when do you expect her back?"

"She said she'd be back in about two weeks. If she could get the reservations she wanted, she might be back a boat sooner. She's going to send me a cablegram as soon as she knows."

"Well," Mason said, "I guess you're entitled to the ten dollars, although I still think . . . oh, well, never mind."

Her face flushed. "You think I'm taking advantage of you? Here, take your ten dollars, I don't want it."

"No, no. It isn't that," Mason said hastily. "I just can't understand how my deductions could be so completely wrong. Just what *does* your sister look like, Miss Whiting?"

"I'll get you her picture," Marian Whiting offered. "You can see for yourself."

Mason glanced at Paul Drake. "Not a posed photograph, please. Something that will show her character and . . ."

"Certainly. Just a minute."

She left them and went into the bedroom. "What does the letter say, Paul?" Mason asked in an undertone.

"All about the Islands, people she met, dances she's attended, a *luau*, native feast, and how they ate with their fingers, and . . ."

"Never mind all that," Mason said. "How about the intimate personal details?"

"She tells Marian she forgot to send her fall suit to the cleaners, to please have it cleaned and pressed, and there's a spot on one sleeve which she's to call to the attention of the cleaner. That she'd like to have her fur coat out of storage when she gets back, and . . . Wait a minute, Perry, she mentions her husband. . . ."

Marian Whiting returned with a photograph album. She placed it on the table. Mason and the detective stood at her side as she turned the leaves. "Here's Evelyn. . . .

There's an old picture of Evelyn and Carl Moar. There's another one of Evelyn. Here we are in bathing suits. . . . Here we are . . ." Abruptly she laughed and turned the page. "I guess you hadn't better see that one. Here we were on our vacation in shorts. Here's Evelyn and a boy friend. Here's . . . Oh, wait a minute. I know . . . I have a dandy picture taken when Evelyn sailed."

She turned over a dozen pages and showed them a mounted, eight-by-ten enlargement. "Here it is. I had the picture enlarged because it was such a good negative. You can see her up there at the rail. See, she's holding on to the strips of colored paper . . ."

Mason said, "Pardon me," picked up the photograph album and took the picture to the light so that he could study it carefully. "I'm something of a nut on photography myself," he said, by way of explanation. "This is a fine piece of work. You must have a very good camera there, Miss Whiting."

"I have," she said. "It was given to me by an uncle who runs a camera store in the East. It takes a sharp negative, has an anastigmatic lens and a focal plane shutter . . ."

"I see you're something of an expert yourself," Mason laughed.

She nodded. "I'm just crazy about it," she said, "and this color photography gives me the biggest thrill of all."

Mason said, "Yes, I bought a miniature camera over in China and snapped hundreds of colored pictures. Perhaps when your sister gets back you'll be interested in seeing those I took in Honolulu and while I was on the ship coming over. By the way, who's this young chap standing just back of your sister? He seems to be acquainted with her and . . ."

Marian Whiting grabbed up the album, started to say something, and then checked herself and said, "Someone on the boat, I guess."

"He seems to be taking quite an interest in your sister," Mason said.

"Oh, Sis just slays 'em when she gets on a boat," Marian Whiting said. "Why, I remember one time—"

"I notice his hand is on her shoulder," Mason insisted.

Marian Whiting looked up and said, "I'm not supposed to tell you about this, Mr. Mason. I'd forgotten about him being in that photograph."

"Of course," Mason said, "I don't want to pry into your sister's private affairs. I take it this is some young man she's friendly with?"

"He's her husband."

Mason remained silent.

"Sis was secretly married and went to Honolulu. She's over there on her honeymoon. That's Morgan Eves, her husband. She's not ready to announce the marriage yet."

"I see," Mason said. "Then she's still over in the Islands on her honeymoon?"

"Yes."

"Her husband still with her?"

"Of course."

"Looks like a nice chap," Mason said. "I would size him up as a bond salesman."

"Well, he isn't," Marian Whiting blazed. "And if you ask me, he isn't any good."

She checked herself abruptly.

Mason said, "Oh, surely, it can't be that bad. He has rather a nice face."

"Ever since he's known Sis," Marian went on passionately, "he's been a bad influence in her life. I was certainly hoping she wouldn't marry him."

"What's he do?" Mason asked.

"I don't know. That's the mysterious part of it. He has plenty of money and a prejudiced, warped, cynical outlook on life. I think he's in some sort of a racket. I don't trust him."

"I take it your sister won't be living with you when she gets back."

131

"Yes, she's going to for at least a couple of months. They can't publicly announce the marriage yet. It's something about an interlocutory decree that isn't final, or something. Sis has been rather mysterious about it all. He's made such a change in her. My heavens! I'd have sworn she'd *never* get married again. She liked men and she liked to have a good time, but we, both of us, decided it was a lot better these days for a girl to have her independence and keep house by herself than to have some man ordering her around, making her work, and spending her money. Sis had one experience with marriage, and it was enough. . . . Now you promise me you won't say anything to the newspapers."

"About your sister's marriage?"

"Yes. I shouldn't have told you that."

Mason said, "Well, I'll make a bargain with you. If you'll let me have a picture of your sister, we'll call it square."

"Is there any particular one you'd like?" she asked.

"How about the one where she's getting into the automobile?" Mason asked. "The one where she has her hand on the door. That's a particularly good picture."

"Yes, I think I have an extra print of that."

She once more entered the bedroom. "That the girl all right?" Drake asked.

"That's the girl," Mason said.

Drake said, "The chap she married is a crook. He's been in two or three scrapes. They had a murder charge against him in Los Angeles two or three months ago; had a dead open-and-shut case, but he squirmed loose. I'd recognize that face anywhere. I saw him—"

Marian Whiting came back with the photograph. "I found it. It's an extra print," she said. "It really belongs to Sis, but I can have another one made for her."

Mason said, "I'll be glad to pay—"

"No, no," Marian Whiting said hastily. "That wasn't what I was getting at."

Mason gestured toward the ten-dollar bill. "Well, it's your money," he said. "You won the bet."

"Oh, I couldn't take the money, Mr. Mason."

"Why not?"

"The odds were too great. My heavens! It was interesting seeing you try to describe Sis, and I'm all wrapped up in mental telepathy and character reading. I'll bet you're a Leo, Mr. Mason. You have—"

"If I'd won the bet," Mason said sternly, "I'd have taken your dime. Now then, young lady, under *those* circumstances, you take that ten dollars."

She picked up the ten-dollar bill, slowly folded it.

"I don't feel right about this," she protested.

Mason laughed, shook hands and said, "Thanks a lot for your co-operation."

"And you'll keep it under cover about Sis?"

"Yes," Mason promised. "I won't say anything about what you've told me. If, of course, I should get the information from some other source, I couldn't guarantee . . ."

"Oh, that's all right. As far as that's concerned I don't think it makes any great difference, except that I don't want Sis to think *I* gave her away. Gee, Mr. Mason, I still don't feel right about this ten dollars!"

Mason laughed, took Drake's arm and moved toward the elevator. Marian Whiting slowly closed the door of the apartment.

Mason said in a low voice, "This photograph shows the license number on the automobile, Paul. It's a recent photograph, and the car's a late model. Let's run around to your San Francisco branch office and chase it down."

"Good idea," Drake said, "they may have something on Evelyn Whiting by this time."

In the taxicab Drake said, "How about the chap she married, Perry? Was he on the boat coming over?"

"No," Mason said, "he wasn't. And I can't get this stall

over the Honolulu end. She must have written letters ahead and left them to be mailed to her sister.''

"What's the idea?" Drake asked.

"Damned if I know," Mason said, "unless she's trying to build up an alibi of some kind."

"That might be an idea, Perry. Two or three months from now the sister would swear up one side and down the other that Evelyn was over in Honolulu, and could produce her letters to prove it."

"The only trouble with that is that she sailed back under her own name," Mason said. "She's on the passenger list as Evelyn Whiting. How do you account for that?"

"She may have had a round trip ticket," Drake said, "or . . . oh, shucks, Perry. I don't know. We haven't enough to go on yet. What do you suppose happened to the husband?"

Mason shrugged his shoulders.

"And," Drake went on, "who was this chap with the broken neck?"

"Wait a minute," Mason said, "that chap with the broken neck was probably her husband."

"What name was he going under?"

"Roger P. Cartman. Give me a description of this chap, as nearly as you can remember him, Paul."

"Well," Drake said, "his real name is James Whitly, and he's gone under the name of James Clerke. He's a small fellow, weighing not over a hundred and thirty-five pounds, with thin features and small bones, and he's deadly as a rattlesnake. He's been mixed up in two or three rackets, has served time in San Quentin, and Folsom. Then he wormed his way out of that open-and-shut murder charge. The judge bawled hell out of the jury when they brought in the not-guilty verdict, but that didn't keep the verdict from standing. He has dark eyes, set rather close together, a thin mouth, high cheekbones and—"

Mason said, "I believe that's the chap, Paul, the one she

was nursing. Of course, I couldn't see his face plainly. He had to hold his head in one position because of that neck brace, so his eyes were shaded against the sunlight by heavy goggles, and the harness came up around his chin. But I remember he was a small-boned chap with high cheekbones and a thin mouth. His forehead was covered with a strip of gauze—it's the man all right."

"He must have been hurt over there."

"And she brought him back to the Mainland for medical treatment."

"He may have pulled something over in Honolulu and is hiding out," Drake said. "Do you want to go any farther with it?"

"You bet we do," Mason told him. "Get this, Paul: Unless we can get some sort of a break, Mrs. Moar is going to be convicted of first-degree murder. She lied about going on deck with her husband. She had her husband's money. There was a large policy of insurance. Two shots were fired. A gun which undoubtedly belonged to Moar was found on the boat deck with her fingerprints on the barrel, and an eyewitness will swear to enough to make the jury feel it isn't a case of circumstantial evidence. It's very possible that she's innocent. *I* think she is or I wouldn't be representing her, but try and sell that idea to a jury. Now then, if you add to that the fact that when she telephoned the operator to notify the bridge she told them a man had been *pushed* overboard, her chances are absolutely nil. They may even return a verdict without recommendation, which will automatically carry the death penalty."

"How strong will this eyewitness go?" Drake asked.

"I don't know," Mason told him. "We're having a preliminary examination tomorrow. I think I can use a technicality which will force the district attorney to put on all of his evidence at the preliminary. That'll give me a chance to rip his witnesses wide open and shoot the case full of holes. By the time that Fell girl gets into the Superior

Court she'll have rehearsed her testimony so much in her own mind that it'll be impossible to shake her. By catching her now, I may be able to find a weak point. In fact, I think I have one—if your men can get that photograph."

"What's that photograph got to do with it?" Drake asked.

"That's a secret," Mason said.

"Well, we can tell when we get to the office," Drake told him. "I have men working on it."

The taxi deposited them at Drake's office. Mason sat in a cubby-hole office while Drake received reports from his subordinates.

Drake skimmed through a typewritten report and said, "Okay, Perry, Aileen Fell is going to be at a party tonight in a formal. Operatives so far haven't been able to locate Evelyn Whiting. The ambulance companies all say they didn't have an ambulance at the dock yesterday."

"Well, an ambulance was there," Mason said. "I saw it."

"I saw it too," Drake said, "but I didn't pay particular attention to it. I saw the word AMBULANCE written on the side under the driver's window. I have an idea it was a private ambulance."

"Well, we can chase down that angle, can't we?"

"Yes, it's being chased down."

"How about her baggage? Where was that taken?"

"Taken to storage," Drake told him. "She gave checks to a storage company, and the address she gave the storage company was the Wavecrest Apartment address."

Mason said irritably, "I never knew a girl to leave such a broad back trail and then have it vanish so completely."

The telephone rang. Drake picked up the receiver, listened and said, "Okay, Perry, we've traced that car. It's registered to a Morgan Eves who lives at 3618 Stockton Boulevard. Do we go there?"

Mason said, "We go there, but first I want to ring up Della and tell her what we're doing and see if the district attorney's released Belle Newberry."

136

Drake passed the telephone over to Mason. Mason dialed the number of the hotel and said, "This is Mr. Mason talking. Connect me with my suite, please."

After a moment, the operator's voice said, "I'm sorry, Mr. Mason. They don't answer. I don't think there's anyone in there."

"There must be," Mason insisted. "Miss Street, my secretary, is there waiting for instructions—"

"Miss Street went out just a few minutes after you left, Mr. Mason," the operator said. "I saw her go past my desk."

"You're certain?"

"Quite certain."

"How was she dressed?"

"She had on a raincoat and hat."

"Carrying a brief case with her?" Mason asked.

"No. There was nothing in her hands except her purse."

"And she hasn't returned?"

"No."

Mason frowned thoughtfully and said, "When she does return, please tell her that I'll be back in about an hour."

He dropped the receiver into place, said, "Okay, Paul. Let's go."

The Stockton Boulevard address was a two-and-a-half-story flat. In the basement floor were two shops. One bore the legend, "F. KRANOVICH, Tailoring, Cleaning and Pressing"; the other, "MABEL FOSS, Picture Studio—Developing, Printing, Framing." The window carried a display of photographic prints and an assortment of picture frames. The second-story flat seemed vacant, while the third apparently was tenanted.

One of Drake's men had driven them out and Mason instructed him to park the car half a block down the street. The lawyer and the detective climbed the half dozen stairs which led from the street and looked at the name on the mail box.

"Here it is," Drake said, "Morgan Eves. This chap may be a tough customer, Perry. He won't fall for any of the usual lines."

"All right, then," Mason said, "we won't give him a usual line," and jabbed his finger against the bell button. They could hear the faint jangle of a bell two floors above.

"Being in trouble doesn't mean anything to this chap," Drake went on. "He's taken lots of raps. If you leave him an opening, he'll take it, and take it damn fast. This is no time for any theatrical stuff."

Mason nodded, pressed his finger against the button once more. "Nobody home," he said, after several seconds had elapsed.

"Now listen, Perry," the detective cautioned, "let's not go snooping around *this* place."

Mason walked to the edge of the porch, stood staring out at the reflecting surface of the wet street. The rain had ceased, but low clouds, splotched with the black markings of potential showers, drifted overhead.

"I have an idea the birds have flown the nest," Mason said.

"If Evelyn Whiting had recognized Carl Moar and had worked some kind of a blackmail racket on him, she wouldn't have stuck around where she could be located— particularly after the murder case broke."

"The more I think of it, the more I want to find her, Paul," Mason said. "Let's find out where they are."

"How?" Drake asked. "This chap had an automobile. He could simply pull out and—"

"He also has a broken neck," Mason said. "Don't forget that."

"Well, the girl could drive."

Mason nodded. "Look here, Paul, there's no garage in

connection with this building. The chances are they didn't take their car over to Honolulu and back. So they must have left it here. Let's look around and see if we can't find where it was stored somewhere in the neighborhood."

"Not much chance," Drake told him. "They'd have put it in one of the big storage garages up town. They'd have driven down to the wharf with it when they left, and stored it where it would be handy when they got back."

"If they'd done that," Mason said, "they probably wouldn't have had the ambulance waiting. Let's look around."

They walked back to the car, circled three blocks, and Mason said, "Let's try this place. Looks like the only storage garage in the neighborhood."

"Is Morgan Eves' car here?" Mason asked the garage attendant.

"No."

"He keeps it here, doesn't he?"

The attendant studied Mason. "Yes," he said, "he keeps it here."

"When's he going to be back?"

"I don't know."

"Look here," Mason told him. "I want to find out something about that car. What condition is it in, do you know?"

"Why do you want to find out?"

"I'm interested in buying it," Mason said. "Eves made a proposition to the agency for a new car. They figured he wanted too much for his old car, but they said if they could sell it at that price they'd make the deal. I have a car I can trade in for a good allowance if I handle this bus. I want to find out if it's in good shape."

"Well, it's in good shape," the attendant said. "He keeps it running like a watch."

"How soon will it be where I can look at it?"

"I don't know. Eves had a whole bunch of baggage piled

in it when he took it out. He didn't say how long he was going to be gone."

"His wife with him?" Mason asked, casually.

"A woman was with him. I didn't know he was married."

Mason said, "I gather it's his wife. The automobile salesman thought it was. You don't know where I could reach him?"

"No, I don't."

"You don't think he went to Los Angeles?"

"I don't know *where* he went. He didn't say how long he was going to be gone. He comes and goes, and we don't ask any questions."

"When did he leave?"

"Yesterday afternoon about three o'clock."

Mason said, "Oh, well, the deal will wait for a couple of days. If he doesn't show up then I'll have to do something else. Thanks a lot."

Back in the car, Drake said, "You won't get anywhere trying to ride that bird's back trail, Perry. He's been through the mill."

Mason said, "I have another idea, Paul. The nurse had a camera. She was taking snapshots of a couple of steamers we met."

"Well?" Drake asked.

"Well," Mason said, "she got in early yesterday morning. They didn't pull out until early yesterday afternoon. She had some films with her. There's a chance she left those films to be developed and printed down at the photographer's place."

"Not if she'd been going away, she wouldn't," Drake pointed out.

"No," Mason told him, "but suppose she didn't know she was leaving? Suppose she thought she was going to stay there in the flat? She'd have taken the films down the first thing. Then, if she'd been called away, she'd have left some word as to when she'd be back for the films or left a forwarding address, or there may be something in the pictures she took which will give us a line on what we want."

Drake said, "You're playing with dynamite on this thing, Perry."

"I know I am."

"And," Drake persisted, "it's something you can't afford to be mixed up in, Perry. We'll send the operative in to pick up the films, and if there's a squawk about it he can take the rap and—"

"Nothing doing," Mason interrupted. "I won't ask a man to take any chances I won't take myself. Drive over there and park. I'm going in and see what I can find out."

It had started to drizzle again by the time Mason walked down half a dozen steps from the street into a little cement areaway. He pushed open the door of the picture shop. A bell tinkled in a back room, and a woman in the late forties, wearing a blue smock, came through a curtained doorway to regard the lawyer with lackluster black eyes.

"I called to pick up the pictures for Mrs. Morgan Eves," Mason said. "They may be under the name of Evelyn Whiting."

"But she wanted them mailed to her," the woman said.

"I know," Mason said casually, "but that was before she knew I was coming in. She asked me to pick them up."

The woman opened the drawer and selected two flat yellow envelopes. "There's six dollars and seventy-five cents due," she said.

Mason produced a ten-dollar bill, glanced at the back of the envelopes. The name, "Mrs. Eves," had been scrawled on the envelopes in pencil. There was no address.

"Wait a minute," Mason said. "She told me they wouldn't be over five dollars."

"I'm sorry," the woman said, "my prices are cheaper than she could get them done downtown. Six dollars and seventy-five cents is the lowest I can make it."

Mason said, "I can't understand it. . . . How were you to receive your money if you'd mailed them out?"

"I was going to send them collect. I was just getting ready to mail them."

"Tell you what you do," Mason said. "I don't want to take the responsibility of paying six dollars and seventy-five cents, but you get them ready and mail them right away because Mrs. Eves is in a hurry for them. You can mail them collect and I'll tell her they're on the way."

The woman nodded, pulled out films and prints, packed them in a box which had been used for photographic paper, wrapped up the box, went to the back of the store and addressed a gummed paper sticker. Mason said abruptly, "Oh, well, I'll take a chance. After all, there's only a difference of a dollar and seventy-five cents, and I'm quite certain it'll be all right. They'd be delayed quite a bit in the mail."

"Just as you say," the woman said, as Mason again offered her the ten-dollar bill. "When will Mrs. Eves be back?"

"It'll be a week or so."

"How's her patient getting along?"

"The man with the broken neck?" Mason asked.

"Yes."

"I don't know. I haven't seen him."

"It certainly is a shame," she said. "Think of having to wear something like that strapped around your head and shoulders. She said he'd been wearing it for weeks. She brought him over on the ship from Honolulu. I've been wondering how he was getting along."

"Brought him out in an ambulance, didn't they?" Mason asked.

"Yes. They carried him up on a stretcher. I've been wondering who's taking care of him. There doesn't seem to be anyone coming or going from upstairs."

"I think they moved him," Mason said.

"I haven't seen nor heard any ambulance."

"You've known her husband long?" Mason asked.

"Oh, ever since he's been here."

"Did you see him before . . . before . . . ?"

"You mean before he got married? Oh, yes, he was in here getting some things and I chatted with him. By the way, how was that picture frame I sent up? Was that what Mrs. Eves wanted? She ordered it over the telephone and I rushed upstairs with it."

"I think I heard her say it was a little small," Mason said.

"Well, it was just the size she ordered. She told me to get her an oval frame for a picture which had been trimmed down from an eight by ten print into an oval size."

Mason said, "I don't know much about it. After all, I'm just a neighbor."

She gave him his change and handed Mason the package. Mason thanked her, tucked the package under his arm and stepped out into the drizzle.

"Draw something?" Drake asked, as Mason opened the door of the car.

"I'll say I did. She not only left her films there but left a mailing address. The chap with the broken neck isn't Eves."

Mason entered the car, placed the package on his lap and he and Drake studied the address.

"Know where the place is?" Mason asked.

"Yes. It's up in the Santa Cruz Mountains."

"How long will it take us to drive it?"

"An hour and a half probably, maybe a little longer if it rains."

Mason said, "Okay, let's go. We'll mail the photos."

"We may be taking a detour which ends in a blind road," Drake told him. "After all, Perry, how do we know she had any connection with Moar?"

"We don't," Mason said, "but outside of Moar's party,

she's the only living person on that ship who knew Carl Moar by sight, and whom Moar knew by sight.''

"How about the Dail girl?"

"The Dail girl evidently found out who he was by tracing Belle. She didn't know him and therefore Moar didn't have any idea she was wise to his alias.''

"Think Celinda traced Belle through the stolen picture?" Drake asked.

"Probably. She probably switched pictures, sent Belle's picture on to Rooney by air mail and had him trace her.''

"That doesn't coincide with what Rooney said," Drake remarked.

"I'm thinking of that, too," Mason said. "Let's get to a telephone where I can call Della. I have an idea we can get something from this nurse. If she left the note which sent Moar up on deck, I'll be certain we're on the right track. Evidently she's been playing around with a bunch of crooks. She went over to the Islands with her husband. He must have been called back and took a clipper plane. She was coming over to join him, and took a nursing job to pay expenses. On the ship she ran into Carl Moar. She recognized him, but found he was traveling under the name of Newberry. Now, that's a perfect set-up for blackmail, and, as a blackmail victim, Carl Moar was a natural. Remember, he was carrying at least eighteen thousand dollars in cash in a money belt. That was hot money.''

"What makes you think it was hot money?"

"From the way he acted.''

"He might have won it in a lottery.''

"He *might* have," Mason admitted, "but eighteen thousand bucks represented what he had left after a couple of months of playing tourist. He probably started with around twenty-five thousand dollars. Now, a man can't win twenty-five thousand dollars on a lottery without leaving some sort of a back trail somewhere.''

"Then there's this other thought you brought up that the money might have been his wife's," Drake said.

"Well, I don't figure that angle so strong right now," Mason told him, as the operative pulled in to the curb and said, "Here's a telephone, Mr. Mason."

Mason telephoned the hotel, only to learn that Della Street was still absent. He walked back to the automobile, frowning. "I don't like it, Paul," he said. "Della's still out."

"Maybe she went to get her hair done," Drake suggested.

"Not that girl," Mason told him. "When she works on a case she's like I am, working day and night, grabbing a bite to eat when she can get it. She's doing something on this case."

"I wonder if that piece of blue silk cloth has anything to do with it," Drake asked.

"Now *that's* a thought," Mason said.

"Maybe she's remembered who wore the gown," Drake suggested.

"Perhaps," Mason said, still frowning, "but it's entirely unlike Della to have left the hotel without letting me know, and making certain it didn't interfere with any of my plans. It's equally unlike her not to have telephoned in a report. And I can't understand what's keeping her so long."

"Oh, well, one thing at a time," Drake told him. "Let's tackle this place up in the Santa Cruz Mountains."

"Think we can locate Morgan Eves once we get up there?"

"Sure," Drake said. "It's just a little post office, general store and cabin proposition. It won't be any trouble at all."

The rain had ceased by the time Drake's operative pulled the car to a stop and entered the general store and post office. Clouds which had been drab and gray had broken into patches of dazzling white, between which showed the deep blue of a clear California sky. Huge redwoods glistened with moisture as shafts of sunlight streamed through the clouds.

Drake's operative came out of the store, climbed in behind the wheel and said, "Follow this road half a mile, take the first turn to the left, and it's the first cabin on the left."

As they traveled over the dirt road, bits of wet gravel thrown up by the tires clattered against the mud guards. Drake said, "Perry, this is once you do *all* the talking. I do all the listening. Remember not to take any chances with this chap. He packs a rod and is dangerous."

Mason nodded.

The driver slowed down, cautiously turned the car, shifted gears and said, "This must be the place."

They inspected a rustic cabin under the trees, slabs of bark covering the outside.

"There's a fire in the fireplace," Drake said, indicating a stream of light blue smoke which drifted upward from the chimney. "Someone's home."

"All right," Mason said, "let's go."

"You got a rod?" Drake asked the operative, and when the man nodded, said, "Well, after we go in you move over toward the wall as though you were trying to keep yourself in the background. Be sure you're where no one can stick a gun in your back. All right, Perry, here we go."

Evelyn Whiting opened the door in response to Mason's knock. Her face showed surprise and dismay. "Why . . ." she said. "Why, you're Mr. Mason, the lawyer."

Mason nodded and said, "Do you mind if we come in, Miss Whiting? We want to talk with you."

She hesitated for a perceptible instant, then held the door open and stood to one side. The three men filed into the cabin.

"You're alone here?" Mason asked.

"Yes."

"I wanted to talk with a Mr. Eves."

146

"Well, he isn't here."

"Do you know when he'll be back?"

"No."

"Do you know where he is?"

"No."

"I'm sorry to bother you," Mason said, seating himself in a chair, "but there's some information you can give me, and I want it."

"I don't know a thing—"

"Let's go back and begin at the beginning," Mason said. "You knew Carl Moar, didn't you?"

"Yes."

"You've known him for some time?"

"Yes."

"How long since you'd seen him?"

"Do you mean before I left Honolulu?"

"Yes."

"It's been years. I hadn't seen him since he was married."

"And you saw him on the ship?"

"Yes."

"I rather gathered that he was trying to avoid you," Mason said.

"I think he was, at first. However, I happened to run into him on the promenade deck Sunday morning."

Mason said, "I'm going to put my cards on the table, Miss Whiting. I've been investigating you because I think you may be a very material witness for me. I know all about your marriage, about your going to Honolulu on your honeymoon."

"It wasn't my honeymoon," she said—"that is, it was and it wasn't."

"Just why did you go?" Mason asked.

"I started to Honolulu with my husband," she said, "but before we'd left the bay a speed launch came alongside the ship. My husband had to go back. They lowered a rope ladder. He went down the side. I couldn't have gone down that ladder even if I'd wanted to. I was never so bitterly disappointed in my life. He told me to go on to Honolulu and he'd follow on a clipper plane."

"Did he?" Mason asked.

"No."

"Why not?"

"I don't think that concerns you in the least," she said.

"And you came back without letting your sister know?"

"Yes. I had a chance to nurse Mr. Cartman. He was injured in an automobile accident and wanted to go to the Mainland. They needed a trained nurse who could be with him. It was a good chance for me to come back, so I did."

"And you didn't let anyone know you were coming back?"

"No."

"Not only that, but you took particular pains to see that your sister thought you were still over there. You left letters to be mailed on the *Clipper* so that—"

"How did you know about that?" she interrupted.

"We've talked with your sister," Mason said. "In fact, we've made rather a complete investigation, Mrs. Eves."

She started to say something, checked herself, bit her lip, looked at the floor and said, "I'd rather you'd wait until my husband comes before I tell you anything."

"Oh, then, your husband is due to return?" Mason asked.

"Well . . . that is . . . I . . . ."

She broke off and was silent. Drake and Mason exchanged glances. Mason said, "I think you understand why I'm asking you these questions, Mrs. Eves. I'm representing Mrs. Moar."

She nodded.

"Aside from the fact that I'm Mrs. Moar's attorney, I have no interest in the matter whatsoever. I'm not concerned in the least in any of your private affairs. I'll respect your confidence."

She blinked her eyes thoughtfully, then suddenly reached a decision and said, "All right, Mr. Mason, I'll tell you the truth. I was married once before. That marriage didn't jell. It wasn't a particularly pleasant experience. It left me rather suspicious of men. Since then I've known a few married men. What I've seen of them hasn't made me care to play the rôle of wife who sits at home while her husband's playing around. After I got over to Honolulu I kept thinking about the way Morgan had put me aboard the ship while he suddenly went back, and I thought perhaps . . . well, I thought perhaps there was another woman. I wanted to come back and find out, but I didn't have the money, for one thing, and I didn't have any legitimate excuse for another. Then, Mr. Cartman, who had been hurt in an automobile wreck, and who had to wear a steel brace for months, wanted to come home. I had been in touch with some of the nurses in the hospital. They knew how I felt. They told me this would be a fine chance for me to make a surprise trip to the Mainland. I could get enough out of it to pay my round trip passage, and, in addition to make a little pocket money. So I decided to go. But, naturally, I didn't want Morgan to know I was coming, so I wrote letters to him and left them to be mailed on the *Clipper* after I'd sailed. And because I thought perhaps Morgan might get in touch with Marian, I did the same with her. Now then, that's all there is to it."

"And what did you do when you came here?" Mason asked.

"I got in touch with Morgan, naturally. I went right to his flat. I thought perhaps he'd have some other woman there. Well . . ."

She broke off as the sound of a speeding automobile motor became audible. They listened while the machine roared into a turn at the foot of a hill, heard the driver shift gears, and then the tires slid over the gravel as the machine was braked to an abrupt stop. A moment later, there was a pound of steps on the porch, and a man flung open the door of the cabin. Mason recognized him at once, from the photograph he had seen, as Morgan Eves.

"All right," the man said, standing in the doorway, his hand hovering near the left lapel of his coat, "what is this, a pinch?"

Mason said, "Take it easy, Eves. I'm Perry Mason, the lawyer."

"That's what *you* say," Eves said.

"He is, Morgan," Evelyn Whiting assured him. "He was on the boat with me coming over. Remember, I told you."

Eves nodded without shifting his position. "All right," he said, "so what?"

"We're asking questions," Mason said.

"Well, you're not going to get any answers. And you," he said, shifting his eyes toward Drake's operative, "be careful what you do with that right hand. If you pull that rod, you're going to have to smoke your way out."

In the moment of tense silence which followed, Perry Mason extracted his cigarette case, leisurely selected a cigarette, tapped the end on the side of the cigarette case, and said, "Let's talk sense, Eves."

"All right," Eves said, "you do the talking."

Mason snapped a match into flame, lit his cigarette and said, "Thanks," when Evelyn Whiting handed him an ash tray. He settled back comfortably in the chair and said, "I'm a lawyer, Eves. I'm representing Mrs. Moar. The D.A. is trying to frame a first-degree on her. Your wife was on the ship coming over, nursing a chap with a broken neck. She knew Moar before he was married. Moar was on the ship under the name of Newberry. I had a hunch she might know something which would help me, so I came out and asked her."

"All right," Eves said, in a flat monotone. "You asked her. What did she say?"

Mason glanced inquiringly at the nurse. She nodded

imperceptibly. Mason said, "Before I came out here I looked her up. I knew you'd been married and had sailed for Honolulu on your honeymoon. She told me you were called off the ship and she went over by herself. She got lonesome, so when she had a chance to come over and join you, and make a little money on the side, she did it."

Eves laughed bitterly and said, "Lonesome, hell! She came over to check up on me. She thought I was two-timing her."

"That's all right with me," Mason told him. "You can straighten out your domestic affairs without my help. I'm interested in protecting my client."

"What else did you tell him, Evelyn?" Eves asked.

"Nothing else," she said. "That's all there is to tell, isn't it?"

Eves thought for a minute. Then he walked forward to sit down in a chair. He lit a cigarette, studied Mason thoughtfully and said, "Okay, Mason, I'm for a good mouthpiece myself. I'll give you a break. We can do a hell of a good turn for you any time you say the word."

"I'm saying the word," Mason told him.

"With what? Money, marbles or chalk?"

Mason said, "I don't buy testimony, Eves."

"Well, why the hell should we come into court and get panned by the newspapers just in order to help you?"

"Probably," Mason said, "because it's the right thing to do. I understand you've been up on a murder rap yourself. You know what it feels like."

"Who was telling *you?*" Eves asked savagely.

"A little bird," Mason said.

Eves smoked in thoughtful silence for several seconds, then said, "Okay, Mason, I'll shoot square with you. I'd told Evelyn to keep out of it, but I'll give you a break. Here's the dope: Evelyn knew Moar before he was married. She spotted him on the ship. Moar gave her the office to keep quiet until he could see her. He waited for her on deck

Sunday. He told her he was dough-heavy, but the money was hot and that the bulls were going to pinch him on an embezzlement charge he hadn't committed, but before he got done beating that rap they'd find out something he *had* done which was just as bad. He said he was crazy about Belle and he was going to give the dough to his wife and take a powder."

"Did he say what he was going to do?"

"He was despondent," Eves said, "so low he could walk under a snake's belly on stilts. He said he was going to give himself the works if he had to."

Mason strove to keep excitement from his voice. "You know," he said, "that'll rip the murder case wide open, Eves."

"I'm not so certain," Eves said. "That's what Moar *intended* to do. His wife didn't know he intended to do it. She wanted him out of the way. He went up on deck to do a Brodie, and she came along and gave him the works first."

Mason shook his head. "You're all wet, Eves."

Eves said, "I may be all wet, but I'm telling you what happened. That's the God's truth."

"How do you know?" Mason asked.

"I've put two and two together. Don't forget that Fell woman saw the whole business."

"I don't think she saw as much as she thinks she did," Mason said. "Your wife's testimony will put my client in the clear. The question is, do I get it?"

Eves said, "You get it. But I'll tell you something else. You're going to run into a surprise on this case, and they're going to convict your client. I'm giving it to you straight. He would have croaked himself if his wife had let him alone, but she beat him to the punch."

"I'll take my chance on that," Mason said.

"You're going to run up against some surprise testimony," Eves insisted.

"What testimony?" Mason asked.

Eves glanced across at his wife. "Think we'd better tell him?" he asked.

She shook her head and said, "Not if he doesn't know."

"Okay," Eves said, "you don't know, so we don't tell you."

"You tell your story on the witness stand," Mason said to the nurse, "and I'll guarantee no jury is ever going to convict Mrs. Moar, no matter how much surprise testimony they bring in."

"You don't know what this surprise testimony is," Eves said.

"That's right, I don't, do I?" Mason grinned.

"How about it?" Eves asked his wife.

She shook her head.

Eves said, "All right, that's twice I got the red signal. We'll quit talking about it."

Mason said, "There are a couple of things I want to clean up. Did you send a note to Moar telling him to come on deck?"

"Me?" Evelyn asked.

Mason nodded.

"Good heavens, no," she said. "I *did* leave an envelope on the purser's desk. I was paying the chits I'd signed on shipboard."

"That's probably it," Mason said. "One of the room stewards saw you leaving an envelope. So much for that. Now, how about the patient you brought over with you? What happened to him?"

She flashed Eves a swift glance.

Eves said, "He doesn't enter into it. He didn't hear the conversation. He had a broken neck and paid Evelyn for bringing him over. She ran into a little trouble. He wanted to hold out some of the money, but she brought him up to my place. His relatives were to come up there and get him. I sent Evelyn up here so it wouldn't cramp *my* style. After the cheap chiselers saw they were dealing with someone who knew the ropes they didn't make any more trouble. They paid up nice and sweet."

"Where's Cartman now?" Mason asked.

"I don't know," Eves said, "and what's more I don't give a damn. His friends took him. I do know they'd never have moved him if they hadn't kicked through and lived up to the agreement they made with Evelyn."

Mason took a folded, blank subpoena from his pocket. "All right," he said, "I'm going to subpoena you. How do you want the supoena made—to Evelyn Whiting or Evelyn Eves?"

"Better make it Evelyn Whiting," Eves said. "My interlocutory ain't final yet. I suppose they could punch the marriage full of holes if they wanted to, and the D.A.'d probably like to get something on me. It'll help your case a lot more if I don't enter into it. I've got a record a yard and a half long, in case you don't know it."

"I know it," Mason said.

"Okay," Eves told him. "Remember this, Mason, we could have closed up on you like a clam and you'd have been out on the end of a limb. I'm giving you a break. Don't forget it."

Mason filled in the subpoena.

"And don't think this is going to be a downhill pull," Eves said. "If the D.A. uses his head you're up against the toughest proposition you ever tackled."

"Thanks for the warning," Mason told him. "I'll take a chance. Evelyn Whiting, you're subpoenaed to appear tomorrow morning at ten o'clock A.M., or as soon thereafter as Counsel can be heard, as a witness for the Defense in the preliminary hearing in the case of the People of the State of California vs. Anna Moar."

"Okay," Eves said. "That's all in due and regular form. Now you guys get to hell out of here. I'm on my honeymoon."

Chapter 12

As Mason entered the lobby of the hotel, he said to Paul Drake, "Paul, I've been doing a little thinking. I'm uneasy about this Eves business."

"Why?" Drake asked. "Eves is a crook. He respects you because you're a mouthpiece. He'll go the limit for you. Moar's statement to Evelyn Whiting gives you everything you need in front of a jury. Even if his wife *did* beat the gun and bump him off, you're never going to get a jury to bring in a verdict against her—not after Evelyn Whiting tells her story."

Mason said, "Just the same, Paul, I want you to look up Roger P. Cartman, find out all about the automobile accident in which he was injured over on the Islands, find out who his friends were, and find out where he is now."

"Okay," Drake said, "I'll get busy on it right away."

Mason paused at the desk for his key. The clerk handed him a key and several messages. Looking them over, Mason found they were messages of his calls to Della Street.

"Hasn't Miss Street come in *yet?*" he asked the clerk.

The clerk said, "I don't think so."

Mason strode toward the elevator. "Come on, boy," he said to the operator, "shake a leg. See how quickly you can get this crate to the fifth floor."

They emerged on the fifth floor. Mason strode down the corridor, fitted the key to the lock, flung the door open. "She hasn't been here since morning," he said. "Look here, Paul, something's happened to her."

"She left under her own power," Drake pointed out.

"But she'd have come back or left a message," Mason

said. "For God's sake, do something. Don't stand there gawking at me."

"What do you want me to do?" Drake asked.

"Get on the phone," Mason said. "Start your men covering the city. Check the automobile accidents. Cover the ambulance calls. Check through the hospitals. Give me some *action*."

Drake nodded, ran through the connecting door to his room and started putting through calls.

Mason's telephone rang. The lawyer scooped it up, placed the receiver to his ear, said, "Hello," and heard Belle Newberry's voice saying, "Is that you, Mr. Mason?"

"Yes. Where are you, Belle?"

"At my hotel. I've been calling you all afternoon. They let me out when they knew you were getting a writ of *habeas corpus*."

"Have you heard anything from Della?" Mason asked.

"No. I've been ringing the hotel every half hour. No one's answered. I didn't want to leave any message because I was afraid some newspaper reporters might get hold of it, and I'm dodging them."

"Jump in a cab and come on up here," Mason said. "I want to talk with you."

He hung up the receiver, walked through the suite of rooms to Della Street's bedroom, then retraced his steps and went through to Drake's room. Drake had just finished putting through telephone calls.

"Okay, Perry," Drake said. "If anything's happened to her, I'll have a report within half an hour."

"If anything's happened to her," Mason said, "half an hour's too long."

"Well, I'll get it just as soon as the information's available. I told the office to put on as many extra men as they needed. It'll take a little while to get them all working, but we'll cover the city with a fine-tooth comb. We'll know within five minutes if there's been any accident reported of if she's in the emergency hospital."

Mason nodded. "Belle Newberry's coming up," he said.

"They let her out, eh?"

"Yes. It was a bonehead move, holding her, in the first place. They wanted to shake information out of her about that money. They're more interested in the eighteen thousand than they are in anything else."

Mason started pacing the floor. "The thing gets me, Paul," he said. "I should have come back here earlier in the day. To think that while we were chasing around, running down clues, Della may have been lying in a hospital somewhere, seriously hurt."

"She had her purse with her, didn't she?"

"I believe so, yes."

"How about calling your Los Angeles office, Perry? If anything had happened to her, they'd have found her Los Angeles address, and—"

"Good idea," Mason said. He jerked the receiver from the hook and told the operator to rush through a call to his Los Angeles office. Once more, he resumed pacing the floor.

The phone rang. Drake picked it up, said, "Hello," listened for several seconds, said, "All right, throw out a dragnet. Cover everything."

He hung up the telephone and said, "No ambulance report on her, Perry. Nothing in the emergency hospital. No report at the police desk."

"What else could have happened," Mason asked, "if it *wasn't* an automobile accident?"

"She might have been rushed to a private hospital somewhere," Drake said. "We'll know on that within half an hour."

"Let's see," Mason reflected. "It was raining when she left here. That means the roads were pretty slippery. Someone might have skidded into her, and rushed her to a hospital. . . . But he'd have reported the accident to the police by this time."

"He would unless he'd have been injured himself," Drake said.

"Even then, the police would have known of the accident."

Drake nodded.

"What else could have happened to her?" Mason asked.

"I don't know," Drake said. "She might have . . . Say, wait a minute, Perry."

"Go on," Mason said, as the detective hesitated, "spill it."

"She went out under her own power," Drake said. "Now, as I understand it, she wouldn't ordinarily have done that without leaving a message for you or giving you a buzz to see if you had anything you wanted her to do. Is that right?"

"That's right," Mason said.

"Well, then let's suppose she went out on something fast, something which couldn't wait."

"What are you getting at, Paul?"

"Just this," Drake said. "We weren't where we were immediately available. Remember, we were going over to Marian Whiting's. Della wouldn't have called you there unless it had been a major emergency, because she knew you were going to try to shake Marian down for some information."

"Go ahead," Mason said. "Get to the answer. Never mind the preliminaries."

"Remember," Drake said, "just before we went over there, this table steward of yours had brought in a piece of blue silk. We'd cut it up into three pieces and—"

Mason nodded, fished the segment of blue silk out of his vest pocket and said, "Yes, you mentioned that before. Do you think she may have located that blue silk dress?"

Drake said, "Suppose she had? She'd have gone out to make sure, if she'd been in doubt. All right, now suppose while she was making sure, she tipped her hand, and someone did something about it."

158

"That wouldn't have happened," Mason said. "It's too unlikely."

"Don't kid yourself it's unlikely," Drake told him. "Let's figure about that dress, Perry. That dress was on a cleat on the *outside* of the rail."

Mason nodded.

"And with the sea that was running, no one would have been climbing around on the outside of the rail."

"What are you getting at?" Mason asked.

"Just this," Drake said. "Suppose that someone gave Moar the works. Suppose the Fell woman is telling the truth, and a woman hoisted him up to the rail and pushed him over. Just as he went, he made a grab at her and ripped a chunk of cloth out of her dress. As he fell, that cloth caught on the cleat and ripped from his fingers."

"That's just a theory, Paul."

"All right," Drake said, "give me some other theory which will hold water, and account for that dress being on the outside of the ship."

Mason squinted his eyes in thought and stared moodily at the carpet. The telephone rang. He picked it up and learned that his Los Angeles office was on the line. Jackson told him they had had no word from or about Della Street.

As Mason was ready to hang up, the hotel operator cut in on the line and said, "Mr. Mason, a Miss Newberry is down here."

"Send her up," Mason said.

He was idly twisting the piece of blue silk in his fingers when Belle Newberry rapped at the door.

Mason let her in, shook hands and said, "How was it, Belle, pretty bad?"

"It was tough," she told him, "but not *too* tough. Poor Moms, I'm afraid she's having a harder time of it."

"I'm going down to see her tonight," Mason said. "I have her preliminary set for tomorrow morning. I wanted to get down this afternoon but I've been busy. I've uncovered a witness who will smash the case wide open. Tomorrow night she'll be a free woman."

Belle's eyes widened with glad surprise. "You're certain, Mr. Mason?" she asked.

Mason nodded. "This witness," he said, "will show that Carl was trapped. He knew the game was up and he'd decided to end it all to save you disgrace."

"You mean he committed suicide?" she asked.

Mason nodded.

"I hate to think of Carl doing that," she said.

"He did it because he cared so much for you, Belle."

"But *why did he do it?*"

"I think the money he had was hot money."

"What do you mean by hot money?"

"Money which had been illegally obtained, and he thought the law was catching up with him."

She shook her head slowly and said, "That doesn't sound like Carl. He was pretty conservative, you know, Mr. Mason. He wasn't given much to taking chances."

"Well," Mason said, "the facts all point to it and this witness will swear to it."

"What's the cloth?" she asked, noticing the piece of silk Mason was twisting in his fingers.

"Recognize it?" Mason asked, handing it out to her.

She looked at it and frowned. "I've seen it before somewhere."

"You saw it somewhere on the ship," Mason told her. "A woman had a dress made of it, probably an evening gown. It was—"

"Oh, I have it," Belle Newberry said. "I remember it now. I remember the pattern in it."

"Good girl," Mason told her. "Whose was it?"

"That nurse wore it."

Mason glanced at the detective. "Evelyn Whiting?" he asked.

"Yes, the one who was nursing the man with the broken neck."

"You're sure?" Mason asked.

"Absolutely positive," she said.

Mason said to Drake, "All right, Paul, there's your answer. Della spotted this material. She went out to check up on it. Remember, Evelyn Whiting had been out in that mountain cabin since yesterday afternoon. Eves had been away all night. Eves is a known crook. He'd stop at nothing. Now, if Della were pinning something on Evelyn Whiting—"

Drake reached for the telephone. "What do we do, Perry?" he asked.

Mason said, "Round up a bunch of hard-boiled dicks with plenty of guns and ammunition. We're going back to that cabin, Paul. Thinking back on it, Eves was altogether too much on the prod when he came in, then he was too anxious to make a play for my gratitude. Get going!"

Drake grabbed the telephone, put through a call to his office and said, "Get me half a dozen tough babies who can dish it out and take it. I'd like to have a couple of special deputy sheriffs in the lot, and I want guns, ammunition and tear gas."

"What is it?" Belle Newberry asked, staring with apprehensive eyes at the grim face of the lawyer.

"Della Street's missing," Mason said. "She went out this morning and we haven't heard from her since. A check-up on the hospitals and automobile accidents shows she hasn't been injured. When she went out, she was trying to trace down this piece of blue silk."

"Is there anything I can do?" Belle Newberry asked.

Mason said, "Yes, you wait here and play secretary. Take all the messages that come in, and be ready to give me a complete report whenever I call in. You, Paul, tell your office to report to Belle and give her all the dope. Keep men on the job."

Mason walked to his suitcase, pulled out a holstered revolver, unbuckled his belt and slipped the strap through the loop in the holster. "Come on, Paul," he said to the detective, who was telephoning. "We haven't got all day, you know. Tell 'em to rush those men down here."

Chapter 13

The two automobiles, filled with grim, silent men, roared up the paved road which wound through redwood-covered mountains. An orange-peel new moon hung suspended against the orange after-glow of sunset. The drivers were men who knew their business, men who kept the cars in second gear, gave plenty of throttle on the turns and used the brakes but sparingly.

Drake said, "Have you any idea how you're going to play this, Perry? We don't want any rough stuff if we can avoid it."

Mason said, "I'm going to find out whether Eves knows anything about Della Street. If he starts anything, I'll finish it."

"He's very apt to start something," Drake warned.

"And I'm very apt to finish it," Mason said.

"How do you figure the nurse in it?" Drake asked.

"I don't know," Mason admitted. "They're holding something back. How the devil did her dress get on the cleat?"

"Well," Drake said, "we can ask her."

"Later on," Mason told him, "after Della Street shows up, I'm going to do some thinking. I have an idea there's a plain, logical solution to this whole business staring us in the face, Paul, but I can't see it right now because I'm too worried about Della."

"You're going to make a mistake if you crowd Eves," Drake warned. "You could do a lot more by putting cards on the table. . . . Look here, Perry, why don't you get Van Densie to approach him?"

"Why Van Densie?"

"He's the lawyer who defended him on that last murder rap. He might be able to square the whole thing up for you."

"Not that shyster," Mason said. "Anyway, he's in bad enough already. He has troubles of his own. He wouldn't cross the street to do me a good turn."

"Why not try it?" Drake persisted.

Mason said, "I can't try anything except direct action, Paul. I can't explain it. When I talk with a man, I form an impression of whether or not he's telling the truth. If I can look Eves in the eyes and ask him about Della, I'll bet money I can tell whether he's lying."

"All right, suppose he's lying. Then what?" Drake asked.

Mason said, "Then I'll take him into custody."

"*You'll* take him into custody!"

"Yes, *I* will," Mason said. "It's not generally known, but under the law a private citizen can make an arrest when a felony has in fact been committed and he has reasonable grounds to believe the person he's arrested has committed the felony."

"Do you have reasonable grounds?" Drake asked.

"I'll make them reasonable," Mason said.

They drove in silence for another half hour. Then Mason said to the driver, "All right, it's this turn. Get up all the speed you can, then cut out the motor and coast. When you come to the turn on the left, you'll find a hill. Shut off your headlights and stop at the foot of that hill. We go up on foot."

The cars roared into speed, then, as the drivers shut off the motors, glided over the mountain road. "Okay," Mason said, "shut off your headlights and stop."

The cars slid to a silent stop. Mason got out, and the men gathered about him in a compact little knot.

163

"All right," Mason told them, "we go up the road, surround the house. Don't shoot unless you're shot at. I'm going in. Don't let anyone out. I have reason to believe a girl has been kidnapped and that the man in the house did the kidnaping. Don't use guns unless you have to. Use tear gas first, and clubs."

"On our way," one of the men said.

They climbed the hill. Mason and Drake paused to let the men deploy out into the shadows. The cabin was dark and silent.

Mason consulted his wrist watch. When five minutes had passed, he nodded to Drake and said, "Okay, Paul, here we go. You keep back and let me go in front."

"Nothing doing," Drake said. "We go in together."

Their feet crunched up the gravel walk. Mason climbed the stairs to the cabin and pounded on the door. There was no answer. Mason kicked on the door and tried the knob. It was locked.

The lawyer stepped to the window, turned on his flashlight, and directed the beam at the interior.

"I wouldn't do that, Perry," Drake warned. "It's dangerous as hell. He could shoot at that flashlight and—"

Mason said, "Save it, Paul. I want action," and kicked in the window.

The crash of breaking glass sounded startlingly loud in the silence of the mountain night. Mason reached in through the broken pane, unlocked the window, raised the sash, and crawled through. "Coming, Paul?" he asked.

Drake hesitated for a moment, then slid through the window after Mason.

The lawyer directed the beam of his flashlight around the cabin, found a light switch, and snapped on the lights.

"You know what a spot we'll be in if we're caught at this," Drake said.

"I know," Mason remarked absently, "and I don't give a damn. I'm going through the house."

164

They searched the cabin thoroughly. At the end of the search, Mason delivered his verdict: "Okay," he said, "they played us for suckers. The business about Evelyn Whiting's testimony was just a stall to get rid of me and keep me from getting suspicious. They packed up and left as soon as we'd gone."

"What do we do next?" Drake asked.

"We find Eves."

"How?"

"I don't know," Mason admitted, "but I do know we're going to find him."

"Where do we go from here?" Drake asked.

"We wake up the man in the store, find out if he saw Eves leave, and put through a telephone call," Mason said.

They summoned the operatives, returned to the cars, and, after some delay, got the man who operated the general store out of bed. He had seen Eves and the young woman, whom he understood was Mrs. Eves, leave within half an hour after Mason had visited him that afternoon. The car, he said, was pretty well filled with baggage.

Drake put through a long distance call to his San Francisco office, talked for several minutes, then drew Perry Mason aside.

"Perry," he said, "this doesn't look so good."

"Do you have some news of Della?"

"Yes."

"Go ahead," Mason told him, "spill it."

Drake said, "After all, Perry, we don't know that she was working on this evening gown business. She may have had reasons of her own—"

"Never mind the preliminaries," Mason said. "What are you getting at?"

"Look here, Perry," Drake blurted, "has it ever occurred to you that Della might . . . well, might walk out on you some day?"

Mason's face darkened. "Damn you, Paul," he said, "if you—"

"Now, take it easy, Perry," Drake said, backing away. "After all, she may have met someone on the ship, or—"

Mason moved toward him belligerently. "Spill it," he said. "Come on, Paul, out with it."

Drake said, "My men have been busy, Perry. They've uncovered a drive-yourself agency which rented a car to Della shortly before noon. She put up a fifty-dollar deposit and paid a week's rent in advance. She used the name of D. M. Crenshaw."

Mason said, "If your men have pulled a boner on this, Paul, I'll—"

"They haven't, Parry. They have a photograph of Della. The man who rented her the car identified it absolutely."

"She was alone?" Mason asked.

"She was alone," Drake said. "Come on, Perry, let's go back to the hotel and get a night's sleep. After all, you'll have to be in court tomorrow, and by tomorrow you may know what it's all about."

Mason stared steadily at the detective for a moment, then turned on his heel. "All right, Paul," he said, "let's go."

Chapter 14

Outside the courtroom windows, the sun was sparkling San Francisco's buildings into clean brilliance. Within the courtroom, daylight waged a losing fight against the gloomy dignity of somber walls of dark mahogany. Electric lights flooded the room with subdued illumination. Not all of the chairs were filled. The thrill-hungry spectators who haunt courtrooms with eager ears, listening for salacious details, could hardly be bothered with a commonplace husband murder.

Perry Mason, lines etched deeply into his countenance, his slightly reddened eyes showing the effects of a sleepless night, said to Judge Sturtevant Romley, "We are ready on behalf of the defendant."

"Very well," Judge Romley announced. "Testimony in the preliminary hearing of The People of the State of California versus Anna Moar, also known as Ann Newberry, will be taken at this time pursuant to stipulation of Counsel. Call your first witness, Mr. Prosecutor."

Donaldson P. Scudder, a slender, anemic individual, with skin which seemed almost transparent, and the precise, academic manner of one who is completely removed from human emotions, said, "Our first witness, if the Court please, will be Frank Remington."

Judge Romley, recognizing from the Prosecutor's voice that there was to be nothing spectacular, a mere matter of assembling the legal red tape with which a murder case must be duly tied, sat back in his cushioned chair and glanced appraisingly at the defendant.

Anna Moar, seated behind Perry Mason, her chin held high, her eyes slightly defiant, as though daring the machinery of Justice to do its worst, sat virtually without emotion.

Remington testified that he was manager of the Products Refining Company of Los Angeles; that the corporation had employed a Carl Waker Moar; that Moar was no longer in their employ; that he had failed to report for duty two months ago and the witness had not seen him since.

Scudder, opening his briefcase, said, "I will show you a photograph, Mr. Remington, and ask you if you can identify it."

"Yes," the witness said, "this is a photograph of the party to whom I have referred in my testimony—Carl Waker Moar."

"The person who was employed by the Products Refining Company?"

"Yes."

"In what capacity?"

"As bookkeeper."

"We will ask that the photograph be marked for identification," Scudder said.

"No objection," Mason said.

"Cross-examine the witness," the Prosecutor invited.

Mason made a gesture of dismissal. "No questions."

"The next witness will be Miss Aileen Fell," the Prosecutor announced.

Aileen fell, in her early thirties, trying to conceal her nervousness beneath a cloak of calm dignity, was sworn and took the witness stand.

"Your name?" Scudder asked.

"Aileen Lenore Fell."

"Occupation?"

"I'm a schoolteacher."

"Where were you on Sunday night, the sixth of this month?"

"I was on a ship, traveling from Honolulu to San Francisco."

"There were other passengers aboard that ship?"

"Oh, yes."

"I call your attention to the defendant, Mrs. Anna Newberry Moar, and will ask you if she was aboard that ship as a passenger."

"Yes, sir, she was, but not under the name of Moar—she was traveling under the name of Newberry."

"And she was accompanied by whom?"

"By a Carl Newberry, her husband, and Belle Newberry, her daughter."

"Belle Newberry is the young woman sitting on the aisle of the first row of spectators on the left?"

"Yes."

"And would you know Carl Newberry if you should see him again?"

"Yes, of course."

"Would you recognize his photograph?"

"I believe so, yes."

"I hand you a photograph which has been marked for identification as People's Exhibit A, and ask you if that photograph is of anyone you know."

She studied the photograph and said with quiet dignity, "It is. That is a photograph of Carl Newberry, who shared the defendant's stateroom as her husband."

"Now, what was the state of the weather on the evening of the sixth on that portion of the ocean which was then being traversed by the ship on which you and the gentleman whose photograph you have identified were passengers?"

"The weather," she said, "was very rough. It was stormy."

"Can you describe the storm?"

"There was a wind which came, I think, from the southwest. It was blowing very, very hard. Rain was falling in torrents. It was absolutely impossible to stand on the right-hand side of the ship without being soaked by both rain and spray. On the left-hand side of the ship, it was possible to stand in the shelter of the decks, and away from

169

the wind, without getting drenched, although water would run along the decks every time the ship rolled."

"And the ship was rolling?"

"Yes, quite heavily."

The deputy district attorney said to the Court, "We will go into greater detail about the weather with the captain of the ship." Then, turning back to the witness, "Now, Miss Fell, when did you last see the gentleman, Carl Moar, or Carl Newberry, as you knew him?"

"On the evening of the sixth."

"Can you tell us about what time it was?"

"It was shortly before nine o'clock."

"Where were you standing?"

"I was standing on the deck below the boat deck, near the stairs."

"And where did you see Mr. Newberry?"

"Mr. Newberry and his wife . . ."

"Now, you are referring to the defendant here, when you say 'his wife'?"

"Yes."

"Go on."

"Mr. Newberry, or Mr. Moar, to use his right name, and Mrs. Newberry stepped out on the deck. They stood there for a moment, looking around them. Then they started toward the stairway which led to the boat deck."

"That was the deck immediately above the one on which you were standing?"

"Yes."

"Did Mr. and Mrs. Newberry walk past you?"

"Yes."

"How close were they to you?"

"Not more than a few feet."

"How were you dressed?"

"I had on a dark beret and a dark rain coat. I was in a sheltered part of the deck directly under the stairs. I was standing in the shadow where they couldn't see me."

"Did you hear them say anything?"

"Yes, I heard Mrs. Newberry—that is, the defendant—say something and I heard Mr. Newberry reply in an angry voice. I gathered that Mrs. Newberry wanted him . . ."

"Never mind what you gathered," Judge Romley said. "Just give us your best recollection of what was said and who said it."

"Well, Mr. Newberry, or Mr. Moar, said, 'I tell you, it has to be handled my way. I've already discounted that. You keep your fingers out of it.'"

"And then what happened?" Scudder asked.

"Mr. Newberry walked rapidly toward the open stairway which led to the boat deck and started up."

"How was he dressed?"

"He was wearing a tuxedo."

"Was he wearing any overcoat or rain coat?"

"No."

"And was this staircase exposed to the rain?"

Mason said casually, "If Counsel is going to lead the witness throughout her entire testimony, I suggest Counsel should be sworn."

The judge said, "You will avoid leading questions as much as possible, Counselor."

"All this is merely preliminary," Scudder retorted. "There can be no question about it."

"We're coming to the point in this young woman's testimony where there's going to be lots of question about it," Mason said. "I don't want Counsel to elicit that testimony by leading questions."

"Counsel won't," Scudder snapped.

"Proceed," Judge Romley ordered.

Aileen Fell said, "Rain was falling in torrents. That staircase was entirely open and unprotected. I could see rain beating down on the shoulders of Mr. Moar's coat as he started up the stairs."

"And what did the defendant do?"

"She ran after him and started up the stairs. Mr. Moar turned and protested. He told Mrs. Moar to go back to her cabin."

171

"And what did Mrs. Moar do?"

"Waited until he had ascended the stairs, and then she ran up the stairs."

"And how was she dressed?"

"She had on a dark dinner dress."

"Any wrap of any sort?"

"No, it was a backless gown. The rain was simply pouring down on her bare skin."

"Then what happened?"

"They went up on the boat deck. I heard the sound of their feet on the deck above me. Then, after a while, I heard a scuffle, the sounds of a struggle . . ."

"I move to strike the words 'scuffle' and 'struggle' as conclusions of the witness," Mason said.

"Motion's granted."

"Just what *did* you hear?" Scudder asked.

"Well, I heard just what I told you. I don't know how to express it otherwise."

"You heard the sound of feet on the deck above you?"

"Yes."

"And what was the nature of that sound?"

"It was a series of rapid scuffs, with dragging sounds in between, just the sort of noises which would be made by two people . . ."

"Never mind that," Scudder said. "I think the Court understands what you *heard*. Now tell what you *did*."

"Well," she said, "after a few minutes of that, I started to go up the stairs to the boat deck to see what was happening. I was half way up the stairs when I heard the sound of a shot. When I got to the top of the stairs I . . ."

"Now, just a minute," Scudder said. "Let's get this all in order. You went up the stairs to the boat deck. Now, by those stairs, are you referring to the same stairs up which Mr. Moar and Mrs. Moar, the defendant in this action, gained the deck?"

"Yes, sir."

"And were there lights on the boat deck?"

"No, sir. The boat deck wasn't illuminated, but there were lights in the hospital section."

"Where is that?"

"It's just forward of the gymnasium. The stairs are at the after part of the ship. There are two stairways, one on the left side and one on the right side. I went up the stairs on the left side. The gymnasium is right at the head of those stairs. Then there is a court for playing deck tennis, and beyond that is a section of the ship set aside for hospital rooms."

"There was a light in this hospital section?"

"Yes."

"Could you see that light through a door or through a window?"

"Through both. A window was open—that is, I mean there was no shade across it—and the door was standing open."

"How far were you from that open door?"

"Oh, perhaps fifty feet."

"Very well. Now tell the Court what you saw."

"I saw Mrs. Newberry—that is, Mrs. Moar, the defendant in this action, the woman sitting over there—standing over her husband's body. Her husband was stretched out on the deck, motionless."

"And what did the defendant do?"

"She reached down and picked the body . . ."

"Now, when you say 'body,'" Scudder interrupted, "you mean the same thing which you have previously referred to in your testimony as the motionless form of Mr. Moar lying there on the deck?"

"Yes, sir."

"What did she do?"

"She put her hands under his armpits, half lifted him, and started to drag him toward the rail."

"Then what happened?"

"When the boat rolled over to the right, she couldn't make any headway. But when the boat rolled to the left, she moved very rapidly. Just then the boat gave a sudden lurch.

173

The defendant ran the body down to the rail, then lifted it, raised the revolver and shot him again. Then she pushed him into the ocean."

"Then what did she do?"

"She ran forward along the boat deck, and I lost sight of her when she ran around behind the hospital."

"What did you do?"

"I screamed."

"Now, do you know what time this was?" Scudder asked.

"I do. I know exactly what time it was."

"What time was it?"

"It was a few moments after nine. Just before I heard the first shot, I had heard the ship's bell ring twice. That's nine o'clock, according to ship time—two bells in the evening."

"You may cross-examine," Scudder said.

Mason got slowly to his feet. "How was Mrs. Moar, the defendant in this case, dressed?" he asked.

"Just as I told you," Aileen Fell snapped back at him, with the quick enunciation of one who fancies herself rather good at repartee and is determined not to be worsted in a verbal exchange. "In a dark, backless formal gown."

"It was the night of the captain's dinner on shipboard?" Mason asked.

"Yes."

"And how were *you* dressed?"

"In my rain coat, just as I've told you. Standing in the shadow, as I was, it was virtually impossible to see me . . ."

"I'm not asking you now about your rain coat," Mason said. "I want to know what you had on underneath your rain coat."

"What I . . . What I had on *underneath* my rain coat?"

"Exactly," Mason said.

"Why . . . I don't see what different that makes."

"What I'm getting at," Mason said, "is that you also

were wearing an evening gown on that occasion, were you not?"

"Yes."

"A light blue silk print?"

"Yes. That's right."

"You were dressed for the captain's dinner?"

"Yes."

"And after the captain's dinner, you decided to go on deck?"

"Yes."

"You went to your stateroom and put on your rain coat and beret? Did you put on anything else?"

"No."

"You're absolutely certain?"

"Yes."

"You didn't pick up anything in your stateroom, other than the rain coat and the beret?"

"Mr. Mason, I fail to see what that has to do . . ."

"Did you pick up anything else in your stateroom?"

"That's none of your business."

Judge Romley swung around in his chair to frown down at the witness and said austerely, "The witness will confine herself to respectful answers to Counsel's questions. The question was whether you picked up anything else in your stateroom. Did you or didn't you?"

"No," Aileen Fell snapped.

"Now," Mason said, "going back to what you saw when you were on deck: You have stated, I believe, that Mr. Moar climbed up the open stairway to the boat deck."

"Yes."

"And you say he protested when Mrs. Moar started to follow him?"

"He did."

Mason said drily, "His protest was a gesture made with his right foot, wasn't it?"

"Well . . . yes."

Someone in the courtroom tittered. The bailiff pounded for order.

"In other words," Mason said, "he kicked at her, didn't he?"

"Yes, I suppose so."

"Why didn't you say so in your direct examination?" Mason asked. "Is it because you are biased in favor of the Prosecution and didn't want this Court to feel Mrs. Moar might have been acting in self-defense?"

"I have no prejudice whatever against Mrs. Moar, other than the normal prejudice a woman has for a wife who will deliberately murder her husband," Aileen snapped, and then settled back in her chair with the triumphant expression of one who has bested a cross-examiner.

Mason was completely unruffled. "Now, Mrs. Moar," he said, "had on a backless evening gown. This gown was rather tight fitting, was it not?"

"Yes."

"And there was no back?"

"No."

"It was rather skimpy in front?"

"Too skimpy, if you ask me," the witness said.

"Well," Mason observed, "I *am* asking you."

"Yes, it was *very* skimpy."

"And fitted her tightly across the hips?"

"Molded to her hips would be more like it," the witness said. "It was what I would call daring—to the point of bad taste."

"Many formal gowns are like that, are they not?" Mason asked.

"It depends on the taste," the witness countered, "and the manner in which they're worn."

"Now, Mrs. Moar followed her husband up the stairs to the boat deck?"

"Yes."

"There's an iron rail running along both sides of those stairs?"

"That's right."

"And as Mrs. Moar went up the stairs, she held to the rail with both hands," Mason asked, "that is, she placed each of her hands on one of the rails?"

"Yes, she . . . no, she did not!" the witness said emphatically, in the manner of one who refuses to be trapped. "Her right hand held to the iron rail. Her left hand had gathered up the skirts of her dark gown."

"Now," Mason inquired blandly, "will you kindly tell us just where a woman clad in a backless evening gown, with a front which was altogether too skimpy, a gown which fit so tightly over the hips that you considered it indecent, with her right hand holding to the iron rail of a flight of steps, her left hand holding up the skirt of her evening gown, could have carried a thirty-eight revolver?"

For a startled moment, Aileen Fell was silent. The tense courtroom was filled with the sound of rustlings as spectators leaned forward, anxious to miss no word. After a moment, Aileen Fell said, "She had it in her left hand."

"You mean she was holding the revolver in her left hand and also holding her skirt?"

"Yes. The gun was beneath the folds of the dress."

"Now, was this dress transparent?" Mason asked.

"It might as well have been."

"But could you see the gun through it?"

"Well . . . well, I don't suppose I could, no."

"In other words," Mason said, "you didn't actually *see* Mrs. Moar take any gun up to the boat deck, and, when she walked past within a very few feet of you, you didn't see any weapon in her possession, did you?"

"Well," the witness said, "I know she had the gun. She must have had it."

"And that's the only way you know she had it—because you think she must have had it."

"Well, yes, if you want to put it that way."

Mason smiled. "I want to put it that way, Miss Fell."

Her mouth was a thin, straight line. Her eyes blazed indignantly.

"Now, when you were half way up the stairs, you heard a shot?"

"Yes."

"And when you arrived on deck, you saw Mrs. Moar standing over the unconscious form of her husband?"

"Lifeless form," the witness said.

"Ah," Mason observed blandly, "then it *was* a lifeless figure?"

"Yes."

"You're certain of that?"

"Yes."

"In other words, you're positive that Mr. Moar was dead at that time."

"I think he was, yes."

"Well now, are you guessing, or do you know?"

The deputy district attorney jumped to his feet, said, "Your Honor, I object. This is not proper cross-examination. This witness couldn't possibly tell . . ."

"I object to the Prosecutor coaching this witness," Mason interrupted. "She's an educated woman and is thoroughly competent to take care of herself under cross-examination. She has said Mrs. Moar was standing over the lifeless form of her husband. She used that word 'lifeless' to prejudice Your Honor against Mrs. Moar, and I'm going to make this witness take back that statement. I am going to make her admit that she doesn't know whether the form was lifeless or not."

"You're not going to do any such thing," Aileen Fell snapped. "I said the body was lifeless, and it was lifeless."

Scudder slowly sat down.

"You mean that Mr. Moar was dead, then, when you came up the stairs to the boat deck?"

"Yes."

"Then, when you state that the defendant hoisted him to the rail and fired another shot into his body, you want the Court to understand that she was firing that shot into a dead man, and that shot had nothing to do with the murder of Mr. Moar, because Mr. Moar was already dead. Is that right?"

The witness started to say something, checked herself, stopped, then said savagely, "I guess Mrs. Moar wanted to make sure he was dead. That's her type!"

"In other words," Mason went on, smiling, "your idea is that Mrs. Moar, standing within three feet of her husband, wasn't certain he was dead when she dragged him to the rail, whereas you, standing some fifty or sixty feet away, took one look at him and are willing to *swear* that he was dead. Is that right?"

"He was dead," she said.

Mason continued to smile. "Now then, just before Mrs. Moar lifted her husband to the rail, the ship had rolled far to the left, hadn't it?"

"Yes."

"By the way," Mason said, "weren't your stockings torn when you came down off the boat deck?"

"One of them was, yes."

"What caused it to tear?"

"I skinned my knee and tore my stocking when I fell down."

"Oh," Mason said solicitously, "you fell down, did you?"

"Yes."

"That was when the ship took that heavy roll to port, was it?"

"Yes."

"You lost your footing, fell to the deck, and started to slide?"

"I nearly went overboard."

"How did you check yourself, Miss Fell?"

"I clung to the deck as much as I could and finally came to a stop against the rail."

"You must have been a pretty busy young woman for a few minutes," Mason suggested.

"I was," she assured him.

"And it was when the ship took this roll to port that Mrs. Moar lifted her husband to the rail, shot him and dropped him overboard. Is that right?"

"Yes."

"Did you roll over and over as you slid down to the rail on the port side?"

"I rolled over a couple of times, then I slid the rest of the way."

"On your face?"

"On my hands and knees."

"Yet, notwithstanding all of this, you didn't take your eyes from Mrs. Moar, but actually *saw* her lift her husband to the rail, shoot him and drop him overboard?"

"Well," she said, and hesitated.

"Isn't it a fact," Mason asked, "that immediately after this occurrence, you talked with the young woman who shared your cabin and then and there told her that when Mrs. Moar started to drag her husband to the rail you had lost your footing and hadn't seen what happened, but had heard the second shot and then saw Mrs. Moar running down the deck alone?"

"Well, if she didn't shoot him and pitch him overboard, who did?" she asked.

"That," Mason said, "is the point the Court will be called upon to determine. Now, isn't it a fact that *you* didn't see what happened there at the rail?"

"Well . . . no, I saw it."

"But didn't you state at a time when the occurrence was more fresh in your memory that you hadn't seen it?"

"Well, perhaps I did."

"Which is right?" Mason inquired. "What you said then or what you say now?"

"Well . . ."

"Answer the question," Mason insisted as she hesitated.

"Well," she said, "I didn't see . . . that is, I didn't actually see with my own eyes Mrs. Moar lift her husband to the rail and drop him overboard. But I did hear the shot."

"And you didn't see Mrs. Moar shoot her husband the first time, did you?"

"Well . . ."

"That shot," Mason reminded her, "was fired when you were half way up the stairs."

"Well, no. I didn't see her shoot him."

"Then you don't know of your own knowledge that she fired either one of the shots, do you?"

"Well, I guess that when a woman . . ."

"Of your own knowledge," Mason interrupted. "You don't know, do you?"

"I don't know absolutely, no."

"Now then," Mason said, "let's check up for a moment on the manner in which you were dressed at the time." He walked over to the table where his briefcase was reposing, took from it a photograph, offered it to Scudder for inspection and then passed it to the witness. "I show you what purports to be a flashlight photograph of a group in evening clothes, and in which you are standing the second from the left. Is that the dress you wore on the night in question?"

"Why . . . yes," she said, staring at the picture. "I remember when that picture was taken, but I didn't have any idea . . ."

"Save only and solely for a beret and a rain coat, that's exactly the way you appeared when you were on the deck at the time Mr. and Mrs. Newberry walked past you?"

"Why . . . yes, I guess so."

"And that photograph shows you exactly as you were at the time of the captain's dinner?"

"Yes."

"To all practical intents and purposes, that photograph of you might have been taken at the time of the captain's dinner?"

"Yes."

Mason said, "By the way, Miss Fell, may I see your glasses?"

"You may not," she snapped.

Judge Romley said, "What is the purpose of this, Mr. Mason?"

Mason said, "Your Honor, this witness has testified that this photograph shows her exactly as she was at the time of the captain's dinner. She has also testified that she went to her stateroom and there picked up a beret and rain coat, but did not pick up anything else. She swears that this photograph also shows exactly the manner in which she appeared, save for a cap and rain coat, when Mr. and Mrs. Moar walked past her on deck. Now then, if the Court will notice this photograph . . ."

Mason passed the photograph up to Judge Romley, who studied it for a moment, nodded, and said, "Very well, Miss Fell, you will please let Mr. Mason inspect your spectacles."

With an air of outraged dignity, the witness removed the glasses and handed them to Mason.

"Ah, yes," Mason said, "I see the resemblance now. The reason I hadn't thought it was such a good photograph before, was that you weren't wearing spectacles in the photograph. I believe it's your invariable custom to leave off your spectacles when you dress formally, isn't it, Miss Fell?"

"Well," she admitted, "I don't think a woman looks as attractive in spectacles when she's attending a formal function. In my own case, I think my appearance is . . ."

"Exactly," Mason said. "And, of course, you weren't wearing your glasses when you went on deck after the captain's dinner?"

"Well, I . . ."

"Because, if you had been," Mason went on to point out, "with the rain beating down in torrents, the lenses would have been covered with moisture and you couldn't have seen things clearly."

"No," she said emphatically, "I was *not* wearing my glasses."

182

"I thought not," Mason said, still holding her glasses in his hand. "Now then, Miss Fell, about how far were you from Mrs. Moar when you climbed the stairs to the boat deck?"

"You mean when she was standing over the body of her husband?"

"Yes."

"I said fifty or sixty feet."

Mason backed away from the witness, to stand just in front of the deputy district attorney. "This far?" he asked.

"Certainly not," she said. "I said fifty or sixty feet. You're not over twenty feet away from me. You can't trap me that way, Mr. Mason."

"Then I am standing at only about a third of the distance at which you saw Mrs. Moar, is that right?"

"Yes."

"Now, was there as much light on the deck as there is in this courtroom?" Mason asked.

"Of course not."

"Well, how much was there?"

"Not very much," she said, "but enough came through the hospital door so you could see objects."

"Would you say a third as much light as there is here in the courtroom?"

"Probably not that much."

Mason nodded. "Now you've identified a photograph which has been introduced in evidence as being that of the gentleman who was traveling on this ship under the name of Newberry, the man who was the husband of this defendant."

"Yes."

"I'll show you another photograph," Mason said, "of Mr. . . . er . . . I never can get that name straight. . . . Paul, where's that photograph?"

Drake handed Mason a rolled photograph.

Mason, still standing in front of Scudder, said, "This is a life-size photograph, Miss Fell. I'll ask you if you can identify *it*."

He unrolled the photograph; she glanced at it and nodded her head.

"And this is the man whom you saw pushed overboard?" Mason asked.

"Yes."

"And it was this man's *lifeless* figure which you saw lying on the boat deck, with Mrs. Moar, the defendant in this action, standing over it?"

"Yes."

Judge Romley suddenly frowned and leaned forward to stare at the photograph, glanced from Mason to Scudder. A smile twitched at the corners of his lips.

Scudder, noticing the expression on the judge's face, became instantly suspicious. He said, "It is customary, if the Court please, to let opposing Counsel inspect a photograph before a witness is examined on it."

"I beg your pardon," Mason said urbanely, "I *did* overlook that, didn't I? It happens, Mr. Scudder, that the photograph I hold in my hand is a life-size photograph of Mr. Donaldson P. Scudder," and Mason turned so that the photograph was visible to Scudder and to the courtroom.

The bailiff vainly pounded with his gavel, seeking to restore order. Judge Romley fought to keep a smile from his lips, while Scudder, his face red, shouted indignant protests which went unheeded.

When order had been resumed, Scudder shouted. "Your Honor, I object. This is not proper cross-examination. It's unethical. It takes an unfair advantage of the witness. Counsel distinctly told her that he was showing a life-size photograph of the decedent, Mr. Carl Waker Moar."

"Counsel told her no such thing," Mason said.

"I think Mr. Mason is right," Judge Romley ruled. "I remember particularly that he said, 'Mr. . . . er . . .' and hesitated, then said, 'I never can get that name straight.' Of course it was an attempt to entrap the witness, but, as Counsel has so aptly pointed out, this witness is educated and should be able to take care of herself on cross-examination. Her identification of the photograph has been most positive."

Mason turned to the witness. "Will you kindly explain, Miss Fell, how it is that you have now testified that it was Mr. Donaldson P. Scudder, the deputy district attorney, whom you saw lying lifeless on the deck, whom you saw thrown overboard, whom . . ."

"You had my glasses," the witness said acidly. "You lied to me about that photograph, Mr. Mason. I took your word for it."

Mason, still holding the photograph, said, "But you didn't have your glasses on the night in question, Miss Fell. Whose word are you taking for what happened then?"

She was silent.

"Now, will you kindly tell us how it is that when I show you a life-size photograph, standing within one-third of the distance at which you have testified you saw the defendant on the deck of the steamship, in a room which you admit is more than three times better lighted than that deck, under conditions, therefore, which are far more favorable than those which existed at that time, you are unable to distinguish between a life-size photograph of Mr. Scudder and a photograph of Mr. Moar?"

The witness said, "If you will kindly return my glasses, Mr. Mason."

Mason said, "In other words, Miss Fell, without your glasses you can't identify faces at this distance, can you?"

"I can identify figures."

"Exactly," Mason said, "by the way they are dressed. Is that it?"

"Well, that's partially it."

"In other words," Mason went on, "while Mr. and Mrs. Moar passed closely enough to you when you were standing on the lower deck so you could recognize them, by the time you had gained the boat deck, you were *not* close enough to them to recognize their faces. You could see figures. You only knew that there was the figure of a man in a tuxedo and a woman in a dark formal gown. Is that right?"

185

"That's all I needed to know under the circumstances," she said.

"But that's right, isn't it?"

"I could identify those figures, Mr. Mason. I *know* the woman was Mrs. Moar. It couldn't have been anyone else."

"She was wearing a dark formal gown?" Mason asked.

"Yes. I've told you that two or three times already."

"And isn't it true," Mason asked, "that someone wearing a formal gown of any other dark color—for instance a dark blue—would have appeared to you under those circumstances to have been Mrs. Moar?"

"Those were the only ones who had gone up to that deck."

"But there were other means of gaining that deck?"

"There were other stairs, yes."

"And someone must have been in the hospital section, to have turned on that light."

"I don't know *how* it was turned on."

Judge Romley said, "Just a minute, Mr. Mason." He bent forward to regard the witness with frowning disapproval. "Miss Fell," he said, "this is a murder trial. You're in a court of justice. You are testifying under oath. This is not a game of wits which you are playing with opposing Counsel. This is a serious matter. Apparently your vision without your glasses is very much impaired. Now then, I want you to answer Mr. Mason's question."

"What question?" she asked.

"If the only thing you can absolutely swear to is that you saw two figures on the boat deck, but that you can't positively identify either of those figures."

"Well, I guess I saw them when they walked by me on the lower deck . . ."

"I'm not talking about the lower deck now," Judge Romley said. "I'm talking about the boat deck."

"No," she admitted after a moment's consideration, "I can't identify the figures I saw on the upper deck."

"That," Mason said, surrendering her glasses with a bow, "is all. Thank you very much, Miss Fell."

Scudder hesitated for a moment, then said, "That's all."

Aileen Fell adjusted her glasses, glowered at Perry Mason, and, chin in the air, marched across the railed enclosure to take her seat in the courtroom.

"Call your next witness, Mr. Scudder," Judge Romley said.

"Captain Joe Hanson."

Captain Hanson, big-bodied, heavily-muscled, clear-eyed, took the stand and regarded Perry Mason with steady gray eyes.

"We will stipulate, to save time," Mason said, "that this is the captain of the ship on which Carl Newberry, or Carl Moar, as the case may be, sailed from Honolulu; that he was at all times the captain of the vessel; that he is acquainted with Carl Moar, and will identify the photograph identified as that of Carl Moar by the previous witnesses as being that of the passenger who had taken passsage on his ship under the name of Carl Newberry, and who occupied cabin three twenty-one."

"Very well," Scudder said. "Now then, Captain, can you tell us the condition of the weather on the night of the sixth, at approximately the hour of nine o'clock P.M.?"

"It was blowing a gale from the so'west," Captain Hanson said. "The rain was coming down in torrents. Visibility was very poor."

"What was the position of the ship at nine o'clock on that night?" Scudder asked.

"We were just a-beam of the Farallon Islands."

"And you were within three miles of those islands?"

"Yes, within a mile and a half."

"What about the sea?"

"A heavy sea was running, hitting us on the starboard quarter. The vessel was rolling rather heavily."

"Had you taken any precautions to keep passengers from the decks?"

"On the windward side, yes. However, it wasn't rolling heavily enough so passengers couldn't go out in roped-off

187

areas on the lee side. All doors on the weather side had been locked, and the exposed portions of the lee decks were roped off."

"Shortly after nine o'clock, did you have occasion to go to the cabin of the defendant?"

"I did."

"Who was present at the time?"

"The Purser, the defendant, Mrs. Moar, Mr. Perry Mason, Miss Della Street, Miss Belle Newberry, the daughter of Mrs. Moar."

"Now then, at that time and place," Scudder said, "did the defendant make any statement as to when she had last seen her husband?"

"She did."

"What did she say?"

"Just a moment, your Honor," Mason said, getting to his feet, "the question is objected to as incompetent, irrelevant and immaterial, and no proper foundation laid."

Judge Romley stared over his glasses at Perry Mason. "I'm not certain I understand the objection, particularly the part about no proper foundation having been laid."

Mason said, "May it please the Court, it is necessary for the Prosecution to prove the *corpus delicti*, before there can be any testimony connecting the defendant with the commission of the crime. In other words, in this case, the Prosecution must prove, first, that Carl Newberry, or Carl Moar, as the case may be, is actually dead. Secondly, the Prosecution must prove that he met his death as the result of some criminal agency. When this is done, the Prosecution can then seek to connect the defendant with the crime. But until that has been done, there can be no testimony of confessions or admissions on the part of the defendant.

"Now, in this case, the most that the Prosecution has been able to show is that a witness heard a shot and saw two figures standing some sixty feet away. She cannot identify those figures."

Scudder said, "Your Honor, if I may say just one word."

Judge Romley nodded permission.

"This is merely a flimsy technicality," Scudder said. "But I will meet Counsel on his own ground. Let us suppose that no one can testify that Mrs. Moar shot and killed Carl Moar, but someone did drag a man to the rail and throw him overboard. Now, I will show by Captain Hanson that the condition of the sea was such at that time that a man couldn't live for ten minutes, even if he were a most expert swimmer in . . ."

"But no one has testified that any man was thrown overboard," Mason said.

"Miss Fell saw . . ."

Mason smiled as the trial deputy suddenly lapsed into silence.

Judge Romley said, "This is a most peculiar situation, Counselor."

Mason said affably, "Isn't it, your Honor?" and sat down.

"I can reach it in another way," Scudder said desperately. "Let me ask Captain Hanson a few more questions."

"Very well," Judge Romley said. "Go ahead."

"What happened on that ship, so far as you know, of your own knowledge, shortly after nine o'clock in the evening of the sixth?" Scudder asked.

"The operator telephoned the bridge that a man was overboard. I immediately took necessary steps to do everything in my power to find this man, and, if possible, rescue him. I swung the ship in a sharp turn back onto the course which we had been following. I threw over light flares and life buoys with light flares attached. I continued to search the water for more than an hour and a half, and then proceeded into San Francisco."

"Did you take steps to ascertain the identity of any person who might have been missing from the ship?"

Captain Hanson scratched his head and said, "Well, we did and we didn't."

"What do you mean by that?"

"Well, we started to call the roll," Captain Hanson said. "We ordered all the passengers to their staterooms. Then this Miss Fell came to me and told me that it was . . ."

"Never mind what some one told you, Captain," Judge Romley interrupted, "just state what you did."

"Well," Captain Hanson said, "before we'd checked all of the staterooms, we started checking on Mr. Newberry, or Moar, I suppose his real name is. We couldn't find him, and we did find evidence that his wife . . ."

"Never mind any of that evidence now," Judge Romley interrupted. "What we are trying to do now is to prove the *corpus delicti*."

"Well," the captain remarked patiently, "I don't know what that is; all I know is what I did."

"Then you never did check all of the staterooms and all of the passengers against the passenger list?"

"Not then," Captain Hanson admitted.

Scudder, desperately worried, said, "Your Honor, I have not concluded. I appreciate the position in which the Prosecution finds itself. It's rather a unique position. I may say, of course, that as a Prosecutor, I have no sympathy with a criminal who seeks to hide behind a technicality . . ."

"That will do," Judge Romley interrupted. "You will confine your remarks to the proper subjects, Counselor. You know such remarks are improper."

"I beg the Court's pardon," Scudder said. "My feelings got the better of me. May I ask, if the Court please, that we have an adjournment until three o'clock this afternoon? There's one more witness I hope to be able to produce at that time."

Judge Romley nodded. "The request is rather unusual, but the circumstances are equally unusual. The Court will take a recess until three o'clock this afternoon," he said.

Chapter 15

Drake pushed his way through the spectators, to reach Mason's side. "Okay, Perry," he said, "I think we have something."

"On Della?" Mason asked.

Drake nodded.

Mason bent over the chair in which Mrs. Moar was sitting. "That," he told her in a whisper, "just about blows up their case. Judge Romley doesn't believe in binding defendants over when it will be impossible to obtain a conviction in the Superior Court. He'll give you just as fair a hearing here as though you were on trial before a jury, and Aileen Fell's testimony isn't going to carry very much weight. All she saw was two figures struggling on the deck, and she saw them rather indistinctly."

Mrs. Moar squeezed his hand gratefully.

"I have to run out on an important matter," Mason said. "I'll see you at three o'clock this afternoon." He turned to Drake and said, "Okay, Paul, let's go."

Belle Newberry grabbed his hand as Mason started to leave the courtroom. "You darling!" she exclaimed.

Mason smiled down at her, patted her shoulder, and said, "You'll have a chance to visit with your mother for a few minutes before the matron takes her back. I'll see you later, Belle."

Drake had a car waiting in front of the courthouse.

"All right," Mason said eagerly, "what have you found, Paul?"

Drake said, "I don't know, Perry. I don't want to be the one to tell you. I'd rather you'd see for yourself."

"What the devil are you getting at?" Mason asked.

Drake shook his head and said, "Get in, Perry. It won't be long."

"Where is it?"

"Over in Berkeley."

"Well then, let's get started," Mason snapped.

The car dashed across Market Street and turned to the left, to speed down the boulevard leading to the bridge which crossed the bay.

"Look here," Mason said, "there are only three of us. If we're going to have trouble with Eves—"

"We're not going to have any trouble with Eves," Drake said. "He didn't have anything to do with Della's disappearance."

"How do you know?" Mason asked.

"I'll tell you more about it in a few minutes," Drake said. "In the meantime, I think I know what was the trouble with Eves."

"Go ahead and spill it," Mason said. "Or do you want to be mysterious about that, too."

"Now, take it easy, Perry," the detective cautioned. "I'm just trying to be fair all around. You'll understand my position when—"

"Forget it," the lawyer interrupted savagely. "Tell me what you can tell me and quit beating around the bush."

"Well, about Eves," Drake said. "I think Eves was planning some sort of a big bunco game, and this murder knocked him out of it."

"Go ahead," Mason told him impatiently.

"Well, when I looked up Roger P. Cartman in Honolulu," Drake said, "I found he'd been injured in an automobile accident, all right, and had suffered a broken neck. But that was three months ago. He was a wealthy visitor from the Mainland who was caught in a skidding car on the Pali, and—"

Mason interrupted, to say to the driver, "For God's sake, get some speed out of this bus. I'll pay the fines."

192

The driver lurched the car into speed. Drake glanced apprehensively through the rearview mirror and said, "A car tagging along behind, Perry. It may be a prowl car."

"I don't care if it is," Mason said irritably. "I said I'll pay the fines. You were talking about Eves and Cartman. What about him?"

"Well," Drake said, "Cartman had a lot of money. Doctors put a brace on him, which held his head absolutely rigid and he came over to the Mainland—"

"I know that already," Mason interrupted.

"No, you don't," Drake said, "because Cartman came over to the Mainland six weeks ago."

"He did what!" Mason asked, staring at the detective.

"Came over to the Mainland six weeks ago, and he came over on a clipper plane."

"Then why did he go back to Honolulu?" Mason asked.

"He swears he didn't," Drake said.

"You've talked with him?"

"My operative located him in a private sanitarium. He says he's been in the sanitarium ever since he arrived, and, what's more, the nurses and doctors all swear he has."

"Then this wasn't the real Cartman that Evelyn Whiting brought over?"

"No."

"Well, what was the idea?" Mason asked.

"Don't you see," Drake said, "it was some sort of a bunco game. Put one of those harnesses around a man's head, put on a large pair of smoked goggles, and it's just about the same as a mask. Cartman has money. He can't move around, and he doesn't care about publicity, so he's been careful to keep his whereabouts from becoming generally known. His friends, however, his bankers and associates, knew all about his accident and knew he had to wear his head in a brace.

"Eves wasn't going to the Islands on his honeymoon. He sent Evelyn Whiting over there to pick up this ringer. She was to build up his identity on the ship, and also her identity as his nurse. Then, after they'd arrived on the Mainland, she and Eves were going to put through some major swindle. But the murder on the ship attracted too much attention, and they had decided to lie low until it blew over. Then, as an unfortunate coincidence, it happened that she knew Carl Moar, and he ran into her on deck and told her *his* troubles. Nothing could have upset her more. It was exactly what she didn't want. Then when you discovered that she was a witness, traced her to that place of concealment and served that subpoena on her, she knew the jig was up."

"Then why didn't she obey the subpoena and be in court this morning?" Mason asked. "She can be fined for contempt of court—"

"Because the swindle has gone so far they didn't dare show up. Eves may have intended to let her testify in your behalf when he was talking with you yesterday. But after he studied the situation a bit, he realized how suicidal that would be, because it would be brought out in the trial that Evelyn Whiting had been escorting Roger P. Cartman; that Cartman had had his neck broken over on the Islands. The newspapers would mention it. Someone would see it who knew Roger P. Cartman was in a private sanitarium near Glendale. Then the fat would be in the fire. The police would investigate and quietly move in."

Mason narrowed his eyes, bringing into view a network of fine wrinkles at the corners, as he stared into space. "Yes," he said slowly, "I see the sketch now. But I want Evelyn Whiting's testimony. It's the one thing I need to bust this case wide open."

"Well," Drake said, "those are the facts. You can make a showing to the Court if you want to."

"I'd a lot rather locate Evelyn Whiting and force her to testify," Mason said.

"How did you know that the Fell woman would blow up?"

"I'd noticed her in the dining room," Mason said.

"Whenever she wore an evening dress she left off her glasses. I'd noticed her rather particularly, because it seemed to me such an absurd gesture for a woman who had that wall of reserve thrown up around her, and who seemed to be so completely immune to emotion to sacrifice the comfort of her vision to make herself more attractive. I noticed from the way she walked that she seemed rather careful of putting her feet down, and had an idea she depended pretty strongly on her glasses. But she's one of those opinionated persons who will cheerfully commit perjury rather than admit they're wrong. And I knew that unless I had a photograph to show her and could definitely prove her custom of not wearing glasses with a dinner gown, she'd swear she had her glasses on that night."

"Just how much do you suppose she actually *did* see?"

"She had a blurred conception of figures struggling. She heard shots but she didn't see any gun, and she doesn't know what gun fired the shots," Mason said. "She's opinionated, obstinate, and hates to lose an argument. She didn't take the stand as a witness, but as an adversary. She was just dying to give me a 'piece of her mind,' and particularly anxious to show me that no smart lawyer was going to rattle her. We run up against witnesses like that every so often, both men and women, people who will do anything rather than admit the possibility they may have been mistaken. . . . Come on, Paul, tell me where we're going. Have you found Della, or someone who knows where she is, or what?"

"I'd prefer not to talk about it right now, Perry."

"She isn't hurt?"

"No, she's all right."

"If she isn't hurt physically," Mason said, "something's wrong with her mentally, Paul."

Drake remained silent.

"Isn't that true, Paul?"

"I don't think so."

Mason said irritably, "Well, go ahead and be mysterious, then."

The lawyer turned from the detective to the driver.

"Won't this car make any better speed than this?"

"I'm dong fifty right now, Mr. Mason."

"All right," Mason told him, "do sixty."

Drake flashed a glance back through the window and said, "That sure *is* a prowl car, Perry. They're dishing out jail sentences for doing sixty."

"I'll take the responsibility," Mason told the driver. "Go ahead and step on it."

They dashed through Berkeley, came to the outskirts, and the driver swung the car sharply to the left. He braked the car to a stop in front of a long line of cabins in an auto camp. A man jumped to the runningboard. "Okay?" Drake asked.

"Okay," the man said.

"You show us the way," Drake said.

"Straight down here. The second cabin on the left."

The driver moved the car forward, then brought it to a stop in front of the second cabin.

Drake said, "All right, Perry, she's in that cabin."

Mason jerked the door open, pushed past the operative, twisted the knob of the cabin door, and banged it open.

Della Street was seated in a wicker rocking chair, reading a magazine. She looked up with apprehensive eyes, then half-stifled a scream. "Chief!"

Without a word, he crossed the room and opened his arms to her.

"Chief," she said, snuggling against him. "Oh, Chief! . . . Why *did* you have to do it?"

"Do what?" Mason asked.

"Hunt me out. . . . Now I'll have to tell you. . . . I didn't want to."

"Tell me what?" Mason asked.

"Haven't you guessed?"

Mason shook his head. "Don't ever leave me like that again, Della," he said, his voice choking. "I need you."

"But, Chief, I had to. I couldn't . . . Oh, I simply can't be the one to put you on the spot!"

Mason stared at her, comprehension showing in his eyes. "Della," he said, "you couldn't . . . you wouldn't . . ."

She nodded. "I couldn't go against you, Chief, and after all, it didn't make any difference as far as the case was concerned. I knew that the law couldn't make me testify, but I was afraid the newspapers could play up my refusal . . ."

"The law *can* make you testify," Mason said.

"Why, I thought a lawyer's secretary was in the same position as a lawyer in being a witness against a client."

"She is," Mason told her, "but that applies only to confidential communications. It doesn't keep a lawyer's secretary from testifying things she's *seen*. And you know how I feel about suppressing evidence, Della. Any time I have to win my cases that way, I'll quit practicing law. Now tell me just what it was that you saw."

She clung to him. "Chief, I'm so darned sorry! I wouldn't have done it if I hadn't thought they couldn't make me testify. But you know how it would look in the newspapers. . . . I wasn't hiding from the law, Chief, I was hiding from the newspaper men."

Drake said, "The more I hear, the less I know. I wish you two would come down to earth and tell me what the devil you're talking about."

Mason said, "Don't you see, Paul, she's the . . ."

There was a commotion on the outside of the cabin. One of Drake's operatives said, "Beat it, you," and a man's voice answered, "Take a look at this, smart guy." Then two men pushed into the room.

Mason whirled to face them. "What the devil," he asked, "are *you* two trying to do?"

"Take it easy, Mason," one of the men told him, flashing a badge. "We're taking this young woman into custody as a material witness in the case of The People of the State of California versus Anna Moar."

197

Consternation showed on Mason's face. One of the men took Della Street's arm and said, "Come on, sister, you're going places." The other, huskier of the two, stood with his arms swinging free. "Don't start anything, boys," he warned.

Mason said, "You can't get away with that stuff."

"The hell we can't," the other man said. "You just think we can't. This is a material witness. She ducked out when we were trying to serve a subpoena on her and she's been a fugitive ever since, living under an assumed name. We're taking her into custody right now, as a material witness on an indorsed subpoena and as an accessory after the fact. If you have any kick to make, go get a writ, and if you want to talk with her, you'll talk with her on the witness stand in San Francisco."

Mason stepped forward, ominous purpose in his face. Della Street said, "Please don't, Chief! It's bad enough, the way it is . . ."

The men hurried her through the door. Drake, looking at Mason, said, "What do you say, Perry? Do we take her away from them?"

Mason slowly shook his head. "This is the pay-off, Paul. Let her go."

The two officers hustled Della Street to an automobile which roared into speed. Mason sat dejectedly down in the chair which Della Street had just occupied. He stared about him, at the furnishings of the shabby cottage, the new suitcase, the underwear drying on a clothes line which had been stretched from the shower bath to one end of the bed.

"That wasn't a prowl car," Drake said bitterly. "They were tagging us. And like a fool, I played it wide open."

Mason said gloomily, "I could kick myself all over the lot for not understanding. Why the devil didn't I have confidence in her?"

"What do you suppose she knows, Perry?" Drake asked.

Mason put his chin on his hands, propped his elbows on

his knees, stared at the floor and said, "Hell, she's the one who telephoned the bridge. I should have known it all along."

"What can we do?" Drake asked.

"Nothing."

"Well, she won't hurt your case much," Drake said. "They can't drag anything out of *her*. She . . ."

"She's going to tell the truth," Mason said. He got to his feet and stared at Drake. "She's going to tell the truth," he repeated, "because I'm going to *make her tell the truth*. If my client's guilty of murder, she's guilty of murder. No client is going to make Della Street get on the witness stand and take a chance on a perjury rap in order to give *me* a break. Do you get that?"

Drake said soothingly, "Okay, Perry. I'm not arguing with you. I was just asking, that's all."

Mason said, "All right, then, you know the answer."

He got to his feet, crossed the cabin, hoisted the suitcase on the bed and started packing it. "Go down to the office, Paul," he ordered in a husky voice. "Find out what her bill is, and pay it. We're checking out of here."

"Will you have a chance to talk with her before she goes on the witness stand?" Drake asked.

Mason shook his head. "I don't want to, Paul."

"We could have taken her away from them," one of the men said.

"And what a sweet mess *that* would have been," Mason said. "Played up right in the newspapers, it would have made her testimony sound ten times as bad as it's really going to be. My only remaining chance is to show she was hiding from me as well as from the D.A."

"How bad do you think it'll be, Perry?" Drake asked.

"It'll knock my technical defense into a cocked hat," Mason said grimly. "What the hell do you think she ducked out for? She actually *saw* Carl Newberry go overboard. God knows what else she saw. Get busy and pay that bill. I want to get out of here."

Chapter 16

A crowd jammed the courtroom when Judge Romley reconvened court at three o'clock. Word had been passed through the courthouse of what was to happen. Telephone wires had buzzed with the news, and, by two-thirty, every seat was taken. By three o'clock, people, standing elbow to elbow, were flattened against the walls. The crowd overflowed into the corridor.

Judge Romley, apparently unaware of the cause for the sudden interest, glanced curiously at the crowd, then said to Scudder, "Have you any further evidence to prove the *corpus delicti?*"

Scudder arose, his manner triumphant. "I have," he said, "evidence which will not only prove the *corpus delicti*, if the Court please, but which I expect will connect the defendant directly with the crime. Before placing that witness on the stand, however, I would ask permission to call one witness slightly out of order. It is for the purpose of laying a foundation."

"Foundation for what?" Judge Romley asked.

Scudder said dramatically, "The witness whom I expect to place on the stand, your Honor, is Miss Della Street, the secretary to Perry Mason. She has refused to make any statement whatever as to what her testimony will be. It is, therefore, necessary for me to treat her as a hostile witness, and in order to do this, I wish to lay a foundation for the questions which it will be necessary to ask . . ."

"Put on your witness," Judge Romley interrupted.

"Miss Adele Adams," Scudder said.

A trim-figured young woman walked forward, held up a gloved hand, was sworn, and took the witness stand.

"Your name is Adele Adams? You are a telephone operator, and on the evening of the sixth instant you were employed as telephone operator and were, at that time, in the discharge of your duties, sailing on the ship of which Captain Joe Hanson is the captain, and on which there were traveling as passengers one Carl Newberry and wife?"

"Yes, sir."

"I will call your attention to the defendant and ask you if you have ever seen her before."

"Yes, sir, she was on the ship as Mrs. Newberry."

"Now, directing your attention to the evening of the sixth, at approximately the hour of nine o'clock in the evening, did anything unusal happen at that time?"

"Yes, sir, a woman called in on the line from the social hall and said . . ."

"Just a moment," Mason interrupted,"we object to anything which was said over the telephone as hearsay."

"I don't wish to ask for any conversation which took place over the telephone outside of the presence of this defendant," the deputy district attorney said, "which will be binding upon the defendant. I am only asking now, if the Court please, to show the *identity* of the person placing the telephone call."

"The Court will not permit the witness to testify as to what was said," Judge Romley ruled.

"Would you recognize the voice of that person who placed the telephone call which you have characterized as unusual if you heard it again?"

"I would."

"Have you heard that voice again?"

"I have."

"Whose voice is it?"

"Objected to," Mason said. "Incompetent, irrelevant, immaterial. Apparently this entire procedure is either for the purpose of intimidating the witness the Prosecutor is about to call, or else for the purpose of impeaching his own witness."

"I think it is of the *res gestae*," the Porsecutor argued.

"The objection will be sustained," Judge Romley ruled. "As the Court sees it, this testimony should be received only by way of impeachment."

"Very well," Scudder said with bad grace, "you may leave the stand, Miss Adams."

Mason's voice was clear and steady. "If Della Street put in that telephone call," he said, "you have only to ask *her* and she'll tell you the truth."

"I don't need your advice," Scudder snapped.

Judge Romley said in a tired voice, "That will do, gentlemen. If there is to be any more repartee between Counsel, the Court will restrict all remarks of Counsel to examination of witnesses and arguments made to the Court."

"Miss Della Street," Scudder said savagely.

A door opened, and a deputy escorted Della Street into the courtroom. Her face was expressionless. Her eyes avoided those of Perry Mason as she was being sworn.

"Your name is Della Street, and you are employed by Perry Mason, as his private and confidential secretary, and have been in his employ for several years last past?" Scudder asked.

Della Street said, "Yes."

"You accompanied Perry Mason on a trip which he made to the Orient, acting as his secretary, taking down data on the police systems of China and Japan?"

"Yes."

"And you were returning with Perry Mason on the ship which Mr. and Mrs. Moar took out of Honolulu?"

"Yes."

"And you were acquainted with Mr. Moar and Mrs. Moar, knowing them under the name of Newberry?"

"Yes."

"I show you a photograph which has been marked 'People's Exhibit A,' and ask you if you can identify that photograph?"

"Yes."

"Whose photograph is it?"

"That of Mr. Newberry."

"The same one who was on the ship with you?"

"Yes."

"Now then, do you remember the night of Sunday, the sixth of this month?"

"I do."

"Where were you at approximately the hour of nine o'clock that evening?"

"I was on the promenade deck."

"What were you doing there?"

"I was looking for Mr. Mason."

"Mr. Mason had asked you to join him on deck?"

"Yes. Mr. Mason had an appointment with Mrs. Moar for nine-thirty. He told me to meet him at nine o'clock and we would have a *liqueur*."

"And previous to that, you had been at the table with Mr. and Mrs. Moar—or Mr. and Mrs. Newberry, as they were known aboard the ship—Belle Newberry, and a Roy A. Hungerford?"

"Yes."

"Now, can you fix the exact time when you appeared on deck?"

"Yes. It was approximately nine o'clock."

"How do you know?"

"The ship's bell struck twice within a second or two after I stepped out on deck."

"Now, which deck was this?"

"The deck just below the boat deck."

"Did you see anyone on that deck?"

Della Street hesitated for a moment, then said, "Looking

203

aft, where the stairs went up to the boat deck, I could see the skirt of a woman's dress, a woman's feet and ankles. This woman was ascending the stairs."

"Did you hear anything?"

"I heard peculiar thumping sounds from the deck above me."

"Did you hear anything else?"

"I heard a loud noise."

"You heard a shot, didn't you?"

"I presume it was a shot, yes."

"Then what happened?"

"I started to walk back toward the stairs, up which I had seen the woman climbing. The ship was rolling heavily. Shortly before I reached the stairs, it took a *very* heavy roll to port, and I slipped on the wet deck."

"What did you do?" Scudder asked.

"I tried to regain my balance, and ran toward a stanchion on the port rail. I caught hold of it and hung on."

"What did you see?" Scudder asked.

"I saw something above me," she said, "something hanging over the rail of the boat deck."

"Did you see what this was?"

"At first I saw it as a vague object. I didn't have my eyes focused on it. I had an impression of—"

"Never mind your first impression," Scudder said. "You did focus your eyes on the object, didn't you, Miss Street?"

"As nearly as I could, under the circumstances. As I looked up, I was looking directly into the rain. The drops flooded my eyes."

"But you *did* see something. What was it?"

"It was a man," Della Street said, avoiding Mason's eyes.

"And was this man hanging to the rail?"

"I couldn't see."

"He was partially over the rail?"

"Yes."

"And did you see anyone else near him?"

"Yes. A woman was near him."

"That woman was the defendant in this action, wasn't she?" Scudder asked, pointing dramatically at Anna Moar.

"I don't know," Della Street said.

"*Why* don't you know?"

"Because I couldn't see all of her. I saw a pair of bare arms and a stretch of back. I saw a dark colored dress over the woman's right breast. The driving rain interfered with my vision."

"This woman was wearing a black dress?" Scudder asked.

"It was dark in color."

"It might have been a black dress?"

"Yes."

"In your judgment, it probably was a black dress?"

"Either black or dark blue."

"Did you notice anything about the arms of this woman which would enable you to identify them?"

"Not definitely, no."

"Did you see anything distinctive about them?"

"Yes."

"What?"

"There were two bracelets on the right arm."

"Could you see those bracelets clearly?"

"No."

"Could you recognize their design, workmanship, color or material?"

"No, I just saw two bracelets."

"Now, you have testified that you were at the table with Mrs. Moar, the defendant in this action, earlier in the evening?"

"Yes."

"At that time, was she wearing bracelets?"

"Yes."

"How many?"

"Two."

"Now, referring to what you saw taking place on the deck above you: Was there anything in either of the woman's hands?"

"Yes. There was an object in the woman's right hand."

"It was a revolver, wasn't it?"

"I think so, yes."

"And you saw her fire that revolver into the man's body?"

"Yes," Della Street said.

"And then what happened?"

"The man fell into the ocean."

"Falling past you?"

"Yes."

"As a matter of fact, the woman pushed him into the ocean, didn't she?"

"She may have."

"Could you see the face of this man?"

"No."

"Could you see how he was dressed?"

"I saw that he had on dark clothes."

"And a white shirt front?"

"Yes."

"And, as a matter of fact, this woman shot him and pushed him overboard, didn't she?"

"I can't swear that she pushed him overboard."

"What did you do after you saw the man go overboard?"

"I dashed into the social hall and telephoned the operator to tell the bridge there was a man overboard."

"Didn't you tell the operator that a man had been *pushed* overboard?"

Della Street hesitated, wet her lips with the tip of her tongue, and said, "Yes, I think I did."

"And your best recollection is that the man *was* pushed overboard?"

"Perhaps he was, yes."

206

"Could you recognize the man who went overboard as Mr. Moar?"

"No."

"Could you recognize the woman who shot him and pushed him overboard as Mrs. Moar?"

"No."

"Did you," Scudder demanded, pointing a finger at her, "see anything about the figure of the woman who shot this man and pushed the body overboard which would enable you to swear it was *not* Mrs. Moar?"

For a long moment, Della Street was silent. Then she said, "No."

"That," Scudder announced triumphantly, "is all."

Mason arose to cross-examine.

"Della," he said, "did you tell me about what you saw?"

"No, I didn't. I didn't tell a living soul."

"Why?" he asked.

"Because," she said, "I thought that, as your secretary, I couldn't be called as a witness. I thought that the testimony of Aileen Fell would cover everything I had seen and that therefore it was best for me to say nothing. I was afraid that if the newspapers knew of what I had seen, they would exaggerate it because of my connection with you, and perhaps make it seem you were suppressing evidence by not calling me to the stand. . . . So I kept quiet."

She turned to face Judge Romley.

"I really and sincerely thought, Judge," she went on, "that no one could make me testify if I didn't want to because I understood it to be the law that a lawyer's secretary couldn't be called to testify against the lawyer's client."

"That is only as to privileged communications," Judge Romley said kindly.

"I understand that now," Della Street said. "I didn't at the time. That's why I kept quiet."

A man pushed his way up the aisle of the courtroom, hurried to Scudder's side, whispered in his ear.

Scudder listened, arose with a triumphant smile, and said to Judge Romley, "And if the Court please, as still further proof of the *corpus delicti,* the Prosecution will be prepared tomorrow at ten o'clock to produce the testimony of physicians who have conducted a post-mortem on the body of the deceased. If the Court please, I am just advised that the body of Carl Moar has been discovered and is being taken to the morgue."

The courtroom became a hubbub of excited noise.

"Under the circumstances," Judge Romley said, "this case will be continued until tomorrow morning at ten o'clock."

As the spectators milled into an excited crowd, Della Street left the witness stand. Mason pushed his way past Scudder. Newspaper photographers vaulted the mahogany rail separating the portion of the courtroom set aside for attorneys from that reserved for spectators.

"Chief," Della Street said, "I'm so d-d-d-darned sorry."

Mason held her close to him. "Poor kid," he said.

A newspaper reporter yelled, "Hold that pose." Flashlights etched the scene into brilliance.

Chapter 17

Mason had had dinner served in his room. As waiters cleared away the tables, the lawyer grinned across at Della Street. "Don't ever do anything like that again, Della," he said. "I was frantic with worry."

"I'll say he was," Paul Drake chimed in. "He snapped my head off every time I spoke to him."

"I'm sorry, Chief, but I was afraid the newspaper reporters would exaggerate it and I knew everyone would think that I was holding something back."

She motioned to the late edition of an evening newspaper and said, "You can see what they've done. Notice this headline:

'LAWYER'S SECRETARY CLAIMS SHE CANNOT IDENTIFY MURDERESS.'"

Mason said, "I know. But anything is better than that suspense. Why didn't you tell me before, Della?"

"I tried to, Chief. I dashed all over the ship, trying to hunt you up. Then, when I found you, you'd already agreed to see Mrs. Newberry through. Honest Injun, Chief, I don't know whether she was the one who pushed him overboard or not. I couldn't tell at the time and I can't tell now. But I *did* realize how easy it would be for people to say I was suppressing evidence, so I just made up my mind I'd say nothing about it to anyone.

"Then, when I heard Paul tell you that the district attorney was on the trail of the witness who had telephoned the bridge and that the telephone operator claimed she could

209

recognize the voice . . . well, I felt certain that sooner or later they'd suspect me, and then the newspapers would make a great fuss over it. So I thought it would be best to lie low for a few days until the preliminary was over."

Drake said solicitously, "Where does that leave the case, Perry? Aren't you in a spot?"

Mason said, "I guess so, but I've been in spots before. When will you get a report on that post-mortem, Paul?"

"Just about as soon as the statement is released to the press. They—"

He broke off as the telephone rang, and said, "That must be it now."

He held the receiver to his ear, said, "Drake speaking," then looked across at Mason, nodded, and said, "This is it." After a few moments he said, "All right. Thanks, and thanks particularly for that tip on the bullet."

He hung up the telephone and said to Mason, "Well, Perry, there it is. The body's that of Moar all right. A bullet was fired into his back, just below the right shoulder blade. It ranged downward and lodged near the left hip. Death apparently wasn't instantaneous. He'd managed to keep afloat for some few minutes. He'd stripped himself down to his underwear and managed to swim to one of the life rings which had been thrown out. He'd wedged himself inside that life ring, and died within a few minutes. Death was caused by the gunshot wound, and not by drowning.

"Apparently, he was a strong swimmer, and had removed his coat, shirt, collar, tie and pants. He couldn't get off his shoes because they were high-laced shoes. The knot on one was jammed as though he'd tried to get it off. He evidently died within fifteen or twenty minutes of the time he reached the life ring. It's funny they didn't see him from the ship."

Mason said, "There was such a sea running and such a driving rain it was impossible to make any thorough search. The ship was bobbing around like a cork, and the rain was coming down in torrents. It seemed to bolt up the light from the searchlights."

"Well, Drake said, "here's something else: He was shot with a thirty-eight caliber bullet, but that bullet wasn't fired from the revolver they found on deck."

Mason snapped to startled attention. "It wasn't?"

"The ballistics expert says it wasn't."

"And he was only shot once?"

"That's right. Just the one wound which entered in the back on an angle. That probably was the shot which was fired into him as he was balanced on the rail."

"Wait a minute," Mason said, "there were *two* shots fired. Aileen Fell says she heard *two* shots, and there were two exploded chambers in the gun."

"That's right," Drake said. "But the bullets from that gun didn't kill Carl Moar. He must have been killed by a bullet fired from another gun."

"Then there should have been *three* explosions," Mason said.

Drake nodded.

Mason abruptly got to his feet, pushed his thumbs through the armholes of his vest and started pacing the floor. After several minutes, he turned to stare thoughtfully at them.

"I know what may be a solution," he said. "It makes sense, and it's the only thing which does make sense. But I can't unscramble it until I can get Eves and Evelyn Whiting into court."

"Well, you can't get them into court," Drake said. "I've had men running down every clue, Perry. It's hopeless. Eves is no amateur. He knows the ropes, and he's gone into hiding. It would take the concerted efforts of an organized police force to land him."

Della Street said, "Chief, couldn't you go to the district attorney and tell him what you have in mind and have him put the police on the job?"

"Not so you could notice it," Mason said. "If Scudder thought he could help me dig up witnesses to prove Mrs. Moar innocent, his lack of enthusiasm would be utterly astounding."

"Well," Della Street said, "he showed plenty of enthusiasm when it came to finding *me*."

Mason nodded. Suddenly a twinkle appeared in his eye. "Now, Della," he said, "you've given me a real idea."

"What?" she asked.

"We'll make Scudder think that *I'm* concealing Eves and Evelyn Whiting. Once he gets that idea, he'll move heaven and earth to uncover them."

"And just how are you going to make him think *you're* concealing them?" Drake asked.

Mason looked at his watch. "Got a set of skeleton keys, Paul?" he asked.

Drake said, "Oh, my Lord! I should have known better than to have brought this up in the first place."

Mason grinned, "Get your burglar's outfit, Paul. We're going to do a little high-class house breaking."

"What are you getting at?"

"Has it ever occurred to you," Mason asked, "that we've overlooked the most significant clue in this entire business?"

"What?" Drake inquired.

"The fact that the woman in the picture shop mentioned that Evelyn Whiting had purchased a picture frame, an oval desk frame which would take a picture which had been trimmed down from an eight-by-ten print?"

Della Street grabbed his arm. "Chief, do you mean that *she* was the one . . ."

Mason grinned at Paul Drake. "I'm commencing to feel natural again, Paul," he said. "Scudder has been so smug and complacent throughout this entire business that it's time we exploded a dynamite bomb under him."

"And I take it," Drake said, "we're going to violate a law?"

"Well," Mason told him, "the legality of our position is going to be rather technical, Paul. We're going to break and enter, but not for the purpose of committing a felony."

"For what purpose, then?" Drake asked.

"For the purpose of leaving a choice assortment of fingerprints," Mason told him.

Drake said, "Good Lord, Perry. If you only knew how nice and peaceful it was when you were in Bali!"

Mason climbed the wooden stairs which led up the back of the flat on Stockton Boulevard. Behind him, Paul Drake was a silent shadow. Della Street, seated in a rented car, with the motor running, was parked in the alley.

Drake muttered, "I don't like this a damn bit, Perry. If we get caught it's a felony, and if he comes in he'll spray us full of lead."

Mason whispered, "You have a cheerful mind, Paul."

They climbed to the service porch on the rear of the third-story flat. Fog which drifted in from the ocean blanketed the city, lowering visibility, distorting sounds. The mournful drone of fog signals could be heard at intervals. Fog-bred moisture dripped from the eaves.

Mason inserted a skeleton key. The lock clicked back. Mason gently opened the door.

Drake said, "If he *should* be in there, Perry—"

His voice trailed into silence. The men stood waiting.

Mason took a flashlight from his pocket. "Come on, Paul."

The beam of the flashlight sent a long, white pencil of illumination stabbing through the darkness. It showed a kitchen, with its windows tightly closed. An odor of stale cooking and rancid frying fat clung to the room.

Mason led the way through the kitchen to a dining room and living room, then into a bedroom. His flashlight showed a wheel chair. "That's Cartman's wheel chair, Paul," Mason said. "And you'll notice that someone did some hurried packing here. Notice the way things have been pulled from the drawers. Look at the empty coat hangers in the closet. See the imprint on the bed where a suitcase has been placed."

"Well," Drake said, "Eves had a lot of baggage and his wife had been over in Honolulu—"

213

"His wife," Mason said, "wasn't living here with him. She'd been living with her sister. Her clothes weren't the ones which were taken from those hangers . . . Hello, what's this?"

The beam of his flashlight reflected from a rounded strip of wood enameled and polished to a high brilliance. The bit of wood was perhaps an inch and a half in length, splintered at both ends and partially curved.

Drake inspected the piece of wood and said, "A piece of wood from a molding somewhere. He probably——"

Mason abruptly dropped to his knees, sent the beam from the flashlight sliding along the floor. "Look for splintered pieces of glass, Paul," he said. "See if you can find——"

"Here's one," Drake said, picking up a small fragment of glass.

"And here's another," Mason told him.

"What's the idea?" Drake said. "Do you think there's been a fight here, or——"

Mason said, "Let's take a look at the garbage can on the service porch, Paul."

Drake said, "Listen, Perry, I don't like this. I don't know what you're getting at, but we're going at this thing all wrong. We're——"

Mason walked toward the service porch, taking the flashlight with him. Drake, perforce, followed, Mason lifted the lid from the garbage can, took out several opened tin cans, some halves of orange peel, then a long sliver of glass. "We're on the right track, Paul," he said, and a moment later handed up a long, curved segment of enameled, rounded wood.

"This must have been a picture frame," Drake said.

Mason nodded, fished from the garbage can a crumpled, cracked, oval photograph. He smoothed it out. The likeness of Belle Newberry laughed up into the flashlight. The beam of light showed the words inscribed on the photograph in ink, *To Daddy, With Love, from Belle.*

Mason pushed the photograph back into the can, took

Drake's arm, led him back into the flat and said, "That's all we need, Paul. We'll leave a few fingerprints and get out."

"Why fingerprints?"

"So the district attorney can know you've been guilty of breaking and entering," Mason said. "He'll probably stick you on a kidnaping charge, as well. Here's a good place on the dresser mirror, Paul. And you can put some fingerprints on that table."

"Now wait a minute, Perry. If you—"

"Go ahead," Mason said, pressing his hand against the mirror on the dressing table.

Drake gingerly touched the top of the table as though it were hot.

Mason laughed, lowered his shoulder, pushed his weight against Drake and snapped off his flashlight. The detective, stumbling about in the darkness, grabbed at the table to keep himself from falling, then clung to a chair.

Mason switched on the flashlight and said, "Come on, Paul, you old criminal. Let's get out of here."

Drake said, "Perry, will you *please* tell me what's the idea of all this horse-play?"

"Wait until you hear the D.A. describe it in court tomorrow," Mason said. "Come on, Paul. Do you want to leave, or do you want to stay here and argue?"

"I want to leave," Drake said, "and you can't make it too snappy for me."

Mason led the way out the back door, locking it behind them.

"Okay?" Della Street asked, as Mason reached the alley.

"Okay so far," Mason told her. "You've memorized the story you're to give Scudder?"

"And how!" she told him.

"Let's go," Mason said, settling back against the cushions.

Drake closed the door. Della Street lurched the car into motion. They left the alley for the boulevard, drove half a dozen blocks and slowed in front of a drug store.

"Come on, Paul," Mason said, "you might as well get an earful of this."

Drake said, "I always get suspicious when you throw it in high and don't tell me what you're doing, Perry. You and Della take more chances than any airplane stunters in the world."

Mason took Drake's arm, led him into the rear of the drug store where there was a telephone booth. Della dropped a nickel, dialed a number with swiftly competent fingers and said, "Hello. . . . Hello. . . . Let me talk with Mr. Scudder, please, at once. . . . This is very important. . . . Tell him I have some information for him. . . . It's about a case he's trying tomorrow."

She glanced up from the transmitter and nodded to Perry Mason. A moment later she said into the telephone, "Hello, Mr. Scudder. This is Mrs. Morgan Eves talking. I'm the *real* Mrs. Eves; but I don't want you to ever tell anyone that I called you. My husband's a crook. You'll find his record under the name of James Whitly or James Clerke. . . . Now, wait a minute, don't interrupt me, please. This is something about the case you're trying. . . . My husband's now going under the name of Morgan Eves. He's divorcing me, but he only has an interlocutory decree. The final decree hasn't been entered yet. But that hasn't stopped *him* any. He's gone through a marriage ceremony with a nurse. Her name's Evelyn Whiting. They have a flat at 3618 Stockton Boulevard. Evelyn Whiting is the nurse who came over on the ship on which Carl Moar was murdered. She was nursing a man named Roger Cartman who had a broken neck, and he saw the whole murder. . . . Yes, I say he *saw* it. The nurse had to give him some treatment. She took him up to the hospital quarters and he was sitting there in the wheel chair when Carl Moar was killed. He saw the whole thing.

"Roger Cartman paid Evelyn Whiting to take care of him. He didn't know she was married. She took him to the flat on Stockton Boulevard and told him she was renting it for him. She and Morgan Eves were just planning to knock down a little money on the side. Then they found out he was a witness, and they got in touch with Perry Mason, and Perry Mason paid them five thousand dollars to get the witness out of the country. . . . Cartman wanted to testify, but he's helpless. Yes, I know what I'm talking about. Mr. Mason and Mr. Drake, the detective, were up there and they moved Cartman out. He has a broken neck and can't do anything by himself. . . . In case you want an eyewitness who can testify to exactly what happened, all you have to do is to get Mr. Cartman and if it's against the law for Mr. Mason to pay money to have a witness put into hiding, you can get Mr. Mason, too. . . . But don't you ever mention my name or they'd kill me."

She slammed the receiver back on the hook and said, "How did I do, Chief?"

"You did swell," Mason said. Drake shook his head mournfully. "My God!" he said. "I *always* lead with my chin."

"What's next on the program?" Della Street asked.

Mason said, "We have a couple of hours to kill. How about a picture show?"

"Suits me," Della Street said.

"How would you like a good mystery play, Paul?" Mason asked.

Drake said, "That's the first really smart thought you've had all evening, Perry. I suppose you have some sort of a plan in mind, but it's more than I can figure. *I* think you've gone plumb crazy."

"Not quite that bad, Paul," Mason told him. "There's a method in my madness."

"I'm glad you think so," Drake said. "To me it seems like one of those goofy dreams, where everybody does cuckoo things. Honest to God, Perry, when Della was telephoning to Scudder, I expected any minute to have you chime in with a station announcement and ask the D.A. how he liked the amateur hour."

Della Street drove to a neighborhood picture show, and parked the car. The three of them entered the lighted foyer. Mason bought tickets. Drake said, "Well, at least I can have a few minutes' relaxation. . . . Oh, Lord, Perry, I've seen this picture before and didn't like it."

Della Street parked her rented car near the hotel. Mason took Della Street's arm, started across the pavement with her, heard Drake say, "Oh-oh!" and felt a hand grip his shoulder. He whirled around, to confront a tall man who loomed to enormous proportions in a heavy black overcoat. Thick-lensed spectacles distorted the man's pale green eyes.

"Where you been?" he asked.

Mason turned back toward the entrance of the hotel, the hand of the big man still on his shoulder.

"Who wants to know?" he asked.

"The D.A. does."

Mason said, "Tell him I've been to a picture show."

A chunky figure materialized from the doorway, to stand at Paul Drake's arm.

"Inspector Bodfish," the big man introduced.

Mason unexpectedly reached across in front of Della Street, grabbed Bodfish's right hand, pumped it up and down, and turned to the big man. "What's your name?"

"Borge."

"Nice name," Mason said, shaking hands.

"We *could* get along without your wise cracks," Borge told him.

"So many people can," Mason complained. "The trouble is that *I* can't. Where do we talk?"

"The D.A.'s waiting for you."

Mason said, "Do you know, I think it would be a swell idea to let him wait."

Borge said, "I don't."

"Is this a pinch?" Drake demanded.

"You're damn right it's a pinch," Bodfish told him.

"On what grounds, may I ask?" Mason inquired.

"On suspicion of murder."

Mason raised his eyebrows.

"Accessory after the fact, I believe," Inspector Bodfish announced.

"Kidnaping," Borge added.

"That all?" Mason asked.

"That's all so far. Perhaps we can add resisting an officer by the time we have you booked."

"Got a warrant?" Mason inquired, lighting a cigarette.

"We don't need one."

"All right," Mason said to Della Street, "you go up to the room and wait, Della. Paul can keep you company. I won't be . . ."

"They're coming right along," Inspector Bodfish said.

"What grounds?"

"The same grounds."

"All three of us?"

"All three of you."

Mason yawned, "Let's get it over with."

Borge called a taxi. They drove silently, Mason, Della Street and Paul Drake in the back seat, Inspector Bodfish and Borge seated on the folded backs of the jump seats, facing the trio. The cab turned into Stockton Boulevard, ran several blocks, and stopped.

"The D.A. live here?" Mason inquired.

"You know damn well who lives here," Borge remarked.

Mason said to Bodfish, "I'd like to have your unbiased opinion, Inspector. Do you think it's necessary for an officer to ape this hard-boiled style in order to be efficient?"

"Shut up," Bodfish ordered.

Mason nodded to Drake. "He does," he told the detective.

Borge led the way up a flight of stairs, across a porch, rang a bell, received a buzzing signal, pushed the door open, and said, "Upstairs, you three."

They climbed the stairs, with no word. Mason pushed past Della Street, so that he was the first up. Scudder, who

219

had been standing by a window, walked across to meet Mason, and said, "Perhaps you can tell us what happened here."

"Oh, did something happen here?"

"You know it did."

"When?"

"When you were here."

"And when was that?" Mason asked.

"Not very long ago."

Mason looked at the powder which had been dusted over various objects, and said to Paul Drake and Della Street, "Don't touch anything. Paul, stick your hands in your pockets and keep them there. They've been frisking the place for fingerprints. It looks like a frame-up."

Scudder's face flushed. "You're not in Los Angeles now," he said. "You can't pull that stuff and get away with it."

Mason shrugged his shoulders.

"A man by the name of Roger P. Cartman was here," Scudder said. "You have him concealed somewhere. I want him."

Mason said, "You're crazy."

"You were here earlier this evening. You and a man named Eves decided to hide him so he wouldn't have to testify."

"Have you," Mason inquired solicitously, "looked under the bed?"

"Take his fingerprints," Scudder ordered.

"This," Mason remonstrated, "is a damned outrage!"

Borge slipped out of his overcoat, draped it across the back of a chair, wiped perspiration from his forehead with a handkerchief. Inspector Bodfish moved in on the other side.

"Is this the way you do things in San Francisco?" Mason demanded.

Scudder said nothing.

Borge grabbed Mason's right wrist. Mason jerked back.

Borge twisted Mason's arm under his own, pivoted his body so that Mason was pulled up against the big man's hip.

"Wrestler, eh?" Mason inquired.

Borge, saying nothing, twisted Mason's arm so that the fingers were spread out. Bodfish put ink on Mason's fingers and took a series of impressions. "Hold out your other hand," Bodfish ordered. Mason held it out.

Silently, Inspector Bodfish took the fingerprints from the other two.

"Now then," Scudder said, "we want to know when you last saw Mr. Cartman."

Mason said hotly, "You started this party, now go ahead and run it. Tell your big bruiser to try and make me talk—or do you use a rubber hose in this jurisdiction?"

"You mean you're not going to answer questions?" Scudder demanded.

"I mean I'm not even going to give you a pleasant look," Mason said.

"Perhaps *you'll* tell us something," Scudder said, facing Della Street. "You're mixed up in this thing deep enough already. Loyalty is an excellent thing in its place, but you're carrying it too far . . ."

"Don't answer a single question, Della," Mason ordered.

"You remember a man by the name of Cartman who sailed on the ship from Honolulu with you?"

"Don't answer, Della," Mason warned her.

Della Street clamped her lips together.

"You're not answering?"

She shook her head.

Scudder swung to Drake. "You," he said, "are on a spot. In some ways, I don't blame you—Mason's a client of yours. He gives you all of his business. You naturally want to protect him. But you have a living to make. They revoke the licenses of detectives who . . ."

"You can save it, Scudder," Mason said grimly. "Drake isn't going to talk. If you'd gone at this thing in a decent

221

manner, we'd have been glad to answer questions. As it is, you can go jump in the lake."

Scudder regarded Mason with sullen hostility. "Mason," he said, "you're all finished. You have a reputation for pulling fast stuff and getting away with it. This time you can't do it. Other times, district attorneys have been willing to let things drop when you blew their cases up. This time I'm going through to a finish. I have all the evidence I need, and I'm going to get more."

Mason lit a cigarette, and said tauntingly, "I thought you were a better lawyer than that, Scudder. You can't make a case against me."

"What do you mean?" Scudder demanded.

Mason said, "I'm a practicing lawyer. District attorneys don't like me, but I have a good reputation with the public. How the hell are you going to get a jury to convict me on the testimony of an ex-convict?"

Scudder's face was a mask. "You're kidding yourself," he said.

Mason went on, "Furthermore, a man can't be convicted on the uncorroborated testimony of an accomplice. Turn that over in your mind and see where it leaves you—if you want to get technical."

Scudder's eyes narrowed as he regarded Mason in thoughtful appraisal. "So your accomplice was an ex-convict," he charged.

Mason, instantly wary, said, "Now, wait a minute. Let's not have any misunderstandings about this. I haven't admitted having an accomplice. I've merely quoted some law."

Scudder said, "Let him go, boys."

Inspector Bodfish said, "You mean book him on an open charge or . . ."

"I mean let him go. Let him walk out of here," Scudder ordered. "Turn all three of them loose."

Mason's bow was sardonic.

"Do I," he asked, "get my fingerprints back?"

222

Scudder said grimly, "Try and get them."

Borge wiped his forehead, blinked through the thick-lensed glasses, and said, "We aren't done with this guy."

Scudder said, "Shut up, Borge. That's all, Mason. Get out."

Mason led the way down the long flight of stairs to the street.

En route to the hotel, Mason turned to Drake and said with a grin, "Well, Paul, that wasn't so bad as you thought it would be, was it?"

"Your grammar's all shot to hell," Drake said mournfully. "You mean to say, 'Well, Paul, this isn't as bad as you think it will be, is it?'"

Mason said, "I think we're in the clear now, Paul."

"You mean the district attorney's going to quit?" Della Street asked.

"Lord, no!" Mason told her. "He's just starting. That was the idea back of all this, to get the district attorney started."

"Well," Drake said, "you've got him started now."

Charles Whitmore Dail was waiting for Mason at his hotel. "May I see you for a few moments, Counselor?" he asked.

"You can if you have that ten thousand dollars," Mason told him, grinning.

"I have it," Dail said, "and there's another matter I wish to take up with you."

"Come on up," Mason invited.

When they were seated in the lawyer's room, Dail looked significantly at Della Street and said, "In addition to this settlement I am making with Mrs. Moar, Mason, I had another matter I wanted to discuss with you."

"All right," Mason said, "go ahead and discuss it. I have no secrets from Della. Let's get this ten thousand dollars out of the way first."

"You have an agreement prepared?" Dail asked.

Mason nodded, and passed over a typewritten paper

which contained Mrs. Moar's signature. Dail studied it a moment, then folded it, slipped it in his pocket, opened a wallet, took out ten one-thousand-dollar bills and passed them over to Mason.

"Go ahead," Mason told him.

"It's about my daughter, Celinda."

"What about her?"

"She has been subpoenaed as a witness in this case. It's rather a minor matter. She happened to see Mrs. Newberry running down the stairs from the upper deck. Mrs. Newberry was carrying a chamois-skin money belt in her hand, and her gown was soaking wet."

"How long was this after the whistle sounded its five blasts?" Mason asked.

"Celinda doesn't remember clearly," Dail said.

"What did you want to see *me* about?" Mason asked. "If the district attorney has subpoenaed Celinda, she should talk with him, not me."

"I wanted to discuss Celinda's temperament with you," Dail said. "The child is rather nervous. She's never been in court before and she's read in the newspapers something of your vigorous cross-examination of Aileen Fell. I thought that perhaps we might reach some arrangement, Mr. Mason, by which Celinda wouldn't be subjected to such a grilling cross-examination."

Mason said, "What agreement did you have in mind?"

"Well," Dail said, "of course the matter is rather delicate and I wouldn't want you to misunderstand what I have in mind, but as I understand it, five thousand dollars of the money I have just paid goes toward your fees, five thousand goes to Mrs. Moar. Now, it seems to me that the very clever and adroit representation you are giving Mrs. Moar should entitle you to a larger fee. And, because she was a fellow passenger on the ship, I might be willing to interest myself somewhat in her behalf."

"You mean to the extent of adding to my fees?" Mason asked.

"Yes," Dail said.

Mason's mouth twisted in a fighting grin. "I think I understand you perfectly, Dail," he said, "and it happens I'm very glad your daughter is going to be a witness."

"Why?" Dail said. "I thought the fact that she had seen Mrs. Moar carrying that money belt might . . . well, might be damaging."

Mason said, "Never mind that. When Celinda gets on the stand, I'm entitled to show, by way of cross-examination, her bias toward the parties.

"I happen to know that Celinda found out from Belle that she'd graduated from the University of Southern California; that she sent a wireless to Rooney asking him to look up a Belle Newberry who had graduated from the University of Southern California. With that to go on, it didn't take Rooney long to find out that her stepfather was Carl Moar. Celinda wanted to humiliate Belle Newberry. She thought the best way to do it would be to have detectives waiting at the gangplank to take Moar into custody. I have reason to believe she had made all the arrangements. Now then, on cross-examination I am entitled to show all of that in order to show bias on the part of the witness."

"But," Dail said, "I don't see what that's going to gain you. After all, it's rather petty, it certainly doesn't affect Mrs. Moar—"

"No," Mason said, "but it affects Belle. When Roy Hungerford learns that Celinda was on that ship posing as a friend of Belle Newberry, asking her to attend week-end parties after the ship had docked, and all the time planning to humiliate her at the gangplank by showing that her stepfather was an embezzler, Hungerford will have a very accurate appraisal of just what your daughter considers fair play."

"Oh, I say," Dail protested, his face flushing, "isn't that hitting below the belt?"

Mason said, "Dail, when I'm fighting for a client, I hit

225

where it's going to hurt the most. You might tell Celinda what to expect in the line of cross-examination."

"I'd like very much to avoid this," Dail said.

Mason got to his feet and crossed to the door. "I feel quite certain that you would," he said. "In fact, Mr. Dail, thinking back on it, I have a very clear recollection of the charming urbanity with which you signified *your* willingness to discuss a monetary settlement with Moar. Knowing the plans which you had in the back of your mind, I can only call your attention to the old proverb about chickens coming home to roost."

Dail tried to make his exit dignified. He turned on the threshold and said, "You can't get away with it, Mason. You'll find that I draw some water around here. Good night!"

He slammed the door.

Mason grinned across at Della Street.

"You shouldn't have done that, Chief."

"Why not?"

"Celinda will get in touch with Roy Hungerford and bring things to a head tonight. She's clever, and she wants him. She's a shrewd campaigner."

"That," Mason said, "is exactly what I figured she'd do. Now, I happen to know that of all the things Roy Hungerford detests, a woman who tries to force things is his pet abomination. Designing females have been trying to give him the rush act ever since he was old enough to wear long pants. If he's hesitating between Celinda, who's in his set, and Belle, who's not, Celinda will wreck all of her chances trying to rush things—and the beautiful part of it is that it will be all her doing."

Della Street said, "Well, *I* hope she cooks her goose to a cinder!"

Mason opened the door to Paul Drake's room and said, "Paul, I have something else for you."

"What is it?" Drake asked.

"You said that Morgan Eves was acquitted of murder about two months ago in Los Angeles?"

"Yes."

"And," Mason went on, "Baldwin Van Densie defended him?"

"Yes."

"Well," Mason said, "Moar was on a jury in Los Angeles about two months ago. It was a murder case. Van Densie was defending. Moar took a dislike to Van Densie, claimed he was putting up a sell-out defense. The D. A. had a pushover with the other jurors, but Moar went to the bat in the jury room and whipped them into line. You might have your Los Angeles office look up the records and see if Moar was on Morgan Eves' jury."

The detective twisted his forehead into a frown. "Gosh, Perry, if *that* was the case, then Eves would be bound to Moar by a debt of gratitude, and if Evelyn Whiting had been going with Moar for some time, she must have . . . Why, dammit, Perry, as soon as she found out Moar was on the jury, trying the man she loved, she'd have brought all sorts of pressure to bear to get an acquittal."

Mason grinned and said, "You're doing fine, Paul. Go ahead and put through that call. And in the meantime, I'm on my way to the morgue where I will loudly proclaim that the body is not that of Carl Moar."

"You mean to say they've identified the wrong body?" Drake asked.

"I mean to say," Mason replied, "that I am going to give an interview to the press in which I will positively deny that the body is that of Carl Moar."

"There'll be newspaper reporters there?" Della Street asked.

"There will be before I get through talking," Mason said grimly.

Drake, reaching for the telephone, said, "Gosh, Perry, if you'd only stayed in Bali!"

Chapter 18

Donaldson P. Scudder entered the courtroom with the air of a crusader, armed in the cause of righteousness and intent on routing the forces of evil. He failed to speak to Perry Mason. Judge Romley took the bench. The bailiff intoned the usual formula for opening court.

Scudder arose as soon as court had been convened, cleared his throat and said with the distinct articulation of one who is carefully weighing his words, "Your Honor, it has reached my knowledge within the last few hours that there is another eyewitness to the murder who was within a few feet of the defendant when she fired the first shot. I have endeavored to locate this eyewitness and have failed. While I can make no promises, I sincerely hope to be able to have this witness in court within forty-eight hours. I can assure your Honor that the circumstances necessitating the making of this motion are *most* unusual. I therefore ask that the case be continued for two days."

Judge Romley shifted his eyes toward Perry Mason.

Mason was on his feet, his manner indignant, his voice booming through the courtroom. "Your Honor, not only do I oppose the motion and object to it, but I characterize the making of it as prejudicial misconduct. I characterize the statements made in regard to that witness as pure propaganda intended for newspaper consumption and comparable in every way with the statement released to the press yesterday that the body of Carl Moar had been recovered!"

Scudder took a deep breath, stood very erect, and said, "Your Honor, the only reason I cannot produce this witness now is that Perry Mason has concealed him. I even have reason to believe that the witness is being concealed against his will."

Mason jumped to his feet. "Your Honor," he shouted, "that is the most dastardly accusation which can be made against a practicing attorney. The deputy prosecutor . . ."

"Just a minute, Mr. Mason," Judge Romley interrupted, his voice crisp and businesslike. "I wish to ask Mr. Scudder a few questions. Mr. Deputy District Attorney, are you aware of the grave implications attending your statement?"

"I am, your Honor."

"Are you prepared to substantiate those statements?"

"I am not only prepared to do so, your Honor, but I would welcome the opportunity of doing so. At this time, I cannot produce the evidence which my office hopes to produce at a later date, when criminal action will be taken against the attorney for the defendant, but I can at least produce sufficient evidence to justify your Honor in granting this continuance."

"And I demand that such proof be produced!" Mason shouted.

Judge Romley said, "Very well, the Court will at this time entertain proof in support of a motion made by the Prosecution that the case of The People versus Anna Moar be continued for forty-eight hours. Proceed with your proof, Mr. Deputy District Attorney."

"Call Mabel Foss to the stand," Scudder said.

The woman who had waited on Perry Mason and delivered the photographs to him, came forward and was sworn.

"You reside and have a place of business in a little storeroom at 3618 Stockton Boulevard?" Scudder asked.

"I do."

"Are you acquainted with Perry Mason, the attorney sitting here?"

"I have seen him, yes."

"When?"

"Day before yesterday."

"Did you have any business transactions with him?"

"I did."

"What?"

"Mr. Mason asked for some pictures which had been left to be developed by a Mrs. Morgan Eves. He said that he was a neighbor and friend."

"And who is Morgan Eves?"

"He resides in the flat on the third floor."

"Of the house in which you have your shop and place of business?"

"Yes."

"How long have you known Morgan Eves?"

"Some two months."

"I will show you a photograph and ask you if that is a photograph of Morgan Eves."

Scudder produced a printed placard showing a man's face, both front view and profile. A prison number was printed across the man's chest. Below appeared a series of fingerprints.

Mason said, "I object to this. There is no need to introduce a man's criminal record in this indirect manner."

"The objection is overrulled," Judge Romley said. "I'm going to get to the bottom of this, Counselor."

"Do you know the man whose picture is shown here?" Scudder asked.

"Why, yes, that's Mr. Eves. I had no idea he was a—"

"That's the man you know as Morgan Eves, the man who lives in the flat on the third floor of the house at 3618 Stockton Boulevard?" Scudder asked.

"Yes."

"And Mr. Mason called and secured pictures which had been left to be developed by Mr. Eves' wife?"

"Yes."

"Now, do you know a Roger P. Cartman?"

"I have seen him," she said. "He came over from Honolulu with Mrs. Eves. She's a nurse. He was suffering from a broken neck."

"And was removed from an ambulance and taken up to the flat rented by Mr. Eves?"

"Yes."

"That's all," Scudder said.

"No questions," Mason announced.

"My next witness," Scudder announced, "is Christopher G. Borge."

Borge, looking decidedly bored, raised his huge frame from his chair, walked to the clerk, was sworn, eased himself into the witness chair, crossed his knees and looked at the deputy district attorney.

"Your name is Christopher Borge, and you are now, and for several years have been, a criminologist connected with the homicide detail of the police force in this city?"

"I am."

"And what has been your training for your position?" the deputy district attorney inquired.

Mason raised his eyebrows in surprise, inquired, "May I ask if you're endeavoring to qualify this man as an expert?"

"Yes!" snapped the deputy, without turning his head.

Borge paid no attention whatever to the comments of Counsel. He glanced indifferently down at the reporter's desk, where the shorthand reporter was making his pen fly across the paper, and said, "I studied chemistry, fingerprinting, forensic medicine, and toxicology, ballistics, handwriting, photomicrography and several other allied subjects."

"When you say that you studied fingerprinting, what do you mean?" the deputy district attorney asked.

"I mean that I took a regular course in fingerprinting and all of its phases, learned the methods of indexing and filing fingerprints, of identifying men from fingerprints, of developing what are known as latent fingerprints, photographing them, checking and comparing them."

"I call your attention to the photograph which has been identified by the witness who preceded you as that of Morgan Eves and ask you if you have ever seen that man."

"I have."

"Do you recognize him?"

"I do."

"Who is he?"

"He's James Whitly, also known as James Clerke."

"Does he have a criminal record?"

Mason jumped to his feet, his manner that of one who is cornered and fighting desperately.

"Your Honor, I object. This is incompetent, irrelevant and immaterial."

"It is on a motion only, your Honor, addressed to the discretion of this Court," Scudder said, "and this is preliminary. I intend to connect it up."

"Overruled," Judge Romley said.

Borge took a silk handkerchief from his pocket, wiped his perspiring forehead and the back of his neck and said in a bored voice, "Yes, he has a criminal record."

"What is it?"

"Twice to San Quentin for burglary. Once to Folsom for assault with a deadly weapon. He's been arrested three or four times and was tried for murder in—"

Mason jumped to his feet and said, "Your Honor, I object. Any man may be arrested—"

"Sustained," Judge Romley said.

"Did you," Scudder went on, "take this man's fingerprints, Mr. Borge?"

"Yes."

"When?"

"In 1929, in 1934, and in 1935."

"You have his fingerprints here?"

"I have."

"Produce them, please."

Scudder took the placard which Borge handed him, and said, "I would like to introduce these fingerprints in evidence."

"No objection," Mason said.

"Now then, Mr. Borge," the deputy district attorney

said, "I will ask you if you went last night to a flat rented by Morgan Eves."

"I did."

"And what did you do there?"

"Objected to," Mason said perfunctorily, "incompetent, irrelevant and immaterial."

"It is a preliminary merely. I wish to connect it up," Scudder remarked, without arising from his chair.

"Overruled," Judge Romley snapped.

"I used various powders on various articles for the purpose of developing latent fingerprints which might be found in that apartment."

"And did you develop latent fingerprints?"

"I did."

"And photographed them?"

"I did."

"Have you photographs of those latent prints with you?"

"I have."

Borge pulled a thick file of photographs from his pocket.

Scudder pushed back his chair and got to his feet. He spoke slowly and clearly, so that the audience would have no difficulty in following him or appreciating the significance of his question. "Now, then, Mr. Borge, I will ask you if among those latent fingerprints which you developed and photographed, you found any fingerprints made by the man about whose criminal record you have just testified?"

"I did."

"Where did you find those prints?"

"I found them in various and sundry places, in the bathroom, on the table, on a mirror, on a doorknob, and on a discarded safety razor blade."

"Did you photograph those prints?"

"I did."

"Do you have these photographs with you?"

"Yes."

"I would like to introduce them in evidence."

"No objection," Mason said, as Scudder handed the sheaf of photographs across to the clerk.

"Now then, did you find any other fingerprints in that flat?"

"I did."

"Whose were they?"

"Objected to," Mason shouted. "This is incompetent, irrelevant and immaterial—"

"Overruled," Judge Romley said.

Borge grinned at Mason. "I found fingerprints of Perry Mason," he said. "I found fingerprints of Paul Drake, a detective employed by Perry Mason. I found a wheel chair, and on the wheel chair I found prints of the man who had evidently occupied that wheel chair. I also found some fingerprints of a woman."

"And did you photograph these fingerprints and mark upon each photograph the place where the prints had been found?"

"I did."

"I'm going to ask that these be introduced in evidence."

Mason sat back in his chair with the air of having been defeated. After a moment, Judge Romley said, "It appearing that there is no objection, the photographs will be received in evidence."

"Now, Mr. Borge," Scudder went on, "were you present at that apartment last night at the hour of approximately ten-fifty in the evening, at a time when Perry Mason, Paul Drake, a certain Della Street, Inspector Frank Bodfish, and myself were present?"

"I was."

"And at that time and at that place, did you hear me accuse Perry Mason of having spirited away the said Roger P. Cartman, who had temporarily occupied that flat or apartment? And did I then and there accuse the said Perry Mason of having kidnaped and abducted the said Roger P. Cartman and of holding him where he could not be found by the deputy district attorney, and could not be brought into this court to testify as an eyewitness in the case of The People versus Anna Moar, otherwise known as Ann Newberry?"

"I was there," Borge said. "I heard you make that accusation."

"And at that time and at that place, what statement did the said Perry Mason make in connection with that accusation?"

Mason jumped to his feet, his manner desperate. "Your Honor, I object! This is incompetent, irrelevant and immaterial. This has nothing whatever to do with . . ."

Judge Romley cut him short. "Objection overruled," he snapped.

Borge looked at Mason and said, without raising his voice, "He said you could never convict him because his accomplice had been an ex-convict, and no jury would convict him on the testimony of an ex-convict, and anyway you couldn't convict him because you couldn't corroborate the testimony of his accomplice."

"You may cross-examine," Scudder snapped.

Mason watched Borge wiping his moist forehead with a handkerchief. "How many men have you ever fingerprinted, Mr. Borge?" he asked.

"I can't see that this is material," Scudder objected.

"It goes to his qualifications," Mason insisted. "You've qualified him as an expert, I certainly am going to cross-examine him, to show his qualifications."

"I think the question is perfectly proper," Judge Romley ruled. "Counsel did not stipulate to the qualifications of this witness, and he has a right to ask any reasonable number of questions touching upon his qualifications as an expert. The objection is overruled."

"I couldn't say," Borge said. "I've fingerprinted thousands."

"Who was the first man you ever fingerprinted?"

Borge smiled and said, "Why, I couldn't remember."

"When was it?"

"I can't even tell you that—it was probably fifteen years ago. I can't remember."

"Who was the last man you fingerprinted?"

An expression of satisfaction animated Borge's pale green eyes. "The last man I fingerprinted," he said, and paused dramatically as he flashed a look of triumph at the deputy district attorney, "was Carl Moar. I took his fingerprints at two o'clock this morning in the City Morgue, shortly after you had told the newspapers the body wasn't that of Moar, but of some other person."

Mason hesitated for several awkward seconds, then said, "You're stating positively that this man *was* Carl Moar?"

"Of course I am," Borge said. "The body had been in the water for a couple of days, but I was able to get his fingerprints without any trouble. A man's fingerprints never change, not even in death. They're absolute means of identification."

"And can't the fingerprints of one person possibly be confused with those of another?"

"No," Borge said scornfully. "Every high school kid knows that."

Judge Romley rapped with his gavel. "The witness will confine himself to answering the questions," he said. "The witness is being interrogated as to his qualifications as an expert. The Court will not permit the examination to be unduly prolonged, but if Counsel wishes to inquire concerning the qualifications of the witness as an expert, he has a perfect right to do so, and the witness will observe a respectful attitude in answering such questions."

"Then you must have had Carl Moar's fingerprints," Mason argued. "That is, you must have had something with which to compare the fingerprints of the corpse."

"I did. Moar was bonded by a bonding company when he worked for a bank fifteen years go. The bonding company required that fingerprints be filed with the application for a bond."

"Oh," Mason said, as though the information had knocked the props from under him.

"Any further cross-examination?" the Court asked.

Mason walked slowly forward, picked up the sheaf of fingerprint photographs which had been filed with the clerk, said to Borge, "And do you have photographs of the fingerprints of Carl Moar, deceased, with you?"

Borge slipped a perspiring hand in a voluminous pocket and pulled out an envelope of photographs. "They're all marked," he said, grinning at Mason. "Help yourself."

Mason studied the photographs for a minute, shuffled them around in his hands. Abruptly, he picked out one and said, "Now, the fingerprint shown in this photograph, Mr. Borge, what is that?"

"That," Borge said, "represents the fingerprint of Morgan Eves. It's evidently the fingerprint of the man who leased the apartment. I found lots of those fingerprints over various articles, bottles, glasses, on the wash stand in the bathroom, on shaving things, on suitcases, mirrors. . . . The one which you have reference to was one of several taken from a pane of window glass. I found virtually a complete set of fingerprints there, where a man's hand had pressed against the glass, in raising the window."

Mason slipped the print to one side. "And these?" he asked.

"Those are the fingerprints of Carl Moar, the ones taken from the corpse."

"These?" Mason asked.

"Those are fingerprints of the woman I assume was acting as nurse for Roger P. Cartman."

"And these?"

"Those are the fingerprints taken from the wheel chair. I assume they are Roger P. Cartman's prints."

Mason said suddenly, "Look here, you're basing your testimony, not upon what these fingerprints really are, but on memoranda which you've written on the bottoms of the prints."

"Well, of course," Borge said, "I had to find some way of keeping the photographs all straight. But I could take a magnifying glass and identify any of those fingerprints."

"Could you," Mason asked, "do that here in court?"

"Of course."

Mason took a sheet of paper from his pocket, tore a hole in it, and placed it over one of the photographs, so that only the portion showing the fingerprint was visible.

"Now then," he said triumphantly, "let's take that photograph, covered so that you can't see the printing on it, and this photograph," and Mason tore another hole in another piece of paper, covered another photograph, "and this one," taking a third, "and see if you can identify those three fingerprints."

"It would take a little time," Borge objected.

"Take all the time you want," Mason announced triumphantly.

Borge took a magnifying glass from his pocket, leaned over to study the fingerprints.

"And I'd have to consult certain data which I have in my notebook," he said at length. "Two of these fingerprints are the same. I think they're the fingerprints of Roger P. Cartman, I'm not certain."

"Go right ahead," Mason said.

The witness consulted his notebook, took a finely marked scale from his pocket, then looked up at the judge and nodded. "These two," he said, indicating two photographs, "are both photographs of prints made by the right index finger of the man I assume was Roger P. Cartman, since I found his fingerprints on the wheel chair."

Mason said, "Will you mark these right on the photographs, so there can be no mistake, with a cross in pen and ink?"

The witness, looking bored and contemptuous, took a pen from his pocket, made a cross on each of the photographs.

238

Mason triumphantly removed the paper and said, "Now, then, Mr. Borge, since you've qualified as an expert, and since you've said that any high school pupil knows that it's impossible to confuse the fingerprints of two different people, will you kindly tell me how it happens that you have just identified a fingerprint made from the right index finger of Carl Moar, deceased, as being identical with a print of the right index finger of the man whom you have stated was Roger P. Cartman?"

Borge stared with incredulous eyes at the annotations on the two photographs. Scudder, jumping to his feet, hurried to the side of the witness.

Judge Romley regarded Mason with a puzzled frown. "Do I understand, Mr. Mason, that it is your contention the witness has confused two photographs?"

"No," Mason said with a grin, "what your Honor should understand is that when my learned friend, the deputy district attorney, discovers the true significance of the testimony of this witness, the case against Anna Moar will be dismissed. Otherwise, the Prosecution will find itself confronted with the necessity of explaining to a jury in this case just how it happens the man the witnesses have sworn this defendant murdered on the night of the sixth instantly left fingerprints in a San Francisco flat on the afternoon of the seventh."

"There's trickery here someplace, your Honor," Scudder said.

Mason smiled. "If Counsel is interested in discovering just where the trickery lies, I can give him two clues. One is that when Della Street stepped out on deck on the evening of the sixth, she inadvertently took a position almost exactly where Aileen Fell had been standing before she ran up to the boat deck. The second one is that at the time when the decedent, Moar, was about to sail from Honolulu, someone opened Moar's locked suitcase and substituted a picture of Winnie Joyce, whom Miss Newberry greatly resembles, for a photograph of Belle Newberry. As for the rest, Counsel will have to figure it out for himself."

Scudder bent forward to engage in a whispered conversation with Borge. Then, in a voice which showed all too plainly his bewilderment, said, "May I ask the Court for a brief recess? I wish to correlate certain facts."

Judge Romley said, "Under the circumstances, I am quite certain there will be no objection to a brief continuance, Mr. Mason?"

Mason said, "I will not object to a continuance on only one condition, your Honor. The deputy district attorney has accused me of concealing witnesses. However, I have reason to believe that the deputy district attorney may have in custody a witness who has heretofore been subpoenaed by me as a witness for the Defense. I refer to an Evelyn Whiting, who acted as nurse for Roger Cartman."

Judge Romley glanced at Scudder. "Do you have such a witness in custody?" he asked.

Scudder was visibly embarrassed.

"Why, your Honor," he said, "I have been searching for Miss Whiting. She was apprehended by officers something over an hour ago. She is in my office. I have been interrogating her, but so far have had little success. I had no idea that she was a witness for Mr. Mason."

"You will find that she has been regularly served with a subpoena," Mason said, "and a return of service has been made and is on file with the clerk of this court. Under the circumstances, I demand an opportunity to examine her before this case is continued."

"Is there any objection?" Judge Romley asked Scudder.

"Why, no, your Honor. I can only repeat I had no idea this woman was a witness."

"How long will it take to get her here?" Judge Romley asked.

"Just a moment or two. She is at present held in the witness room. I think the bailiff can bring her here almost at once."

While the bailiff was summoning Evelyn Whiting, Judge Romley regarded Perry Mason in puzzled scrutiny.

"Do I understand, Mr. Mason," he asked, "that it is your contention that the body which I understand was found yesterday, and which has been indentified as Carl Moar is not really the body of Carl Moar?"

"No, your Honor," Mason said. "I gave an interview to the press last night in which I asserted that the body could not be that of Carl Moar. I did this solely because I wanted to force the Prosecution to use every means possible to get Moar's fingerprints."

"Then, if that was Moar's body, how do you account for the fact that Moar's fingerprints also appear on the wheel chair in this flat—and, I take it, upon other objects in the flat?"

"Unless this witness can explain matters," Mason said, "I think I will leave it to my learned friend, the deputy district attorney, to do the explaining. After all, it's *his* case."

Scudder said testily, "I think counsel understands that the district attorney's office will welcome any information which will throw light upon this mysterious affair."

Judge Romley was about to say something when the bailiff brought Evelyn Whiting into the courtroom. She was sworn by the clerk and took the witness stand, her face showing plainly that she was laboring under a nervous strain.

Mason glanced up at Judge Romley and said, "I think if Court and Counsel will bear with me in what may perhaps be a somewhat unusual form of examination, we can clear this matter up. Miss Whiting, you understand that you have taken an oath to tell the truth; that any failure to do so may subject you to a perjury prosecution?"

"Yes."

Mason said, "You have been keeping company with a man whom you knew as Morgan Eves for some time?"

"Yes."

"Did you know that he had a criminal record?"

She hesitated for a moment, then said, "Yes."

"And you had previously known Carl Moar for some considerable period of time?"

"Yes."

"He had, on at least one occasion, asked you to marry him?"

"Yes."

"Now, Morgan Eves was arrested in Los Angeles and tried on a murder charge?"

"Yes, he was," she said quickly, "and he was acquitted."

"Yes," Mason said, "and Carl Moar was on that jury, wasn't he?"

"Why . . . yes, he was."

"And when you saw that Carl Moar was on the jury, you thought that you could do the man you loved a good turn by approaching Carl Moar and asking him to do everything he could to get a verdict of acquittal?"

She hesitated.

"And," Mason asked, "didn't you offer Moar a bribe? Come now, Miss Whiting, the facts are all available. Your part in this matter has been rather culpable. You had better tell the truth."

"No," she said, "I did not."

"Now," Mason went on calmly, "after Moar discharged his duties on this jury and after Morgan Eves had been acquitted, Mr. Moar found himself in the possession of some twenty-five thousand dollars. He went to the Hawaiian Islands and was enjoying a vacation in Honolulu. Unfortunately, however, Mr. Moar was rather naïve in some respects and had made no effort to conceal his sudden acquisition of wealth, or to account for it. He merely changed his name and proceeded to take up a new life.

"Now, Mr. Van Densie, the attorney who represented Morgan Eves, found himself under investigation on a charge of jury bribing. The district attorney launched a sweeping investigation. It became important to Mr. Van Densie, as well as Mr. Eves, to keep the grand jury from calling on Mr. Moar as a witness. Mr. Moar's attempts to take a new identity were sufficient, so far as a mere neighborly interest was concerned, but would hardly have withstood the investigation of trained detectives. Therefore, you were selected to go to Honolulu and arrange with Mr. Moar for a more effective disappearance. In order to explain the trip you were making to your sister, you told her you were going on your honeymoon. Mr. Eves, whom you secretly married, found himself very busy at the moment, assisting Mr. Van Densie conceal matters from the investigators. He actually sailed on the ship with you, but after it had left the dock, climbed over the side on a rope ladder and returned on a speed launch. You went to Honolulu, explained that situation to Mr. Moar, and arranged with him for a complete disappearance.

"This scheme had been carefully thought out by Van Densie, Morgan Eves, and perhaps in part, by you. You knew that a Roger P. Cartman had been in an automobile accident and sustained a broken neck. You purchased a ticket in the name of Roger P. Cartman on the same steamship as that on which Mr. Moar traveled under the name of Carl Newberry. From time to time, Mr. Moar would surreptitiously visit your cabin. You would place a steel and leather harness, or brace, upon his neck so that it concealed much of his face, put on huge dark glasses which concealed his eyes, and wheel him about the deck in a wheel chair.

"On the night of the sixth you, having familiarized yourself with the custom of Aileen Fell of being on deck immediately after dinner, and feeling that this was a propitious time because of the storm, arranged to have Mr. Moar commit a supposed suicide by shooting himself and jumping overboard. You expected that the sound of revolver shots would attract Miss Fell's attention so that she could see what apparently was the body of a man hurtling into the ocean.

"However, Miss Fell's curiosity brought her up to the boat deck; so in place of having Moar apparently a suicide, he seemed to be the victim of a murder, and his wife was accused of the murder.

"After Moar's supposed plunge over the side, he went to your stateroom, where he became Roger P. Cartman, the invalid, and was actually carried off the steamer in a wheel chair, and taken to the flat on Stockton Boulevard.

"However, where the supposed suicide of Mr. Moar would have passed with only a small amount of notoriety, the supposed murder of Moar was an entirely different affair, and the situation became complicated when I dashed to Los Angeles and proved that Mr. Moar had not embezzled money from his former employer, the Products Refining Company. Therefore, Mr. Eves decided it would be better for you to leave the flat at Stockton Boulevard, since he felt some attempt might be made to trace Roger P. Cartman.

"Now, he took you to a cabin up in the Santa Cruz Mountains, Miss Whiting. But did you know that after he had taken you there, he returned to the flat at Stockton Boulevard; that he then told Mr. Moar he had arranged for another place of concealment, placed him aboard a yacht, took him out by the Farallons, cruised about until he found one of the life rings which had been tossed overboard from the steamer the night before, shot Mr. Moar, stripped him of his clothes, placed his body in the life ring, and left it floating on the ocean, knowing that it would be discovered within a day or two."

Mason paused, and Evelyn Whiting, gripping the arms of the chair with her gloved hands, moistened her lips and said nothing.

"You *must* have realized what had happened," Mason went on, "when you read that Moar's body had been found. Now then, Miss Whiting, it's one thing to resort to jury bribing to shield a man whom you love. It's quite another thing to become involved as an accessory on a murder charge. I think it's time for you to tell the truth."

She half rose from the chair, dropped back into it, looked helplessly about her, then slowly nodded her head. She raised her eyes to Judge Romley and said, "It's true. I thought Morgan was innocent when he was being tried in Los Angeles. I thought the case was a frame-up against him, so I was willing to do everything I could. Mr. Van Densie said that if Morgan should be convicted, the district attorney would be able to frame a lot of Morgan's business associates. He said these men had made up a purse to help my husband, and would give five thousand dollars for a hung jury, or twenty-five thousand for an outright acquittal. I explained the situation to Carl. I gave him my word that Morgan was innocent, and he managed to swing the jury. I made Carl Moar think the whole case was a frame-up, because *I* thought it was a frame-up."

Mason said, "Now, you purchased a picture frame on the seventh, Miss Whiting."

"Yes," she said, "Carl was very much attached to his stepdaughter. In order to keep from being called as a witness, it was necessary for him to pretend to commit suicide and he knew that it would be years before he could ever see Belle again. He wanted her picture to keep with him. But he didn't want his wife to know he'd taken this picture because that might make her suspicious of the suicide. So he switched pictures in the frame. Unfortunately, Mrs. Moar found out the pictures had been changed almost as soon as Carl had made the switch."

"And you were the one who sent Carl Moar the note on the evening of the sixth?" Mason asked.

"Yes. We had it all planned. You see, we rigged up a dummy which we could throw overboard, and I left it up in the ship's hospital. On the night of the sixth I waited until Miss Fell had come out on deck. Then I sent word to Carl. He was to come on deck. We were to drag the dummy to the rail and fire a couple of shots from a revolver to attract Miss Fell's attention. Then we were to pitch the dummy overboard and leave Carl Moar's gun where it would be found on the boat deck. Carl was to come down to my stateroom, climb into bed and put on the goggles and head brace, which would make it almost impossible to recognize him, particularly since we'd made such a careful build-up."

"And how did it happen your dress got caught on one of the cleats?" Mason asked.

She said without hesitation, "Mrs. Moar made a mistake, leaving her wet clothes where they could be found. It showed she'd been on deck. If they searched my stateroom, I didn't want them to find my wet clothes as evidence. I threw my dinner dress out of the porthole. By that time, the ship had turned around and the wind was blowing a gale. It caught my dress, tore it out of my hand, and sent it flying up in the air. I suppose a part of it caught on the cleat and the rest tore loose.

"Miss Fell had seen me dragging the dummy across the boat deck and your secretary, Miss Street, happened to be standing just below. She looked up and saw me as I pushed the dummy overboard and fired the second shot. I knew that she had run in and telephoned that a man was overboard, and I knew that sooner or later she'd be made to tell what she'd seen. You see, she was looking *up* into the rain, and therefore couldn't see my features, but I was looking down and could see hers. The rain was in her eyes. It wasn't in mine.

"Please understand me," she pleaded, "I was willing to help the man I loved because I thought he was innocent. Then this morning when I read the papers, I knew why he'd left me up there in the mountains. He'd gone back and tricked Carl to his death. He figured that would keep Carl's testimony from ever being given and that the murder would be charged to Mrs. Moar. I was sick. I loved him—I still love him—I can't protect him now, though I see him for what he really is—even—I can't stand back of him any more— Tell me, Mr. Mason, since you seem to know all about it, he did—kill Carl, didn't he?"

Her eyes, pleading and anxious, hoping against hope, rested on the lawyer's face.

"Yes," Mason said, "and he made the fatal mistake of leaving high-laced shoes on Moar's body. You see, when Carl Moar was supposed to have gone overboard, he was dressed in a tuxedo. As soon as I saw the high-laced shoes on Moar's body I realized what must have happened. The fact that the bullet in the body had been fired from a gun other than Moar's gun was further convincing evidence. I'm sorry, Miss Whiting, but that's what happened. And I'm not altogether blameless. I should have deduced the truth sooner than I did. Knowing that Moar had been on a jury in Los Angeles, that he had been instrumental in getting the defendant acquitted; that Baldwin Van Densie, a notorious jury briber, had been the attorney representing that defendant and discovering that Carl had come into the unexplained possesion of approximately twenty-five thousand dollars immediately after the verdict had been returned, should have been all I needed, particularly when one adds to that the fact that Belle Newberry's picture had disappeared from a suitcase to which only Mr. Moar had the key, and the lock showed no evidence of having been tampered with. I'm afraid, Miss Whiting, that the peculiar manner in which the case developed threw me off the track and prevented me from saving Carl Moar's life."

She nodded. Her lips quivered. "I loved Morgan," she said. "I believed in him. I . . . trusted him." She started to sob.

Mason's voice was filled with sympathy as he said to Judge Romley, "If the Court please, won't it be more merciful to take a recess?"

247

Chapter 19

Mason, Della Street, Paul Drake, Mrs. Moar, Belle Newberry and Roy Hungerford sat in Mason's suite at the hotel, champagne glasses on the table, the neck of a ceremonial bottle of champagne protruding from a bucket of cracked ice.

"What I don't see," Hungerford said, "is how the devil you ever figured it out."

Mason shook his head and said, "It will always be a matter of humiliation that I didn't figure it out sooner. Marian Whiting told us her sister had seen Carl on the street in Los Angeles. Evelyn Whiting said she hadn't seen him for years until she recognized him on the ship. She said he had told her he was going to commit suicide when she met him on deck. Della Street said she had seen him coming from Evelyn Whiting's cabin. Mrs. Moar, herself, told me that whenever Evelyn Whiting appeared on deck with her patient in a wheel chair, Carl Moar was nowhere to be found. You, Belle, told me that your stepfather had been on one of Van Densie's juries in Los Angeles and had been able to swing the jury into a verdict of acquittal. You said that had been two or three months ago, and it was at just about that time Carl suddenly became affluent. But, above all, I should have known the truth when Morgan Eves warned me there was a surprise witness who would jeopardize my case. Then, when I discovered Della was that witness, I should have known at once what had happened. Eves could only have known it through Evelyn Whiting and she could only have known it because she looked down and saw Della Street at the rail on the lower deck.

"Carl Moar tried to take the easy way. As is so often the case, it turned out to be the hard way, yet we must not judge him too harshly. He had confidence in Evelyn Whiting. He was a thinker, something of a dreamer. He didn't have a great deal of what is known as worldly wisdom. He lived in an artificial world peopled largely by his own ideas and administered largely according to his own ideals. Evelyn Whiting had but little difficulty in convincing him that Morgan Eves was innocent. She had less difficulty because she herself really believed it. It looked like a good chance for Moar to do the right thing and at the same time pick up enough money to give Belle her chance . . ."

Belle Newberry, her eyes filled with tears, said simply, "I loved him."

Mrs. Moar avoided Belle's eyes. "I, too, loved him," she said, "in a way. I don't think I had a proper appreciation of his character. I was too ready to believe that he'd embezzled that money. But there was no other explanation I could think of. Carl loved Belle. I don't think he loved me. I think he'd been a bachelor too long to ever fit into the give and take of married life. What he did, he did for Belle, to give her a chance to travel, to meet people of a different class. . . . It was a terrible mistake—but he thought he was planning for the best."

Mason pushed back his chair. "Well," he said, "I don't want to rush things, but Della and I must be leaving. My Los Angeles office phoned me an hour ago. A client is impatiently waiting to see me on a matter of the greatest importance. We're flying down to Los Angeles in a chartered plane. How about it, Della, are you ready?"

She nodded.

Hungerford said, "Just a moment, if you please. I have an announcement to make. It won't be made public for some time because of the tragic circumstances which have gripped us all, but . . . Well . . ."

Della Street raised her glass. "You don't need to tell us the rest of it, Roy," she said, laughing. "It's a toast we'll gladly pledge."

In the plane flying southward, Della Street snuggled close to Perry Mason, slipped her hand down into his. "Didn't she look beautiful, Chief?"

"Belle?" he asked.

"Yes. Her eyes were all starry and she was so radiantly, quietly happy, so sure of her love—and of his."

"She's a mighty fine girl," Mason said. "There's only one I know of who can beat her. I'm hoping that sometime she'll—"

She withdrew her hand from his. "Now wait a minute, Chief," she protested. "Let's not get too sentimental. You know as well as I do that you'd hate a home if you had one. You're a stormy petrel flying from one murder case to another. If you had a wife you'd put her in a fine home—and leave her there. You don't want a wife. But you do need a secretary who can take chances with you—and you have another case waiting in Los Angeles."

Mason's eyes squinted thoughtfully. "I wonder," he said, "just what that case is. Jackson said it had an unusual angle he thought would interest me."